GLIMMER

Also by Phoebe Kitanidis:

Whisper

GLIMMER

PHOEBE KITANIDIS

BALZER + BRAY

An Imprint of HarperCollins*Publishers*

For my parents,
Ranna and Peter Kitanidis,
with love and gratitude

Balzer + Bray is an imprint of HarperCollins Publishers.

Glimmer
Copyright © 2012 by Phoebe Kitanidis
All rights reserved. Printed in the United States of America.
No part of this book may be used or reproduced in any manner whatsoever
without written permission except in the case of brief quotations embodied in
critical articles and reviews. For information address HarperCollins Children's
Books, a division of HarperCollins Publishers, 10 East 53rd Street,
New York, NY 10022.
www.epicreads.com

Library of Congress Cataloging-in-Publication Data
Kitanidis, Phoebe.
Glimmer / Phoebe Kitanidis. — 1st ed.
    p. cm.
    Summary: Told in their separate voices, two teenagers wake up in bed together
with total amnesia and must work together to try to recover their memories
about themselves and the eerie Colorado town in which they find themselves.
    ISBN 978-0-06-179928-0
    [1. Amnesia—Fiction. 2. Occultism—Fiction. 3. Magic—Fiction.
4. Ghosts—Fiction. 5. Supernatural—Fiction. 6. Colorado—Fiction.] I. Title.
PZ7.K67123Gli 2012   2011024552
[Fic]—dc23   CIP
                                                                AC

Typography by Erich Nagler
12 13 14 15 16 CG/RRDH 10 9 8 7 6 5 4 3 2 1
❖
First Edition

CHAPTER 1

HER

I COME TO LIFE WITH A GASP IN THE DARKNESS. My heart's hammering, jolted by a strangely familiar sense of dread.

A blank white ceiling stares back at me as reassuring sunlight from a distant window floods my retinas. Must have had a nightmare or something.

I brace with one elbow and try to sit up, but something's pinning my right leg to the mattress. My other hand's gone numb, trapped under something heavy and warm. Someone's breathing next to me, deep regular breaths.

Is someone else . . . *in bed with me?!*

Calm down. Don't scream. Not yet.

Stealthily I turn my head ever so slightly and stare at the blue pillow beside me. What I see is the face of a young guy, a face that's arresting even in sleep. Maple-brown skin. Straight, buzzed black hair that frames his sculpted features. Bold eyebrows quirked like a question, curly long lashes. Soft, full lips above an angular jawline.

I've never seen this guy in my life.

Yet he's here. So close to me, I can feel his body radiating heat onto my skin. His hair smells like sandalwood, like some exotic forest floor. It's his broad shoulder that my hand's caught under.

His bare shoulder. My bare skin. Oh my god. There's nothing between my skin and his. (How? *How?*) Panic tightens my dry throat, nearly choking me. I turn away from him in stunned horror.

I'm naked in bed with a stranger.

CHAPTER 2

HIM

I DIVE INTO CLEAR, ICY WATER AND SINK DOWN deep. Cold shocks my body through my jeans and T-shirt, seeping into my pores as my boots shake dark mud loose from the rocky bottom. Sparse blades of underwater grass wave back and forth in the silence. And there, scattered on the lake bed all around me, lit by soft sunlight from above, I can see them. Hundreds of human bones. Femurs. Vertebrae. Skulls. Each resting on its own like lonely pieces of coral. Forgotten. But to me they're reminders. This is the place where I am going to die too. I know this, but I'm not afraid.

I'm here for a reason.

A sudden vibration blasts my eardrums, a low rhythmic thumping that rattles every rock and bone in the watery graveyard. I flail toward the surface, toward awareness.

———

My eyes are closed, weighed down with sandbags. I'm warm and dry, breathing air, lying flat. My legs are sweating under a too-hot blanket, all tangled up with someone else's. Long hair tickling my bare chest. Someone else's arm is curled around me, skin that smells like peaches and sunscreen, and like girl. *Mmm.* Feels good.

I relax, head sinking deeper into my pillow, and the dreamscape slips back to me. Cold water flowing over me, underwater grass waving back and forth . . . but before the dream can claim me again, I'm floating to my senses. Millimeter by millimeter, my eyelids rise and brilliant yellow sunshine from the open window streams onto my face. It catches gold highlights in the girl's hair, which drifts gently up and down as I breathe. Blond hair. Light blond. Bright, like wheat. I lean my head closer, wanting to bury my hands in that hair, to feel the wavy strands part between my fingers. But I don't because—it hits me like a shot of adrenaline—because *I have no freaking clue whose hair this is.*

I'm in bed with a girl I don't know.

My heart skips. I pull back my hands . . . and zero in on a tiny scab on my right wrist. Like someone poked me with a pin. I prod it, trying to remember how it got there. Nothing comes to me.

Nothing.

Feeling light-headed, I follow the line of one slightly hairy brown forearm up to a defined bicep, a broad shoulder. A jet black squiggle on my chest catches my eye. Huh. What's that? I strain my neck to examine the ink. A tattoo. A stylized, almond-shaped eye, centered between my pecs.

When did I get this? Again: *nothing.* I'm feeling so dizzy now, I want to throw up. The ink eye, the blond girl, this bed, these hands, I've never seen them before.

No. I *must* have—they didn't just appear out of nowhere. Why don't I remember?

My pulse is hammering. *Think back.* But trying to think back is frustrating, painful, like trying to unpack a suitcase in the dark with just your pinkie finger, and then finding nothing but other people's stuff in it anyway. I remember English words. The rules of baseball. That the stock market crashed in 1929, kicking off the Great Depression. But no matter how deep I dig for it, I can't quite get a picture of my own face. Or my home—where am I from? Who are my friends?

The only thing I can recall is my dream. My dream of dying underwater.

Who *am* I?

CHAPTER 3

HER

A LOUD *THUMP-THUMP* SOUND INVADES THE AIR, making my heart leap toward my throat.

But it's only the alarm clock on the nightstand. A tinny male voice joins the thumping bass, crooning, *"We'll nev-er feel bad any-mo-oh-oh-orrrrre . . ."* Then mystery guy's powerfully built arm swings over my head and punches the clock radio. It dies without a whimper.

Son of a bitch, he managed to hit snooze on the very first try.

In his sleep.

This is his bedroom.

My relief at coming up with that brilliant explanation doesn't last. I know where I am, but how did I get here?

Squinting at the sun's glare, I scan the room help-lessly, searching for anything familiar. On the window wall are three Harry Potter movie posters. Framed. Signed. On the other wall, to my right, a row of photos in bottle-green glass frames. A dark-skinned woman, smiling mysteriously from astride a camel, a sweep of endless dunes behind her. That same woman, clutching a small boy's hand as he gazes up at her with a sweet gap-toothed grin. Then a high school portrait of a guy with playful lips and an angular jawline. His dark eyes sly and intense in their gaze. So that's what he looks like when he's awake. Dangerous.

And still unfamiliar.

And yet last night I walked into this boy's house. Crashed on his twin bed with its faded blue-and-green tartan comforter. Stripped my clothes off . . .

Or did I?

My breathing's gone fast and shallow. What if the reason I don't remember is I never did those things? At least not willingly. Not sober. What if . . . ? It's almost too ugly to think about. But my mind's already there.

What if this guy next to me slipped something into my drink, drugged me, and lured me here?

It's sick. It's scary. It makes him a disgusting dirtbag. It's also the only thing that makes sense.

I have to find my clothes—they must be on the floor somewhere—and sneak out. Now. Before dirtbag wakes up.

Only, when I turn back to check on him, his eyes are open wide. Staring right at me.

I let out a shriek, and before I can think, I'm scrambling out of bed. At the sight of my naked body, his mouth gapes open. I back away from him, clapping my arms over my chest protectively, wishing I had more arms. "Stay away from me, don't touch me!" I'm surprised my voice doesn't shake, because I'm definitely trembling.

The boy averts his gaze. "You seem to be cold. Take this." He pulls the comforter off himself and throws it to me.

Only, I don't think he realized the sheet was tangled up in the comforter. It flies away toward me, leaving *him* naked and exposed. Muttering a curse, he grabs a pillow to cover himself and sits back on the bed.

I wrap the covers around myself like a dress, tying them off at my shoulder, and turn toward the door.

"Excuse me. Wait." He sounds older than he looks. Sophisticated. "This is embarrassing to ask, but . . . how'd I get here?"

I spin around to glare at him. "How stupid do you think I am? We both know this is your room."

"*My* room?" He touches his chest as if affronted by the notion.

I point to his family photos on the wall. He's definitely the guy in the high school photo. Dark brown eyes, almost black, hardly any difference between his pupils and irises.

He shrugs his eyebrows, unimpressed. "Am I supposed to know these people?"

"That guy is *you*." Doubt creeps into my voice though. Does he really not recognize himself? "Or I don't know, maybe that's your twin brother."

"I have a twin?" He narrows his eyes at the photo, tilts his head to either side, lets out a low breath, like he's trying to calm himself. He turns back to me. "Tell me he's not evil, 'cause I've got enough problems."

"You're the evil one," I say, though his responses are rattling me. He sounds just as confused as I feel. "You lured me up here," I say, clinging to my story, a story that made sense in my head. "Last night."

"I don't remember last night." He looks me in the eye. "I don't remember anything. At all."

"But you *have* to." I hate the pleading edge in my voice. We woke up naked, tangled. One of us has to remember it, even if it's because he's the one who drugged me. Somehow neither of us remembering is even worse. Then it's just meaningless, random, out of anyone's control.

"I'm sorry," he says quietly. "I don't even know your name."

Furious, I open my mouth, ready to spit my full name at him, first, middle, and last. But nothing comes out. Because I can't think of it.

It's not on the tip of my tongue either; I don't even know what letter to start with. Jennifer? Anne? Esmeralda? No name sounds right. I try to swallow my panic, to focus my mind and think back to the last time someone called me by my name. But it's hard, because I can't picture who that someone would be. My mother, my father? I try to picture their faces, to remember the last time I saw them, or even anytime I saw them. I try to think back on my friends. My teachers. To mentally call up my favorite subject in school, my favorite sport. But it's all a blank.

My vision's blurring a little; I'm feeling so dizzy, I can barely stand.

It's not just the last few hours I don't remember. I also don't remember the days, months, or years that came before them.

"This isn't happening." My shaking hands rush to my face to feel the contours of my nose, my cheeks, my chin. I grab a few stray strands of hair and hold them up in front of me. Blondish. "This can't be happening to me." Me, that's the only name I have for myself. I'm the voice in my head, I'm the heart pounding like a rabbit's. Nameless, faceless Me. I could be anyone.

"Hey, I'm really sorry." He lowers his voice. "Believe me, I know that's not right. That I don't remember your name. If it helps, I . . . I don't remember mine either." He gazes at me searchingly. "Do *you* know my name?"

For a moment I can glimpse the trusting little boy from the picture in his face, and I feel a stab of sympathy despite myself. His terror and confusion match mine. I lean closer, something deep inside me wanting to believe him. "I don't remember anything either," I tell him.

"Serious?"

"Yeah. So . . . if you didn't drug me, how did this happen?"

His eyes widen, then flash with hurt. "Fuck, you thought I roofied you? You think I'm a *perv*?"

A twinge of guilt tugs at me. "Well, what am I supposed to think? I wake up"—*naked*—"in a strange guy's room . . ."

"I told you, this isn't my room. Anyway, what drug could wipe out your whole memory?"

I fold my arms. "How would I know? I don't *remember* anything."

"That makes no sense," he informs me. "I may have forgotten who I am, but I remember all kinds of other stuff, and so do you or we couldn't be having this conversation." He's right. "And there's no drug I know of that does this."

"Then poison, whatever." How else could this happen to two people at the same time?

"What poison?"

I throw up my hands. "I don't care what did this, I just want my memory back!"

"And I don't think we can fix it till we know what it is." He swallows. "It *could* be some new drug. Highly experimental. Classified."

A cool shiver runs down my back. Exactly what are the two of us mixed up in? "Let's find our clothes and get the hell out of here," I say. "We can argue when we know we're safe."

"Deal." He points to a corner by the door, to an untidy mound of white fabric. "That looks promising."

Cautiously, not disturbing my blanket-dress, I bend to investigate. White Keds, a stretchy white top, and a jean skirt. Something pink and lacy slips out of the skirt and tumbles to the floor.

I hold the skirt up to my body. It's tiny. An ultramini. "These aren't my clothes."

"Well, I doubt they'd fit me."

"I would never wear that skirt."

"Hey." He shivers. "Right now *I'd* wear it if I could get both legs in it."

He's right. Who cares if it's mine, it just has to cover me while we escape. "Fine. Could you, um, face the back wall, please?"

"You want me to roll over?" He gives me a look. "I'm kind of naked here."

Like I hadn't noticed. "This may be hard for you to believe, but I have no desire to stare at your ass."

"Okay. Whatever. Not worth arguing over." He shrugs and turns around. And I can't help it. I check out his ass. Just for a second.

Then I grit my teeth and pull the tight little top over my head. I step into the miniskirt, and am shocked when the zipper actually fastens to the top. I slip on the Keds, then look down at myself. The outfit kisses my every curve and contour like a second skin.

It's a perfect fit.

CHAPTER 4

HIM

YOU'D THINK SHE'D BE HAPPIER NOT TO BE
naked anymore, but she's frowning down at herself in
bewilderment, her heart-shaped face looking like it's about
to crumple. She truly hates these clothes, hates that they
fit her like they were made for her. I know why. It means
she can't trust her instincts. I feel a sympathy knot tighten
in my throat.

"Hey." My voice comes out gruff. "It's going to be
okay, all right?" Which means, don't cry. If you cry right
now *I will come apart.*

"Don't." Her head snaps back up. "Please don't go all
macho and protective. This is going to be harder if I have
to babysit your male ego on top of everything else."

Okay, then.

While my male ego is recovering, she starts tearing
around the room. Bending to survey the messy floor,
reporting on every item of junk she unearths. "Extension

cables. Video game packaging." Getting dressed—even in clothes she hates—has changed her from a block of frozen fear into a hurricane. "Hershey's Kisses." Crushing the foils into a ball and hurling them into a beige plastic trash bin. She riffles through the chest of drawers next and tosses me several pairs of black jeans in various stages of fade.

I waste no time in gratefully pulling on the first pair I get my hands on. They're baggy and threadbare, but at least they don't drag under my heels. I spot a gray sweatshirt sleeve poking from underneath the bed, dive for it, and pull it over my head.

I peek deeper under the bed, hoping to find my shoes. In addition to a ton of dust and a metal baseball bat are a pair of black sneakers. Something small under the bed catches my eye. At first I think it's a sock, but when I pick it up I realize it's a dust-covered velvet bag. Heaving with coins, from the sound of it.

I loosen the drawstring and hold up one coin to the light. "Whoa." It's elliptical-shaped, the words embossed on its shiny surface written in an alphabet I don't recognize. "I think this might be Chinese."

"It's possible. . . ." She bites her lower lip. "Whoever drugged us could have taken us to Asia."

I let that sink in. Cold slithers up from the pit of my stomach, spreading toward the eye tattoo I don't remember getting. How are we supposed to get back home when we don't know where we are, or where home is?

Wordlessly I cross the room and join her by the desk. Its surface is stacked with dusty, clothbound books and scraps of onionskin paper with singed edges. A Mac laptop sits open, but it's password-protected. Figures. She holds up a white envelope and shakes it, excited. "Here's a report card from Summer Falls Senior High School in Summer Falls, Colorado."

I let out a breath I didn't know I was holding. We're in America.

She unfolds a tripled-up white page. "It's for someone named Marshall King. Name ring any bells?"

"Zero."

"Not for me either." She shrugs. "He's pulling Ds."

I'm about to say he sounds too *stupid* to be our kidnapper when she pushes the laptop screen shut. Half a dozen fat pillar candles appear behind it, arrayed in a semicircle from lightest (the white one, melted down to a nub) to darkest (the barely used black one).

Fear tightens my chest. A black candle means black magic.

Wait a minute. Black magic? Where'd *that* thought come from—some stupid horror movie? Magic doesn't exist in the real world. Does it? I stand there frozen, suddenly uncertain of which way is up.

But the girl doesn't even notice the black candle. Ignoring it, she lifts the cover of the thickest book on the desk and reads aloud in a sarcastic tone, *"Darkest Secrets of the Occult."* Her nostrils flare in disgust. "Okay, this guy's a nutcase."

Right. Because only crazy people believe in magic; magic isn't real, *duh*. Glad I kept my mouth shut for once. "New theory," I announce. "Psycho here kidnapped us to use as virgin sacrifices." That last quip rolls off my tongue before I've thought it through, and then my face feels hot and I can't look at her. From the silence on her end I'd bet money she's blushing too. Are either one of us virgins? Were we virgins before last night?

She reaches down to the carpet under the desk chair and holds up a gold chalice, its handle carved to look like two snakes embracing. "Where would you even buy a cup like this?"

"DarklordMcSpookyPantsdotcom? Free shipping."

She glares at me. "Stop making jokes. This is freaking me out." It's freaking me out too, which is why I keep making jokes.

I peer down at the dregs of some thick red liquid at the bottom of the chalice. "There's no way that could be blood, right?"

"Jesus." She drops the golden cup.

It thumps softly onto the carpet just as heavy footsteps pound the hall. Then a fist bangs on the door.

"Hey!" a male voice thunders. "You in there?"

Marshall King.

Her startled green eyes meet mine, and the strangest feeling runs through me. The danger's inescapable, just like in my dream. I'm scared, but not for me. For her. I won't let anything happen to her. I jump to my feet, motioning for her to get away from the door. She looks unsure, but slides down into the corner behind the bed. I reach under the box spring and grab the metal bat.

"I said, *are you in there?*"

The door swings inward, and there in the doorway, dressed all in black, stands a mountain-size bald man.

CHAPTER 5

HER

"THERE YOU ARE." I'M FROZEN BEHIND THE
unmade bed, clammy with scared sweat, but the huge
man in the doorway doesn't even see me. He's not really
looking inside the room as he rocks from side to side.
"*Knew* you hadn't gone anywhere." I can barely hear him
over my pounding pulse. "I'm not dead yet." A note of
unmistakable anger enters his voice. "Don't pretend you
can't hear me."

The dark-eyed boy squares his stance. "Don't get any
closer." He's as scared as I am.

"Huh? Why not?" The big man tilts his pale face, rubs
his salt-and-pepper chin stubble in confusion. Then he
finally looks straight ahead. At me, with my obvious bed
hair, my tight, white, slutty look-at-me skirt and top. My
throat seizes. I'm ready to run. But his bloodshot eyes light
up. "Whoa, hey there! Almost didn't recognize you." He
rushes toward me and I let out a scream, but the dark-eyed

boy steps between us, his cool, carved face intense, the baseball bat in his hands.

"Don't touch her," he says, brandishing the bat. "Who are you?" he demands. "What drug did you give us?"

I add my voice to his. "How'd we end up in this place? What's going on?"

The man's mouth opens wide. "I don't believe it," he whispers, fingers twisting the bottom of his faded heavy-metal band T-shirt. "We never should have brought him here," he says, as if he's talking to someone else, someone who's not even there.

With a stumbling step forward, he reaches into the pocket of his jeans.

The dark-eyed boy pivots toward the closed window, aims the bat over his head, and cracks it down, shattering the glass.

"No!" the big man roars, sounding crazed now. "Please, stop it. You don't know what you're doing."

Smash. He brings the bat down again and again. Crystal shards flying free, out into the vibrant blue sky.

The man dives at the dark-eyed boy, trying to take him down from the knees. "Stop it, stop or you'll break down the wards!"

Whatever that means. Not waiting to find out, I slip around them to the window and stare down. Ten feet below is an overgrown side yard. Jagged pieces of glass sparkle from the windowsill. Grabbing the bulky comforter off the floor, I toss it on the sill and jump through the frame.

Behind me I hear a yell of pain, coming from the man, I think. Then I'm dropping, tumbling to the ground outside. I land in tall, soft grass. Flat on my butt.

For a moment I just sit there, dazed by the sunlight, by the sheer beauty of the world outside that bedroom. The lawn is Technicolor green, dewy-soft, thick with dandelions. Drenched yellow petals, cobweb fluff, and bare stems. Then there's a *thump* in the grass, and I turn to see that the dark-eyed boy has landed in a crouch behind me.

"Walk wide, most of the glass fell near the rosebush." He's already on his feet, holding his outstretched hand to me. "Let's go!"

I hesitate only for a moment, looking back up toward the bedroom. The gnarled, thin branches of a rosebush loom over us, its bloodred blooms climbing halfway to the broken window, where the big man still stands watching us, his face a mask of rage and devastation. Then he's gone from the window. No doubt heading for the door.

Groaning, I haul myself up to my feet, and we sprint down the sidewalk. The sleepy suburban street is silent except for birds, and our footfalls echo off the wood-panel houses. We zip down six or seven sunny blocks, burning off adrenaline, then cross one street over and go another ten blocks. Each house looks almost exactly like the one before it: two stories, painted white or yellow, trimmed with brown or dark green shutters. Frantically, my eyes hunt for a landmark to pass on to the police, but there are no street signs anywhere. Where are we?

After each block I twist around to squint behind me through the glittering sunlight, expecting to see the big man gaining on us, his agitated, desperate face in my face. Each time he isn't there, I feel a surge of gratitude, of elation. "He's not following," I say, finally. "We lost him." We slow to a brisk walk.

"Guess I really scared the bastard," he says with equal measures of pride and surprise. "I didn't even have to hit him," he adds. "Once I broke that window he just about fell apart. It was almost too easy."

I resist the urge to roll my eyes. It's not his fault I didn't think to grab that bat myself but stood there panicking like a moron instead. "Breaking the glass was inspired," I admit.

He shrugs. "I did what I had to do." I think back to how hurt and offended he looked when I told him I'd thought he drugged me. Now it makes sense. He's the hero type.

What type am I? Am I a prodigy? A science nerd? A hacker? Why was *I* chosen to be kidnapped and taken from my home? The questions only stir a gnawing hunger in me for the truth, no matter how shattering.

"I'm going to ring these people's doorbell." I point to the nearest house. "We can use their phone to call nine-one-one."

"Great idea."

No one answers though, so we run back down the front steps and move on to the next house. And the next.

The narrow, tree-lined street's empty of cars.

"Everyone's at work," I say, realizing. Duh. "Or school."

He shakes his head. "There's got to be one person in this town who works from home. A stay-at-home parent. A retired person."

At the sixth house, a German shepherd growls at us from a side yard, then hurls itself against the fence. Dark-Eyed Boy puts his arm around me and together we back away slowly.

After twenty-three doors, in an untamed front yard infested by giant sunflowers, a tiny, wrinkled lady with her salt-and-pepper hair in pigtails answers.

"My goodness." She adjusts her glasses with shaking fingers and peers up at us. "Why did I think it was a school day?"

"Ma'am, we need a doctor." Dark-Eyed Boy's voice sounds different, his cool intensity replaced by Boy Scout charm. "Can we please use your phone?"

"Who is it, Hazel?" a grouchy old male voice calls from inside.

Hazel shuffles back and opens the door wider, revealing her faded flower-sprigged housedress and teal terrycloth slippers. She's a lot older than I initially thought. "It's *kids*," she yells back, sounding happy but confused. "But shouldn't you be in school, or, wait . . . Is it summer already? I thought it was fair weekend. What month is it now?" she asks pleasantly.

Dark-Eyed Boy and I exchange a glance as if to say, Did she really ask what *month* it is? Then again it's not like we know either. Senility has lots in common with amnesia.

"We just need your phone," I say, trying to get things back on track. "To call nine-one-one."

"Golly, nine-one-*one*!" Hazel shakes her pigtails and smiles a toothless smile. "You mean like on TV shows?" She mimics a siren.

"Excuse me." Dark-Eyed Boy cuts her off. He sounds impatient now, like himself again. "Do you *have* a phone we can use? Or internet access?"

"Please," I add. "We're stranded. We have no one else to ask."

"Hold on, just let me think on this . . . Phone . . . Phone bill . . ." The woman pauses and tugs at her pigtail. Then she blinks. "Hey, what were we talking about?"

A chill rakes the back of my neck. I may not know my past, but she can't even hold on to the present moment. I'd rather die than live like her.

Dark-Eyed Boy swallows. "Never mind. Do you know where the nearest hospital is?"

"You mean the Main Street Clinic," she says. "If they're still open, that is. I stay away from doctors, that's why I'm healthy as a horse. That's what my daughter says—stay away from the doctor. He'll just make you sick."

I don't bother to tell her she and her daughter have got it backward. "Just please tell us which way is Main Street?" I pray she remembers that at least.

But instead of answering me Hazel chuckles, puts her hand on the door. "I'm real busy today," she says, with a proud smile. "Mayor's wife asked me to bake twelve dozen cookies for the fair. Want a hot snickerdoodle, you come back in an hour. You too, young man." With that, she lets the door click shut.

We trudge back to the sidewalk, somewhat stunned.

"Well, that was weird." I sigh. "She was a lot older and, um, battier than I first thought."

"It's okay, we still learned something." He puts his hands on my shoulders. "All we have to do is get to the Main Street Clinic."

"But we don't even know which way to go."

"We can guess," he says. "I say we start heading north."

"Why north?" I'm starting to get annoyed at the way he talks. His eternal confidence, his lightning-bolt decision making. Let's do this, I say we do that. "Which way is north anyway?"

"I don't know, all right?" He throws his hands up. "It seemed better than standing here arguing, giving Dr. Psycho a chance to catch up with us. You have a better idea? Speak up."

I'm about to say that I *did* speak up, and that having a plan doesn't mean you have a *good* plan, when out of the corner of my eye, I see a moving dot. A block away, a woman in a sundress is pushing a baby stroller up the street. "Oh, thank god! We'll just ask her to point out Main Street."

"What are you talking about?" He spins, not even looking in the right direction.

"Down the hill." I point to her stroller's wheels, rolling

toward us along the bumpy sidewalk.

"I don't see anything." He still sounds irritated.

She's only half a block away now. A tall Asian woman, glamorous-looking, like she stepped out of the pages of a Tokyo fashion magazine. Glossy hair in an updo, iridescent silver eye shadow, blue knee-length dress with a tiny matching shrug over it, and clear high-heeled sandals. I smile at her. Please be carrying a cell phone. Then I look into the stroller's buggy and see only a white rattle resting on the pink blanket. Where's the baby? No baby. She's pushing an empty stroller. A chill twists its way down my spine.

There's got to be some explanation. Maybe she's on her way to loan the stroller to a friend with a new baby. Or test-driving it before she buys it used.

Or maybe she's bat-shit crazy.

The woman's eyes lock on mine with a hungry focus, and that's when her skin starts to shimmer ever so slightly. Tiny hairs rise on the back of my neck.

"Run!" I yell, and I'm half a block away myself before I turn to see Dark-Eyed Boy's still standing there, looking at me quizzically. The shimmering woman reaches out her long ghostly arms toward him. My breath catches in my throat. But before she can touch him, a faint blue light flashes between them, and instantly she's blown back five feet, thrown onto her back.

Holy shit.

CHAPTER 6

HIM

"HEY, WHAT ARE WE RUNNING FROM?" I YELL, but she's already sixty feet away.

That's when I feel the stinging zap in my chest. A soft blue light blinks across my vision.

What the hell?

Am I cracking up, having some kind of flashback?

Slowly I catch up to the girl, dreading telling her the truth, that I failed to see whatever she was warning me away from. That instead I saw some weird blue light. That there's a nonzero chance I'm losing my marbles.

But as I approach she's looking up at me with wide-eyed awe. "What did you do to that woman?"

"Nothing, I . . ." Never even noticed her. I look around, desperately hoping I'll catch a glimpse this time. "She must have gone away."

"No, she's right *there*!" The girl points at the empty street. "She wandered back to her baby-free stroller and now she's shambling away. How can you not see her?"

My heart sinks. Either the woman is there or she isn't. And either way . . . "One of us is imagining things," I say quietly. If it's her, then I'd still have my wits about me to look out for her till we get help . . . but the blue light thing makes me fear we're *both* losing touch. "Come on, let's get back to looking for Main Street." I put my hand on her shoulder, but she pushes it off.

"Don't tell me what to do," she snaps. "There's no way I imagined all that. I'm telling you, the lady started to shimmer. Her eyes went all hyperfocused like she was in a trance, and then she *went for us*."

I blow out my lower lip with my breath. "I'm trying to keep an open mind here. But you realize how crazy that sounds?"

"I'm not going to lie to you just so I don't sound crazy."

I swallow. That one hit home, since I was doing exactly that in censoring my blue-light moment. "If she was going to attack us," I say, "what stopped her?"

"I thought you did, somehow," she says. "There was this blue light all around you and she flew back and landed—"

"Wait a minute, you saw the blue light?"

She nods.

I don't know whether to be relieved or just more confused. If two people see something, does that make it real? I touch my chest where I'd felt the zap. My fingertip's pressing right on the smooth texture of my tattoo, the Egyptian eye. I shake my head. "There's got to be some logical explanation."

"Can you even consider the possibility that I saw something you didn't? Or couldn't?"

"I do believe you that you saw something," I assure her. "Or *think* you did . . ." Wrong thing to say. Error. Massive fail.

"In other words, you think I'm losing it." She burns me with her retinas of judgment. "You think whatever caused our memory loss is eating the rest of my brain. Well, I know what I saw."

"Then why didn't I see it too?"

She shakes her head like it's a stupid question. "Not the point."

"Okay, what is the point then?"

She says nothing.

"I'm sorry, what do you want me to say?"

We're walking three feet apart at this point.

Considering my bleak situation, what should I care if some equally screwed-up but gorgeous girl I just met thinks I'm an ass? But every second she's silent, an aching divide is widening between us.

Finally she turns to me, her anger bubbling over. "The point is, why didn't you run when I said run? *I* would have done it." But I didn't run, I think, and nothing happened. "Why didn't you just *trust* me? Like I trusted you."

I know what she's talking about. How I pushed her down into the corner behind the bed, out of sight of the bald man. Quietly I say, "Why *did* you trust me? You had no reason to."

28

"Why?" The intense look in her eyes melts a little. It's like she knows what I'm really asking. I'm asking her to tell me who I am, in her eyes. It's fucked up, but I'll believe whatever she tells me. "You seemed so sure I would—*should*—trust you at the time," she said, "and that's probably part of why I decided to. Something about you . . . felt safe."

Her saying that makes my chest hurt, and I want to reach over and take her hand. I want to smooth things over, say "I trust you too. I believe you. Next time you tell me to run, I'll run." But after her weird hallucination just now, I really am concerned, and something in me doesn't want to lie to her. Instead I say simply, "Thank you."

She breathes a huge sigh, and I glance up and this time I see exactly what she's seeing: a big green street sign with white letters, the first sign we've seen. Main Street.

We let out spontaneous whoops and high-five each other.

"We made it!" I'm so excited, I throw my arms around her. At first she stiffens at my touch, then cautiously she gives me a small hug back. Though I'm a foot taller, our bodies instantly find a way to fit just right together, making me wonder how many times we've stood this close. Or lain this close. The peaches-and-summer-grass scent of her skin is driving me insane, reminding me of this morning . . .

As if she can read my mind, she pulls away and takes a step back from me. "So, um, which way do you think the clinic is?"

I look out to the right, at a faint row of moss-green hills on the horizon line. The biggest more like a mountain. "Downtown's probably away from the hills, not toward them."

After seven or eight blocks, the road widens and the little wood-panel houses give way to public buildings. A squat, brick, square post office. A church with a spire. A library with Greek columns. I feel a deep sense of relief to be in a town. Even if it's not an especially bustling town. These buildings look new—brand-new—but they're old-fashioned. There are no chain stores. The shops look ancient, independent. Founders Pub. Hinklebeck's Antiques. Mollie's Milkshakes. In the window of Mollie's we linger a second in front of our reflections, which look faint and ghostly.

"My face doesn't look like my face." She frowns at herself, then turns away.

I know what she means. I'm not used to my own face either. The guy in that photo on the wall looked like a jackass, so it bugs me to think she pegged me for him.

The center square features a bronze statue of an austere man in a morning coat and top hat. The square itself is empty except for a young woman lying asleep across a picnic table, pale limbs sprawling, mouth wide, raggedy carrot-colored hair blowing in the breeze.

The girl leans toward me. "You can see her too, right?"

I nod. "Creepy."

We pass a tiny police station with a single squad car in front. Colorado plates.

"Maybe we should go there first," I say, thinking aloud. "Missing-children reports get sent everywhere around the country, and if our families are looking for us—"

"Families." She stops walking, covers her mouth with her hand. "I just realized, I don't even know if I have one."

"You *do* have a family." I pat her back. "You have a name and an identity and people who love you. I'm sure of it."

"Thanks. I'm sure you do too."

It's kind of sad, but it's the nicest thing we can think of to say to each other right now.

Right across from the post office is the Main Street Clinic. She turns toward it. "If I'm going to sound crazy," she says, "I'd rather talk to a doctor than a cop."

"We're not crazy. But you may have a point."

We power walk into the empty waiting room and march right up to the front counter. The receptionist glances up from the pages of her supermarket glossy. She's twenty-something, with fiery eyebrows dyed to match her hair, and the moment she lays eyes on the girl she crosses her arms over her pointy chest. "So what'd you do now, Miss Prom Queen?" she asks in a cheerful drawl. "Bang your knee? Break your little finger? Your ankle seems to be doing okay," she adds.

The girl and I look at each other. First Hazel, now this extra-quirky receptionist. This town has too much character for its own good.

"Excuse me." The girl takes a deep breath. "I don't know what you're talking about—have we met before? I'm having memory problems. I—we—need to see a doctor as soon as possible."

The receptionist swallows. "Now that's not funny," she says finally, her smile fading at the edges, voice tinged with disapproval.

"It's not supposed to be," the girl says, frowning. "We need to see a doctor as soon as possible."

"The doctor doesn't appreciate it when people pull pranks."

Okay, I've had enough of local color. "Lady, this is not a joke!" I bang my fist on the counter. "Look, I can see why you'd be suspicious, given the likely fact you probably watched a ton of soap operas where people got amnesia. But sometimes it happens to real, live people too. And those people need to set up doctors' appointments, which happens to be, you know, *your job.*"

She shuts her mouth and gives me an appraising stare, as if she just now noticed my existence. Then she tosses her hair, lets out an uncomfortable laugh, and turns back to the girl. "Damn, when'd you get yourself a new boyfriend?"

I glare into her eyes and speak slowly and clearly. "We need medical help. Can. You. Help. Us?"

"Don't you worry, hon, I've got the cure for what ails you." She picks up a beige phone receiver and her pink oval nails click on its lit number buttons. "Sheriff Hank, I got a couple of truants here. Yep, malingerers." Fluffing her hair in a flirty way. "Could you please escort Miss Alton to school again?"

Miss Alton? The girl's last name is Alton?

"She's got a partner in crime this time—no, it's another kid. It's . . ." She squints at me. "Well, that's funny, I can't place him." She looks troubled for a moment, then says, "You're right, he's got to be one of Liz's guests." The phone snaps back into its cradle.

The girl, aka Miss Alton, and I stare at each other, both of us shell-shocked.

She recovers first. "So I guess we're going to the police first after all."

CHAPTER 7

HER

ALTON. MY LAST NAME IS ALTON. I TURN THE word over in my head, but repeating it doesn't help ring any bells. "Kerry," I say, reading the receptionist's name tag. "Can you . . . please tell me what my first name is? Where do I live? How old am I?"

The receptionist rolls her eyes, licks her finger, flips a page in her magazine. My face turns hot. What did I ever do to her? But as I watch her fish a compact from her oversize purse and treat her lips to a fresh coat of hot pink, I wonder . . . What *did* I ever do to her? I've been assuming I'm a decent person. A person people would want to help if she were in trouble. But how do I know? Before I lost my memory, I could have been any kind of person at all. For the millionth time my mind flashes back to that moment of waking up: naked, in a boy's bed. Is he my boyfriend, or is there some other explanation for how we woke up? Or . . . my heart sinks . . . was I just the kind of person who went around taking my clothes off in random guys' beds?

We can hear the sheriff's boots before the door swings open. He's a youngish man, with a steady, ice-blue gaze and sandy curls. The star on his mushroom-colored uniform is so shiny it looks fake, like a prop from some old Western. His sleeves are rolled up neatly to show off his biceps, but his uneven, sandy mustache ruins the effect for me.

But not for Kerry.

"Hank, you're a lifesaver!" A whiff of hair spray hits my nostrils as she sashays by to squeeze the sheriff's bicep. You'd think he was rescuing her from cannibals.

"Just doing my job." He gives her an easy smile. "Let's go, Elyse." The sheriff's hand feels intimidatingly large against my shoulder blades. "You are going to school if I have to handcuff you and drag you there."

"Why do you care more about my attendance record than my health?" I clench my teeth.

"Elyse," Dark-Eyed Boy repeats under his breath, and it dawns on me then. That's what the sheriff just called me.

I thought for sure when I heard my own name that I would know it . . . that it would sound *right*. Elyse doesn't sound right at all. It's girly, brittle. I hate it. It's not me. I'm not an Elyse.

I burst into tears.

"I'm not named Elyse," I manage to say between sobs. "And I'm not going to school. I don't even know where the fucking school is. I just want to go home. But I don't know where home is either."

Everyone stares at me, including Dark-Eyed Boy. First the invisible mommy incident and now a hysterical cry-fest—he must think I'm cracking up for sure. Then Kerry and the sheriff lock eyes.

"Sounds like she forgot her own name," he says, and nervously he peeks behind Kerry at the closed door to the clinic proper. "Aren't we supposed to tell the—"

"No, it's not worth bothering him yet." She lowers her voice. "We'll wait and see if she gets better. Kids her age almost never get sent away."

Sent away where? My breathing's gone rapid and shallow. What do these two know that we don't? Dark-Eyed Boy moves to stand in front of me. He must be wondering the same thing I am: What happens if this doctor finds out we have amnesia? Is it some kind of crime around here?

"She's just having a moment," Kerry says. "Just part of life. We all get them."

"Ain't that the truth," Sheriff Hank muses, rubbing his big chin. "Well, I wouldn't want to waste the doctor's time. I'll take 'em both to Liz." Who is this Liz? I think, but I don't say it out loud. I'm scared now. "Get in the car, Elyse." Once again he uses the name that doesn't feel like mine. "Bring your new friend. We're going home."

———

I stare out the window, numb, as Sheriff Hank's squad car barrels past the downtown building cluster and hangs a sharp right toward the hills. Hemlock and fir trees surround us, scenting the air green with their needles.

Strapped into the backseat next to me, Dark-Eyed Boy reaches for my hand. I wipe mine on my skirt, clenching the fabric in my fist, before taking his.

I lean toward him and whisper, "I'm nervous about meeting my own family."

"At least people recognize you," he whispers back. "No one remembers me at all. It's like . . . I never existed."

"You exist, believe me." My life would suck even more without you.

He looks me in the eyes. "I don't even know my name."

"I think of you as Dark-Eyed Boy," I say, blushing before the words are even out of my mouth.

"Gonna have to take your word for it. I've never looked in a mirror." He squeezes my hand before letting go. "Check that out."

I look up to see that the trees have given way to an amazing view. Pouring down the side of a green mountain capped with a shining white glacier is a waterfall. The drop is dramatic, more than a thousand feet down to the lake below. As we get closer the sounds of pounding water grow louder, and I can't stop staring, turning my head to gaze at it even after we've driven past.

There's a turnoff ahead and a green sign with an arrow reading: "To E. Preston State Mental Health Facility, 5 miles." Dark-Eyed Boy and I look at each other. For a terrible moment I'm worried that Sheriff Hank is driving to the insane asylum, but instead he turns onto a long, winding concrete driveway.

A still blue lake looms into view, and the house in front of it looks more like a mini castle.

"Here we are, gang!" Hank announces in his superhero-smug baritone. "Preston House, on the lake."

I blink up at the three stone stories with a tower at each end, then at the eight-foot-high wooden door. "I live here?" All the houses in the neighborhood we walked through would have low self-esteem if they could see this place. "Just . . . me and my family?"

"And all the tourists," Hank says cheerily.

"Oh," we both say, getting it at the same time. It's an inn, a bed-and-breakfast. It isn't just our house.

I'm relieved. I don't think I would want to be that rich.

Hank parks between two new white, midsize cars—rentals, I'm guessing—and we step out onto smooth white concrete. As we cross a picturesque bridge over a man-made stream just to get onto the lush front lawn, I see a woman working on her knees in one of the circular purple flower beds. An elegant woman in oversize sunglasses, light brown hair tied up in a fancy twist. She sets down her weeding tool, yanks off her gloves, and rushes over to us. "What's the trouble now, Hank? Must be bad if you had to pull her out of school."

"Liz." The sheriff takes off his hat. "Sorry to interrupt your busy day."

"It's no interruption." Her voice is silky, reasonable, one of those voices companies use to record phone announcements. "Being a mom is my most important job."

Then why didn't you know I stayed out all night and wasn't even in school?

"Elyse showed up in the clinic again." Hank lowers his voice. "Seems to be having another moment—"

"You mean all this fuss is over a moment?" Liz rips off her sunglasses, revealing tired blue eyes and crow's-feet. "Hank, what are you talking about?"

"Are you actually my mother?" I blurt out. "Because you sound like an idiot right now. Let's be clear, I'm not having a moment. I have no memories. Of anything before this morning. As in, you're a stranger, and if I'm on some experimental reality TV show, I just want to say to the fans out there: *I did not sign up for this bullshit.*"

She pats her forehead with her fingers, like she's checking herself for fever but never takes her eyes off me. "Honey. Are you *trying* to scare me?"

"Of course she is, Mrs. Alton," Hank says, though his sureness sounds forced. "Acting out for attention. I know you'll straighten her out. She's so young, still."

She's only a kid. I feel a chill remembering the receptionist's hushed tones when she said it would be better for the doctor not to know. "It's not, like, a crime to have amnesia, is it?"

"Elyse." Dark-Eyed Boy's eyes scream at me, *Back off on the amnesia.* "Stop pretending, okay?"

Weirdly, Liz takes that moment to notice Dark-Eyed Boy at last. "Oh, hello there," she says, tilting her head and squinting as if she can't figure out how he got to be where he is, so close to us, listening in on our conversation. Finally she snaps her fingers. "Ah, you're Jim. I didn't make the connection before." Jim? "You stayed with us a couple years back, right?" She flashes a friendly, *professional* smile at Dark-Eyed Boy—as if all this ugliness with her troublemaking daughter is now behind us all. "Welcome back to Preston House. How was the flight from New York?"

New York? Baffled, we both stare at the slim-wristed, diamond-ring-fingered hand she's extending.

Then, with barely a moment's hesitation, Dark-Eyed Boy shakes it. "Not too bad," he says, studiously not making eye contact with me. "But then I got lost downtown. Thank goodness the sheriff offered me a ride."

What the hell? I don't know who he is, but I do know he spent the past few hours sleeping and running and searching for help, not flying here from New York. He just lied, cold-blooded lied.

And his lying means he's not backing up my story. Which makes me look crazy. Crazier. So much for us being a team.

"My work here is done." Sheriff Hank tips his hat as he puts it back on.

Liz thanks him for all his hard work and waves him off. "You must be so tired," she says to Dark-Eyed Boy as the sheriff-mobile's engine starts up. "Here, let me give you the grand tour. Oh, where are your bags?"

"Lost at the airport," he adds smoothly. "I've had quite the day."

Quite the day. I marvel at the way he's managed to make himself sound older, mature enough to book a hotel room. Same way he was able to make himself sound more Boy Scout harmless when he was talking to Hazel.

Liz clucks. "They say travel can be so stressful." Her voice is bright again. Either she's really good at hiding her feelings, or the reality of my amnesia hasn't quite sunk in. Or hasn't upset her. I hope she's hiding her feelings.

Dark-Eyed Boy squeezes my shoulder, a silent thank-you for not ratting him out, and together we follow Liz toward the mini castle. Up the stone steps, onto the vine-covered porch, where a carved wooden swing blows eerily in the breeze, into a cavernous, mirrored, marble foyer. Liz shuts the door behind us.

CHAPTER 8

DARK-EYED BOY

SURE. I LIED. I TOLD THAT WOMAN WHAT SHE already wanted to hear, and running that con didn't even make my pulse speed up. But I did it because I had to.

I'm not leaving Elyse alone here, not until I know she'll be safe.

Even if she is glaring at me from the front parlor sofa while Liz—chattering nonstop about the house and its hundred-and-twenty-year history—leads me down a wide hallway toward the room Jim reserved.

The hallway is carpeted in deep blue and lined with blue-painted doors, the wall space between them plastered with black-and-white photographs. Judging from the doors' nameplates, proudly scripted in silver, the rooms are competing for cheesiest name ever: Suite Nostalgia Lane. The Summer Romance. The Happy Family Suite.

"You're going to love the Country Sun," Liz gushes. "It's one of my favorite rooms."

Bullshit. Like she's ever going to tell people, *Sorry, you picked one of the crappy rooms?*

I put on a smile and pray that the real Jim never shows. "Awesome."

We breeze past more doors and more silver frames, some locket-size, some as large as plates and ornately carved, showing austere, unsmiling people who couldn't possibly still be on this planet. Elyse's ancestors? Or just the rich people who lived in this house, before it became an inn? Was the Suite Nostalgia Lane where the butler slept?

The Country Sun is a huge bedroom with a comfy-looking quilt on the king-size bed, a sunburst-orange-painted ceiling that matches the paint on the bed's wooden headboard, and geese on the wallpaper. No phone. No TV. The geese appear to be wearing blue neck ribbons.

"Hey, is there wi-fi in the house?"

"Our computer with internet access is in the library." She sounds disapproving. "But if you're not too tired, I recommend you check out the trails in Waterfall Park today."

"Love to, but . . ." I have way more important things to do than stare at some waterfall. I point to my sneakers. "I'm not exactly prepared to hike."

She clucks over my supposedly lost luggage. "Airlines these days—the pilots are asleep and the bag checkers are a bunch of crooks and thieves. You hear things on CNN . . ." She trails off vaguely. "That's why I don't fly."

I get the distinct feeling she's never been anywhere near an airport, period.

"But the trails are *really* easy to get to." Liz is beginning to sound like a waiter pushing the halibut special. "City people always say they didn't realize how much they loved nature till they walked on our state-of-the-art paved trails with handrails. Why, I could walk up the mountain in these heels!"

Dutifully I glance down at her skinny-heeled pale pink sandals. Doesn't sound much like being in nature to me, but I don't argue. I want her to leave so I can start digging around for information.

A door clicks shut out in the hallway and I hear a man's voice and a woman's trilling laughter.

"That's the Bishops." Liz beams with pride. "They first came here on their honeymoon when Elyse was three. They come back every year for their anniversary."

"That's nice. I—"

"You should meet them!" She walks out into the hall where a thirtysomething couple is kissing and whispering to each other like teenagers in love. "Frank and Lucia, this is Jim's first visit to Summer Falls." She squints at me. "I *think*."

"Oh, a virgin." Lucia smiles. She's model-thin with platinum blond hair down to her butt.

"Only when it comes to waterfalls." I wink at her, hoping she thinks I seem old enough to book my own hotel room.

"Where you from?" Her bald husband reminds me of a pit bull with his reddish-rimmed eyes and alert posture.

I realize that Liz has slipped away, leaving me alone with them.

"New York." Please don't be New Yorkers.

"Chicago." Frank says the word like it's a challenge. He extends a hand and I know before I even shake it that he's going to crush my bones. "We're heading downtown for a pitcher of beer, if you want to tag along."

"Beer?" Lucia nudges him. "Sweets, I thought we were going to go antiquing."

"Baby, tomorrow. Let's just go to Founders and chill out. You in, New York Jim?"

For a moment I'm so deep into my cover of pretending to be Jim that I consider drinking a beer with them. Then I remember: I'd need ID that says I am twenty-one, and of course I don't have ID, period. Because I don't know who the hell I am. Screw beer. I need to get online. "Maybe I'll catch up later," I say, and hook my thumb down the hall in the direction of the library.

"Just remember, all work and no play makes you crazy," Frank cautions helpfully from behind me.

The library is a cozy room with a round blue rug in the center and dark floor-to-ceiling built-in shelves on every wall. There's an antique writing desk in one corner with a tiny laptop on it that looks eerily anachronistic. Hanging over the desk is a retro-style poster, a side view showing an American family in a snazzy green convertible. Dad's driving, with slicked-back hair and glasses, Mom's blond hair peeking from a red kerchief beside him, junior in the backseat, all three aglow with delight as they gaze toward the sunset. "Summer Falls: Have a great weekend, America."

The connection's superslow. Dial-up.

I type "Summer Falls" into Google and skim the Wikipedia entry.

Summer Falls, Colorado, population around 5,000, including the surrounding areas of Green Vista, Eagle's Creek, and Pleasant Valley. Established 1903, first mayor and official founder William Phillips Preston.

Economy

Though it was established as a mill town, poor oversight and numerous fatal incidents involving human error led to the mill finally closing in 2011. Tourism is the remaining source of revenue.

The heat, elevation, and general laid-back vacation culture has led to tourists comparing visiting the town to being high on a pleasant and relaxing drug, and the board of tourism only encourages this myth. The town culture is relaxed to the point where indulging in a midday nap is accepted even in school or the workplace. "Heatnaps," as they're called, happen spontaneously at seemingly random times throughout the day and evening, during any season. (As visitors can attest, the weather remains in the 60s and 70s even when the rest of Colorado is seeing snow and ice. See the Summer Falls Effect.) Townies claim Walt

Disney stole his famous slogan, "The Happiest Place on Earth," from Summer Falls, but there's no evidence to back this claim. <citation needed?>

People nap at any time of day here? Heh, I could see that. But how could it be warm all winter long in Colorado? I click on the Summer Falls Effect.

Some climatologists have theorized that the location of nearby glacier Kiowa, combined with the valley effect, is responsible for creating a unique microclimate that defies all expectations for the region's latitude and altitude.

It goes on for a few more sentences, but they're full of even more terms I don't understand.

Controversy

The Summer Falls Effect has come under criticism by numerous traditional climate scientists, including Megan Coen, Yonatan Zunger, and Hans Andersen, who has famously called it "bunk science." Yet its detractors have offered no competing theory to explain the unusual microclimates in this part of Colorado.

I kind of have to agree with those guys. I mean, how could a freaking glacier—a mountain of ice—make the place warmer?

There's a video embedded; I hit Play.

A slender woman with a blond bob and gold jewelry smiles at the camera from atop a windy hill. "One thing that helps create the fascinating weather patterns in Summer Falls, Colorado," she says, speaking slowly and thoughtfully, "is the paradoxical effect of the nearby glacier's location." The camera pans out to a majestic mountain of ice. I can't help but laugh when I see it. She's a persuasive speaker, but the theory really does sound moronic. "You see, while it is cooling the surrounding air, winds whipping down into the valley will heat up with compression, similar to a drainage wind like the Santa Ana winds in California—" She uses her hands to gesture, and as the wind blows on the neckline of her peasant blouse, suddenly I see something way more interesting than her cleavage.

I turn it back a few seconds and freeze the frame. Just above her pale, elegant collarbone is an Egyptian eye tattoo. I look down at my own. What does it mean that I have the same tattoo as some batty climate scientist? Maybe we're both part of some secret society? Or maybe we just both thought that tattoo design looked cool. But there's no way to know till I get my memory back.

I watch a clip from the Colorado Historical Association next. The camera zooms in and out of a somber black-and-white photograph, men with their hats in their hands, women in veils as they stare at twin caskets. Everyone wearing stiff, formal facial expressions that you just don't see anymore. "We called him Old Man Preston," says a gruff, aged male voice, "because he was the boss, like a father to the whole town. But of course he died pretty young, in his forties. He and Mrs. Preston were on their boat during a rare storm and they both drowned. Never even found the bodies, though with today's search equipment it would have been easier. But our founders had given us one more gift: They'd invested every penny they were worth back into our town, and so the Great Depression never hit us like it did everyone else. The mill kept going, and it kept us going. . . ."

The next site, a travel article, takes forever to load. Impatiently I leaf through a three-ring binder left on the desk. Flyers for local restaurants. The official Preston House glossy brochure features a portrait of Calvin Coolidge and his wife vacationing by the lake. There are also brochures for local attractions. One catches my eye: Summer Falls Ghost Tour.

We're proud of our hauntings here, I read from the brochure. *Explore each spooky, supernatural spot in town. Note: All our spirits are friendly!*

There's a list of nine below, each with a cheesy little graphic. One has a picture of a pair of beaded moccasins. One has a chocolate chip cookie with a bite taken out. One has a baby stroller.

Tomoko Nakamura, 1988. This young mother was visiting Summer Falls from Kyoto, Japan, when she slipped on the trail wearing high heels, and her infant daughter fell from her stroller, tumbling partway down the cliff side. In a mad effort to rescue her daughter, she tumbled to her death. The baby, who had fallen only a few feet and been caught in some tree roots, survived. Mysterious double-wheel tracks are still regularly found in the dirt near the trails.

The woman with the empty stroller.

The woman who wasn't there.

I drop the binder on the desk.

It's got to be a coincidence.

No. It's too specific to be a coincidence. Elyse would have had to know about that story, and if she were lying about that *and* about seeing the woman, that would mean she was lying about everything . . . that she was some kind of con artist.

Impossible. Never mind the fact that I'm conning Liz and the Bishops, pretending to be New York Jim without my conscience feeling much of a pang. Elyse isn't like me, or even like most people. She keeps telling the truth, even when she knows it's going to make her sound crazy or otherwise bite her in the ass.

I believe in Elyse.

And I hate to say this, but now believing in Elyse means I have to start believing in ghosts.

CHAPTER 9

ELYSE

MY ROOM IS IN THE EAST TOWER. IT *IS* THE EAST tower. By the time Liz leads me up the twisty stairway with its creaky old banister, her smile's lost half its wattage. She winces at me in the open doorway. "Sorry, I know you like the door and window closed, but it was just so *hot* today—"

"I don't care," I cut in. "I just need to remember."

I push past her into the room. It's circular, and so tiny it would give me claustrophobia if not for the open window, its magenta curtains billowing out toward the lush green grounds. I have to crane my neck to check out the high, domed ceiling. Like a miniature cathedral.

It could have been such a cool bedroom; it could have been amazing. But it's gross.

For starters there's the bubblegum-pink carpet, soft pile two inches high. Like some kind of shaggy alien grass. A white four-poster bed with a cream-colored canopy—a

Victorian eight-year-old's dream. Candy-striped walls, bare of posters or personality. The only proof that we're still in the twenty-first century is the desktop littered with fashion magazines.

I shake my head, trying not to cry. "I don't remember this place at all."

"But honey, you love your room." She says it in a don't-be-silly voice, gently correcting. "You're always sitting up here, nose stuck in your book . . ." Her smile fades a little around the edges, disapproving. "Going to need glasses soon if you keep it up."

I'm so sick of her denial, and I'm about ready to snap at her that having amnesia is *way* worse than needing glasses, but the news that I like to read stops me silent. It's the first thing I've heard about myself and my life so far that I don't despise. What kind of books do I read? I wonder. Fantasy? True crime? Newsy nonfiction? I scan the room for shelves, but all I see are the magazines arrayed on the desk, a chorus line of teased blond manes, bubble boobs, and exaggerated pink pouts. Maybe I check out novels from the library one at a time. I try to picture myself in this room, reading, sitting sprawled on top of the turned-down pink comforter, propped up on lacy pink throw pillows. . . . Something occurs to me. "Do you always make my bed for me?"

She blinks at me. "I thought you made it."

"When?"

"Well, this morning . . ." Her voice trails off uncertainly.

"Don't you always make your bed in the mornings?"

I look away, sparks of hot shame flaring in my belly. She still doesn't know. My own mother doesn't know that I was gone all night. What would she think of me, if she knew I woke up entwined with a strange boy, at the home of a crazy magician? Screw that, what am *I* supposed to think of *her*, a parent who doesn't care enough to keep tabs on her own kid?

"You haven't even asked much about my memory," I say. "Aren't you worried about me?"

She shakes her head brightly. "Nope. Your memory's going to come right back. I *know* it is."

"Okay, well, I want to believe that too. But it's been hours. . . ."

"Everyone has these moments, sweetie. People don't like to talk about it, but it's normal." She steeples her hands and breathes into them. Letting me know some part of her is worried, despite her cheery exterior.

Instantly I feel guilty for judging her. Liz doesn't seem uncaring, just distracted. She's probably exhausted, what with running this place—and for all I know she's a single parent, raising me alone. "You haven't mentioned my father," I say, looking her in the eye. "Does he live with us?"

Liz flinches, and I know I've offended her. "Daddy's down at Tim's Hardware," she says, a little stiffly. "Getting a new shower rod for the guest cottage."

"Daddy?" I can feel my nose wrinkling. I'm *sure* I

don't call my father that, like some spoiled little princess. Then again I was sure I didn't wear tight, body-hugging white skirts too.

The fashion-mag models' eyes seem to follow me as I cross the room to examine every cleared, shiny surface for a clue of myself. My attention pounces on a pink wastebasket by the desk. What kind of papers did I throw away—essay drafts, notes from friends, love letters? But when I lean closer to inspect its metal bowl all I see is my own blurry reflection. Empty. Damn it.

Every second in this room makes me feel so uncomfortable that I let myself imagine hurling myself out the window just to get out. But I didn't survive one fall and run my ass off to die stupidly now. Instead I let out a groan of frustration and, like a renegade wiper blade, my arm sweeps across the desk hard. The magazines crash into the basket with hollow metallic clunks.

Liz's shoulders seize at the violent sound and her small, pretty face shrinks into itself. "No need to get so upset."

Guilt tugs at a string in my chest. "Sorry to freak you out," I say. "But I am upset. I'm confused. I'm trying to understand. Trying to remember . . . me. My life. And looking at all this stuff isn't helping. This place looks like a little girl lives here." A creepy little girl. The kind who enters pageants.

"Well, you *were* seven when we decorated it. Don't you remember how much fun we had together painting those stripes, trying to get them to line up perfectly . . . ?"

Right. What seven-year-old would find that fun? "The only thing this room reminds me of is a dollhouse. Or maybe a doll prison," I add, thinking that the vertical pink stripes resemble bars. "Liz, I need your help. What else can you tell me, or show me, to jog my memory? Anything that might make this feel real."

"Of course." She nods, twice, and you can just see her trying to compose herself. "Family photo albums are in the front parlor," she says finally. "It'll help remind you of all the good times we've had."

"I hope so."

When she's gone downstairs to fetch them, I open the closet door and flip through dozens of white scented, satin hangers, checking out every outfit. Most of my wardrobe is cotton, like what I'm wearing. It's not skimpy, that's not the problem, but it manages to be tight and revealing anyway. Also I'm color-challenged. Most everything I own is white, though sometimes I branch out into black. It's unnerving. Did I not get the memo that clothes come in real colors?

The shoe selection's more promising. Two pairs of delicate sandals—skinny heels and flimsy straps—arrayed on a shoe tree serve as closet jewelry, but on the floor are hiking boots, rugged rafting sandals with Velcro around the toes and ankles, and three pairs of running shoes in various stages of wear. I'm amused to see one muddy sneaker half hidden under a white prom dress.

As I'm bending to scoop up the shoe and its mate,

some pencil markings low on the closet wall catch my eye. I pull aside the dress and discover the markings start at two and a half feet and reach halfway up the wall to the closet shelves where I store purses and jewelry. Someone—maybe Liz or my father—has been marking my height over time. But the highest mark isn't much over five feet, which means they must have stopped years ago. Unless . . . I stand directly in front of it, my hand following the line from the top of my head to the wall. It matches the level of the marking.

"Oh my god," I say out loud as the revelation hits me. "I'm *short*."

I am, in fact, a shrimp. What a complete and total disappointment. Until I saw that, I had thought of myself as tall and cool and imposing. Who knows why I would assume that; I was aware that Dark-Eyed Boy was taller than me; I had to look up to glare at him for lying about his identity. I just hadn't grasped how serious of a disparity there was between our heights. And now it's too late. I can't keep imagining I'm big and powerful when I know the truth.

Well, crap. I slam the closet door and the full-length mirror on the outside catches me by surprise. I'm greeted by the same oval face I glimpsed in the shop window, framed by long wavy hair. Only now the image is crystal clear, and what I'm seeing makes my stomach sink with disappointment. My cute-as-a-button pointy chin makes me look like a toddler. My bouncy hair's got a life of its own, front pieces constantly falling into my face with wild abandon. But the worst is that now I can see my own expression—the grouchy curve of my mouth, my huge, venomous green eyes. I can see how funny, how ridiculous, my honest indignation looks from the outside. I look like a pissed-off Disney Princess. Adorable . . . and harmless. I just want to chuck myself under the chin and say, *Aw, don't be such a lil' grumpster! Put on a* smile. And if I feel that way about my own reflection, it's pretty much guaranteed that no guy who looks at me will ever take me seriously. No wonder Dark-Eyed Boy didn't run when I told him to.

I turn to the side to check myself out, trying to see what made him stare with that look of awe on his face. But all I feel is disappointment, mingled with disgust. Though I'm small, no inch of my body is flat. Everything tapers, or nips inward, or flares to the side, or pops out in front or back, seeking attention. Round breasts jut out in front of me, practically inviting touch. I put my hand over my sweater and squeeze—it's squashy, yielding. Ugh. How weird . . . I didn't see myself as the busty type. Too bad bodies are issued randomly, not selected to match your personality. Really, really too bad.

Do I have to live in this body . . . forever?

Maybe I could start working out, get ripped like Dark-Eyed Boy, so people would know they couldn't mess with me. But my arms are already fairly toned, suggesting I do work out. It's just that I'm a girl, so my muscles aren't huge and bulky. They're just kind of *nicely shaped*. Like that ever scared off an attacker.

Maybe I should get a sex change.

There's a knock on the already open door. At the sight of Dark-Eyed Boy, I spin away from the mirror, embarrassed to be caught staring at myself.

"How's Room four, *Jim*?"

"Nice lake view." He walks straight over to me and lowers his voice. "I had to come up with a story. Didn't you notice how people reacted when we told the truth?"

"Of course I noticed this place is a little *off*, but—"

"It's more than a little off. What do you think happens here, to people with . . . our problem?"

I think back to the nurse and Sheriff Hank's hushed tones of shock. To the moss-covered asylum sign. A shiver runs from my scalp all the way to my tailbone. "I know we can't tell them *everything*," I say. "But pretending to be someone you're not—that's so devious."

"I did what I had to do."

"In other words, you lied to get what you wanted?"

"If I hadn't lied, I wouldn't have gotten to stay with you." His voice is pleading for understanding. "And I'm not leaving you alone, not till we know it's safe here. I meant what I said—we're in this together."

He reaches out his hand to me, and after a moment or two I take it. Part of me's impressed that he was able to keep a cool enough head to strategize, back there with Liz and Sheriff Hank, when I was too busy being scared and angry and shell-shocked. That other part of me's disturbed that he could spout lies and feel no remorse.

"So what do we do when the real Jim shows up?" I ask.

"Improvise." His eyes go all intense for a moment, and I can see him struggling to stay positive. "This has to work till we figure out what to do next." He brushes the hair out of my eyes. "Now put on your shoes; there's something I need to show you. Downstairs."

For once I don't even give him crap about telling me what to do. I'm just grateful he has a plan, because I'm feeling lost. And somehow I doubt Liz and her photo albums are going to save the day. "Let me find socks." I lean across the bed and pull open the middle drawer of the bedside table with the hideously cute pink lamp on top. Presto, the drawer's full of sock balls.

"Whoa, hold on." Dark-Eyed Boy looks excited. "There's . . ." He counts quickly, pointing in the air at the chest of drawers, desk, and bedside table. ". . . sixteen drawers in this room, and you went right to that one. Maybe your subconscious is remembering something."

"Like where I keep my socks?" I frown and unroll a pair of black ankle socks to break up the all-white look. "It's not exactly a breakthrough."

"You never know." He looks disappointed though. "What else is in that drawer?"

"Nothing, it's wall-to-wall socks." I open the drawer again. "See?" To emphasize my point, I start to pull the socks out and pile them on the floor. Decorating the bottom of the empty drawer is pink-and-white lacey-flower patterned liner paper. Typical.

But the paper isn't glued all the way. I lean in closer and pat the slightly bulging pouch in the middle. No thicker than a few pages. I rip off the liner like a Band-Aid, and we both gape at what's hidden underneath.

It's a small stash of papers. A map of the Los Angeles County Metro. Cutout pictures of models and actresses. Printouts of open casting calls. Craigslist ads for room shares and shady modeling gigs. And money, nine crisp hundred-dollar bills. What the hell?

He gapes at me, a spark of shrewd new respect in his eyes. "You were planning to break out of here."

CHAPTER 10

DARK-EYED BOY

"YEAH . . . FIGURED THAT ONE OUT." LOOKING dazed, she picks up the map and holds it clenched between her fingernails, digging into the paper version of Los Angeles like a cat clawing into a sweater. "Jesus. What a dumb, dangerous plan. Wonder how long I've been saving up for it." And where were you getting all that money? I think but don't say. The seamier possibilities would freak her out, and she's already freaking. Her worried fingers are crumpling the page. I take the map from her hands, try to smooth it. "It's not dumb to have big dreams."

"I guess. But Hollywood?" She snorts. "Small-town prom queen trying be a movie star—what bigger cliché is there?"

She has a point there. "Still, you could have made it."

"No, actually I couldn't have." Her voice is flat as her fingers tick off the reasons. "I'm short, I'm bigger than a size two, and I don't know anyone in Hollywood. What the hell was I thinking?"

"You could have made it, Elyse. You have something." I'm fully serious, but she groans and shakes her head. Something tells me to drop it. "Just don't be down on yourself for dreaming."

"Dreaming." She snaps her fingers. "I just remembered. Before I woke up this morning, I dreamed I was on a white beach with palm trees, celebrities everywhere. I guess I was obsessed."

"Then why hadn't you left yet? What were you waiting for?"

"Graduation, maybe?" She sighs. "Or more money. Or the return of my common sense."

The clack of skinny heels on the hardwood staircase makes us scramble. I launch myself at the stack of papers and cash, hurling it all back into the drawer and sliding my elbow across the sticky paper to reseal it. Elyse tosses an armful of socks over the top just as Liz stumbles in, hobbled by a small mountain of photo albums.

I try for a winning smile. "What you got there, Liz?"

"Oh, *hi*, Jim." She smiles back at me, but it's all lipstick. I can tell she's less than thrilled to discover a tourist in her daughter's bedroom. Then again—I can practically see the wheels turning in her innkeeper mind—I was only talking to Elyse, with the door wide open. Is it really worth her saying something and risking losing my business? "We were just heading downstairs," she says finally. "To look through some dusty old photo albums. Wouldn't want to bore you," she adds.

Since I haven't been lobotomized, I get the point. Tourist Jim is not on the invite list.

I clear out of Elyse's room and follow her and her mother down the stairs. Hoping to hang around within eavesdropping range, I wander into the breakfast room for a snack. The cheery oval table is bare, but there's a bowl of cocoa-dusted dark truffles and a crystal decanter of port on the sideboard. I take a truffle, realize I'm starving, and grab two more. The heat's already melted them a little, and the sweet chocolate liquefies on my tongue.

Weird how I somehow knew these would be here. Maybe I really have stayed at Preston House before.

I hear Liz's and Elyse's voices nearby and stealthily creep back into the hall. In the sunken front parlor, Liz perches on a high-backed striped sofa, plunks down the photo albums, and pats the seat beside her. Elyse sits down, but leaves more space between them.

Seeing them side by side almost takes my breath away. It's startlingly obvious they're related. Liz is Elyse plus twenty years. Both small and curvy and fit, tan-skinned, wavy-haired, with the same sharp chin and big round eyes. They even carry themselves the same way, shoulders down and back, like runway models. I feel a sudden pang of sadness for both of them. It seems absurd to the point of cruelty that Elyse could not remember

Liz. Hopefully seeing these photos will help.

Craving something more substantial than chocolate, I head back through the breakfast room and swing open the kitchen door. And nearly run smack into the Bishops, the thirtysomething couple I talked to earlier.

Before I can say hi, she hisses at him, "Don't call me paranoid, I *heard* her texting you."

"For God's sake, Luci—"

"This trip was our last chance."

They're standing squared off at the counter, their angry faces only inches apart. This is none of my business. I should go. But why haven't either of them noticed me? Frank in particular is facing the door, but he's not making eye contact or lowering his voice.

"The damn text was from work!" His every syllable leaks contempt. "You know, the job that pays for your Botox?"

It's uncanny and weird, just like it was weird when Kerry the receptionist didn't notice me till I got up in her business. Like it was weird when Liz didn't notice me until I spoke up to protect Elyse. Is it just my imagination, or are people not registering my presence unless I speak?

"If it was work, then show me. Show me your goddamn phone." Her skinny bird-talon fist pounds the countertop. Then her eyes grow round and she gasps.

And crashes to the ground in a heap.

"Holy crap!" I rush over to her still form. "What's wrong with her?"

"Oh, hey, Jim." Frank gives me a casual wave.

"Why aren't you helping your wife?" I kneel down on the carpet and grab Mrs. Bishop's wrist. I'm relieved to feel her pulse beating strong, regular. Her breathing's deep, peaceful. "She's fainted."

"Buddy, relax." He whips open a BlackBerry from his pocket, tamps down the volume, snaps it closed again. "It's just a heatnap."

"Really?" I remember that term from Wikipedia, but her sudden spill seems way too violent to have been a nap.

Frank opens his mouth, but only a gasp escapes him. Then he too falls to the ground, his unconscious body landing only three feet away from his wife's.

Adrenaline pumping through me, I burst through the door into the dining room. "Help!" There's no one in here. Liz can't hear me from the parlor. A loud groan—or yawn—behind me sends me tearing back into the kitchen. To my shock, both Bishops are stirring again. Mrs. Bishop is already on her feet and with a smile she offers an out-stretched hand to her husband. He groans and dusts himself off, then pecks her on the lips.

"Ready to go antiquing?" she says. Purrs.

He kisses her hand indulgently. "No man is ever ready to go antiquing, but I'd do anything for you."

Then, as if they'd never fought, they hook pinkies and waltz out the backyard door together. I watch them merrily swinging their arms through the backyard.

What the hell just happened?

CHAPTER 11

ELYSE

LIZ OPENS A PALE BLUE ALBUM. "THIS IS THE first one with you in it," she says, a note of nostalgia catching in her voice, and I lean close to her, hoping to recognize myself.

Hoping to remember.

Instead all I see is a baby who could be anyone, and then a toddler with inquisitive green eyes and blond curls that grow longer over the course of years and pages. Within a few pages, she grows into a small, nervous-looking girl with pale braids bent toward an easel, painting, or hunched over a sketch pad, crayon in her hand. Tongue pressed against the corner of her lower lip.

"You were like our own mini Picasso." The corners of her eyes crinkle with amusement. "When I was a girl, I drew horses and princesses. I tried to show you how to do a horse, but you only wanted to draw one thing. Your imaginary friends."

"What imaginary friends?" My chest tightens as I think back to the woman pushing her empty stroller, the woman who might have been a hallucination. "Did you keep those drawings?"

"Honey, there were so many drawings . . . you had so many imaginary friends, it was hard to keep up. Doc said it was a sign of creativity, but I was still relieved when you outgrew it all." She ruffles my hair. "Those art supplies were getting expensive, whew. And now you're all grown up and well-adjusted and you have real friends . . . coming out of your ears."

I stare at her. What is she talking about, normal and well-adjusted? As far as I'm concerned, I have one friend. Dark-Eyed Boy. Why can't Liz keep her mind focused on the huge, gaping problem before us: *my amnesia?*

I listen to Liz's breathless remembrances of the "good times." Thanksgiving dinner. Christmas morning. Birthday parties; how hard she worked on those cakes; how much fun the kids had breaking piñatas and pinning the tails on donkeys. The middle of the album is all me: first days of school, Halloween costumes, track meets. The elementary-school girl racing across the finish line has the same face I saw in the mirror, but her body hasn't betrayed her yet. It's still normal-looking: lean, straight lines like a boy's.

Then Liz turns the page, and without warning my stomach sinks.

It's just a picture of a family dinner table, decorated

with a centerpiece of Thanksgiving gourds. Liz is wearing a pink dress, smiling up at a man in a blue plaid shirt as he prepares to carve the turkey. "Is that my father?"

She nods and chuckles. "I remember you snapped that shot of Daddy with your new camera, you were so proud of that thing."

Looking at the big, sturdy, grinning man with the cleaver poised over the poor dead bird is sending waves of nausea over me. I avert my eyes. "I think . . . I might be a vegetarian," I say.

"Praise God." Liz lets out a long sigh of relief. "It's coming back to you! I knew it would."

"No, I was just guessing."

The next album is wedding pictures, a beaming young Liz who looks startlingly like the Elyse in the mirror, in a white princess gown. Half the album is empty, though, like someone just pulled out every other picture. I look for a clear picture of the groom, my father's face, but it's mostly Liz and her bridesmaids.

She wants to zip through them quickly because I'm not in them, but I'm fascinated. "Is that the church downtown? Who's that lady standing next to you in that one?"

"That's my mother, your Grandma Bets." She points to the gray-haired lady in the flower-sprigged lavender dress. The woman doesn't look healthy at all; in fact, Liz is helping support her on the left side while on the other side a guest is steadying her right arm. The guest is grinning with obscenely crooked teeth. Grandma Bets's brilliant ruby necklace only makes her neck look more wrinkled. "Said she could rest easy now that she'd seen me walk down that aisle." Liz's ringed fingers drift toward her throat, and I can see the oval ruby resting against her collarbone.

Hesitantly I say, "I'm . . . sorry for your loss."

Liz's eyebrows knit in confusion. "Momma's doing just fine." She snaps the book shut. *Creepy.*

The sound of tires winding up the driveway makes Liz hop to her feet. "Ah, that must be Candace and Aiden, the young couple from California."

Sure enough, when Liz opens the door, there's a college-aged woman in a designer sundress, her chestnut hair in a short, tousled cut, standing beside a thin goateed man in his early twenties, dressed in dark colors. Between them are two black Samsonite suitcases. They introduce themselves to all of us and to each other as Candace and Jim.

You have to hand it to Liz. When the real Jim shows up, she doesn't lose her professional composure for even a second. "Welcome to Preston House," she says with her warm innkeeper smile. "Come in, both of you. Candace, are we still waiting for one from your party?"

Candace gives an impish grin. "Aiden dumped me last week, but we'd already booked the trip, so I decided to go anyway. I mean, I'm not going to miss fair weekend in Summer Falls just because of some guy."

"We'll make sure you have a fabulous time and forget all about him," Liz says, patting the young woman's arm.

"Solo vacations rock," Jim tells her. "You really get to

be one with the place you're staying." He stretches his arms and breathes a sigh of pure relaxation. "See? I think I'm already feeling the drop!"

"The drop?" I say.

"Oh my god, lucky!" Candace squeals with envy. "When my ex and I came last year, it took me, like, *days* before I felt any different. But then when I did it was awesome."

I have no idea what they're talking about 'feeling'—relaxation? But something about Candace's perky laughter bugs me. It's like she's talking up some fabulous Disneyland ride. Not a real town where real people live. People like me.

"This house you're staying in," Liz says, "is the original construction built by our town's founder, William Phillips Preston, in 1897." You can tell she's said it a hundred thousand times, but there's still a pride in her tone.

"God, I'd give my eyelashes to live here." Candace takes off her sunglasses and turns to Jim. "Can you imagine one couple had this whole mansion to themselves?"

"Preston and his wife did have servants," Liz reminds her, a few fibers of disapproval woven into her silky voice as if to say, *Servants are people too*. It's the first sign of independent thinking I've ever seen from her, and it makes me like her more.

While Liz shows them to their separate rooms, I retreat to the kitchen.

Dark-Eyed Boy is leaning against the marble counter. "Sounds like my cover's blown." He stares at the cookie jar. "Think your mother's going to call the sheriff or just kick me out?"

"I don't know her well enough to guess."

"I don't want to leave you here alone."

I don't want to stay here alone. "Who cares if she calls the sheriff?" I say. "We can run away together. Skip town."

"And go where?" It's weird to hear him sound so hopeless. Earlier in the day, I'd poked holes in his cloud-less optimism, just to vent my own frustration. Now I miss it.

"We'll go wherever we have to go." I put my hand over his. "Maybe find a big city, where there's a real hospital. And we'll just keep moving till we get help or our memories come back on their own. We have money now—"

"*Some* money, and that's your safety net. I'm not touching it."

I try not to feel insulted that he's turning down my offer to share what I have. "It's ours, really," I say. "I never even would have found it if it wasn't for you. Don't be such a hero. Let me help you for once."

"All right." Liz wanders in, looking dazed. "If that was Jim I just led into the Country Sun Suite, then who exactly are you?"

"He's my friend," I say. "He's been there for me and he really needs a place to stay for a while. And if you don't let him crash here when we have *plenty* of room . . . then I'm leaving too."

"Elyse—"

"No, it's true. If you can't take both of us, you can't have either of us."

Liz looks from me to him and back. "Well, there's no need to be so dramatic." She sounds exasperated. "A friend of my daughter is a friend of the family," she says, patting his knee. "For now you can stay in the Rustic's Cottage."

"Seriously?" From the way his eyes are shining I can tell that her generosity's making him feel ashamed of lying to her before.

"It's in the backyard," she warns, "and you'll have to be all right with taking a bath instead of a shower since the curtain rod broke last week."

"I don't know how to thank you."

"You just did." She pulls a key ring from her pocket and removes one key.

"Hey, who's renting the Cottage?" says a hearty voice. A big, tall man strides into the kitchen.

"Honey!" Liz runs over to kiss his cheek. "Did you order the new shower rod?"

"They'll have it in day after tomorrow." He thrusts out his hand amiably at Dark-Eyed Boy, who shakes it. "Don't believe we've met, sir. I'm Jeffry Alton." Even though he's being friendly and polite, I can pick up subtle hints of suspicion in his voice. "So, you a student? Staying in that Cottage all alone?"

"He doesn't speak much English," I say quickly. "He's from . . . Brazil."

Whoa, did I just lie?

I spontaneously lied to my own father—just to keep him from asking Dark-Eyed Boy too many questions. How could I do that, after my whole song and dance earlier about how Lying Is Bad and Wrong? What a hypocrite. Sure, I don't want to do anything to risk Dark-Eyed Boy getting to stay here. Still, this is my *father* we're all deceiving, I think, and guilt nags at me. Then I notice several white dots on his chin and pick up on a familiar medicinal smell. Good god, is that . . . pimple cream? My father's face is covered in pimple cream? I hope his acne isn't hereditary. Jeffry Alton's blue eyes, set deep in his ruddy square face, meet mine and I look away.

"Full house, and a rich foreigner to boot." Jeffry smiles broadly and rubs his hands together. "Looks like the season's heating up."

CHAPTER 12

DARK-EYED BOY

"SO, WHAT WAS THAT GUY JIM TALKING ABOUT?" Elyse presses her mom when Jeffry's headed down to the basement to watch TV. "What's 'the drop'?"

"Just a silly slogan." Liz gestures toward a framed poster on the kitchen door depicting a powerful waterfall. "Summer Falls, 1,600 feet." And below that: "Feel your tensions *drop away*."

"Is it true?" I ask. "Do people really relax that much when they come here?"

Liz shakes her head. "Only because they expect to. It's a good sales technique, and with the mill closing we need the revenue from tourism."

Same thing the sheriff said. "Why did the mill close?" I ask.

Liz preheats the oven to 350 degrees. "Some machines malfunctioned," she says vaguely. Either she had no idea what happened or there was a grisly disaster with tons of casualties. Either way she's not talking about it.

Elyse and I decide to head downtown. On the walk we catch each other up. She tells me about the missing photos in the album, and Liz's weird reaction to seeing pics of her own mother, Elyse's grandmother. I tell her about the fainting, fighting couple—her eyes widen—and my theory that I can turn invisible just by not speaking when I first enter a room.

"You're not invisible." She rolls her eyes. "You're just good at blending in. Besides I saw you, this morning in— um, in bed. You definitely hadn't said anything. You were asleep."

"That doesn't fit the pattern," I admit. "But I think it's more likely that there's something weird about you." I tell her about the ghost description of Tomoko. "You were right, okay?"

"So that's who she was." She stares at the surface of the lake, thoughtful. "So weird that you couldn't see her."

"You think *that's* the weird part? How about the fact that ghosts exist and haunt your hometown?"

She tilts her head toward me in surprise. "The idea of ghosts is perfectly natural. They're just spirits of the dead."

"Right," I deadpan, "spirits of the dead. It's all so very natural and normal. Not like crazy, crazy magic, which you don't believe in." She shoves me playfully, and I grab her hand before she can pull it back. She gasps.

"I just want to know, how come you're down with ghosts but not magic?"

She fixes her eyes on me. "How come you're down

with magic but not ghosts?"

I let go of her hand. I don't have an answer.

"Maybe I'm used to ghosts," she says, shrugging. "Growing up in a haunted town and all."

"Maybe," I say, "except . . . that brochure was very *hokey*. Like whoever wrote it didn't seriously believe in ghosts but just thought it would be cheesy, good fun for the tourists. A sales technique, like your mother was saying. Elyse, don't tell anybody else what you saw. Not even your parents."

She shudders. "You're worried they'd put me in the asylum, aren't you?"

"They would literally have to kill me first." But yes.

———

When we hit Main Street we decide to split up, checking out stores on opposite ends of the street and meeting at the fair in an hour, in time for the picnic.

I cross the street to Hinklebeck's Antiques and note the smaller writing under the main signage. "Thousands of Secondhand Goods and Antiques Within . . . and One Relic."

I'd been expecting a bell to announce every customer, but the door makes no sound as I open it. Maybe the door sensed my broke status and knew I wasn't important enough to warrant a staff welcome.

From behind the counter, an older woman is talking to a slightly built young man.

"And what do we have here, Bette?" The man has a British accent. "A fresh catch from the sea of eBay?"

"1923," Bette brags. She plays with her wooden beaded necklace and grins, the over-sixty version of the hair-flip-giggle combo. "That there's an original Dorian Coffer, seller's great-grandma had it down in her basement . . . souvenir from her honeymoon."

I tiptoe forward and lean closer to see what they're looking at. The woman still doesn't notice my existence—I'm getting used to that treatment around here—but the man turns his head and winks at me. Weird. He stands directly in front of the poster, as if he wants to become one with it, but I can still see a smiling white couple in the foreground. When I say white, I mean really white: the woman blond with a bright white face, the man with his blindingly white arm around hers. I read enough of the words at the bottom to guess that it says something like: "Turn your frown upside down with a holiday in Summer Falls!"

The British guy whistles. "Pristine condition too. Hundred bucks is a steal." He pulls out a brown battered wallet. I have a sudden sad feeling for him. How much of his paycheck does that hundred dollars represent?

"I'm surprised you'd want it, Mr.—"

"Joe, please."

"Why, your people aren't even from here, yet you care so much about our history."

"History's my one true love, Bette. Or maybe just my longest successful relationship."

Bette clucks with pity. "I know how you feel, but don't sell yourself short. You could meet a lovely girl right here

77

in Summer F—" She gasps, and I see why. Right in front of her, the man started rolling up the poster, calmly and deliberately, a smile on his face. The antique poster he hasn't yet paid for. "Mr. English. Oh dear."

He reaches over and pats her sloped shoulder. "Bette Hinklebeck, you're the ugliest woman I've ever seen, and you talk too much. That's why Floyd Johnston dropped you for Myrtle Kessler in 1946."

WTF? Talk about cruel, telling a sweet old lady she's ugly and talks too much? Worse, did he just throw an ancient breakup—one she must have told him about in confidence—in her face?

"Oh dear, oh dear." Poor Bette's hand flies to her heart, and her eyes flutter. Her mouth opens, and she clatters to the ground behind the counter, shaking every hundred-year-old plate and glass on her shelves. Another heatnap?

He's just finished stuffing the poster in his briefcase when she groans and stands up again. "Oh, hello, Mr. English—"

"Joe," he says again, with perfect patience. "Please, keep the change."

"Change?" She glances over at the cash register, confused. "So sorry, I must have had a moment. Thank you."

"Pleasure's mine."

Whoa. This guy has some nerve. On top of insulting her, not that she seems to remember—just like the Bishops after *their* heatnap—he just shoplifted a poster from her by pretending he'd already paid.

And it worked too.

When did he first figure out he could do that? Does he pay for anything in this town?

I hustle out the door, but he catches up with me on the street.

"Hey, where were you yesterday?"

Yesterday. This guy knew me yesterday. I turn to face him, not wanting to waste this opportunity to learn more. But at the same time, I don't want to let on how helpless I am. Especially not to this sadist. "Sorry." I stall. "I wasn't feeling well?" I say, hoping it'll work as a catchall excuse.

"Please, I'm not talking about your missing the history test." He snorts. "Like I'd ever fail you. Do me a favor and don't start giving a damn about school all of a sudden— it's unnerving." Whoa, he's my teacher? A teacher who doesn't want me to care about school? Why won't he fail me . . . are we friends?

"You know, you can tell me if you've changed your mind," he says, leaning in. Behind his Coke-bottle glasses, his owl eyes sparkle with concern. "I'd understand."

I can't fake my way through this. "Understand about what?"

"What do you mean about what?" He lowers his voice. "Your mother's work, what else? Her notes."

"Right." Mentally I'm taking down his every word, because all of it's new information. New and intriguing too.

"Do you have them?"

"Not . . . not with me." Technically not a lie.

"Meet me tomorrow after school at Mollie's," Joe says.

CHAPTER 13

ELYSE

FRESH WHITE PAINT GLEAMS ON THE FAUX-Greek columns of the Summer Falls Public Library, making the building look new even though, from the style, I can tell it must be old. *Very* old.

Back when I had my memory, though, I probably took its well-preserved beauty for granted.

I try to picture my pre-amnesia self racing over here every day after school. Browsing the new books shelf, loading my backpack with hardcovers. If I came in here all the time, the librarians must know me pretty well . . . that thought gives me some trepidation. What if one of them guesses there's something wrong with me?

Feeling a tingle of apprehension, I bound up the three marble steps and pull open the heavy door. A narrow shaft of sunlight disappears behind me as the door snaps shut, leaving me in a cool, dimly lit hallway.

Through a glass window, I can see into the library

proper: metal browsing shelves, long wooden tables where patrons sit studying or reading, and the librarian's desk.

The walls in this entryway are lined with cork bulletin boards sprouting colorful flyers announcing summer fair events, from town softball games to pie-baking contests.

But the main focus is a single exhibit behind glass in the center of the room. It's a dollhouse-like model of Main Street, it looks like, and the surrounding town. A "You are here" flag hangs from a pin stuck in the library building. The shop window of Mollie's is painted the exact same shade of orange as it is in real life. Someone's obsessive about their hobby . . . or is this all just more show for the tourists? Outside the circle representing town is a white-capped plastic mountain.

I read the caption below the model. "The Summer Falls Effect. How come the weather is always warm and sunny here? Many scientists believe our perfect weather is a happy accident caused by Kiowa glacier's proximity to our town. You might think a glacier would make things colder, but scientists know better!"

I frown at the plastic mountain, wondering how the hell it could make anything hotter.

The librarian doesn't notice me entering. Her frizzy graying head is bent over a stack of books that she's vigorously ink-stamping.

My hands feel clammy as I approach her desk. "Hi," I say, trying to sound casual and upbeat. Will she know me well enough to guess that something's wrong?

"Heya." The librarian looks up from her stamping and smiles at me. "Enjoying your stay?"

I blink. Wait . . . she thinks I'm a tourist? "I'm from *here*," I say, feeling irked. Just my luck, the normal librarian must be sick today.

"My mistake. I've never seen you in the library before." The woman slips off her reading glasses and lets them hang around her neck from their string of beads. "Of course," she says, and pops her glasses back onto her nose. "I do recognize you now, from the Sunrays games." She wiggles her shoulders and waves her arms, mimicking pom-poms. "Go, Rays!" She turns back to her ink-stamping.

"Go, Rays," I repeat dumbly, trying my best to hide my disappointment. So my bookworm status, the one thing about my former self that sounded right to me, turns out to be bull. I've never set foot in the library. I don't get it. Why would Liz say I had a reading habit if I didn't? How am I supposed to remember my life if she can't get her facts straight about her own daughter? Does she have a memory problem too or what?

Is *everyone's* memory scrambled in this town?

That thought makes the hairs on my arms prickle to attention.

I wander into the stacks, still pondering. Clearly there are major problems with memory loss here. That would explain the whole conversation between Kerry and the sheriff. Is there just something in the water here, a chemical that makes people slowly lose their memories?

Until . . . until they end up like me? And get shipped off to an asylum?

Not if they don't find out.

"Excuse me," I say to the librarian. "Where are the computers?"

"Researching some new cheers?" she says brightly. "Down the hall."

I don't bother to tell her there's more to me than being a cheerleader. First I need to make sure it's true. I'm planning to Google myself and see if anything comes up.

On my way down the hall, though, I get derailed, distracted by a rich, sweet, female voice in one of the other small rooms. The door's ajar. I peek in and see about a dozen preschool-aged children sitting in a squirmy horseshoe, their parents hovering at the edges of the room. The girl reading from a rhyming picture book looks about my age, but she's about as far from my reflection in the mirror as you could get. She looks more the way I imagined I would look—the way I thought I should look.

Tall. With long, slender limbs. Small breasts that barely disturb the clean line of her blue flower-sprigged sundress. You can tell her glossy chestnut hair would never dream of waving without her permission, let alone tangling and falling into her face like mine's doing right now. Most striking of all is her serene smile, so innocent, so sure, the exact opposite of how I feel inside.

"Time for one last story today," she announces in her even, hypnotic tone.

Several small voices clamor back, "No! More!" and their parents gently shush them.

She gifts the audience with one more poised smile and holds up another picture book. "*The Legend of the Tribe with No Name.* 'Long ago,'" she reads from page one, "'there lived all over this valley a tribe of Native Americans. They hunted deer and rabbits in our big pine forests. When the deer and rabbits weren't plentiful or easy to catch, the tribe gathered mushrooms instead. Or fished for trout in our big, calm lake. They lived happy and easy lives, protected by the spirit of the giant waterfall.'"

This is a girl who's happy and content. Who knows exactly who she is, who's never for a moment felt unsafe or scared. She's beautiful, in all the ways I'm not . . . and never can be. It hurts to look at her, but I linger in the doorway, unable to look away.

"'The waterfall was their holy place, and the tribe's medicine woman lived as close to the water as the spirit would allow her. Once, and only once, the spirit even let her swim in its waters without harm.'"

Great, a story encouraging kids to go swimming in a waterfall. That's when it occurs to me to wonder: Is the story supposed to be about *this* valley? A local legend about *this* waterfall?

"'But one day a strange man and his wife came to the valley. The man told the medicine woman that he had brought gifts for the water spirit and needed her permission to get near it. Now, the tribe knew something wasn't right about this man. His smile did not reach the corners of his eyes. But they also knew the spirit was powerful, powerful enough to devour any mere man who tried to get the better of it, so they all agreed to let him build an underwater stone labyrinth on the condition that he pay the tribe in grains and metals.

"'When the man's labyrinth of stones was finished, he laughed with delight. Holding his wife's hand, they dove together underneath the surface of the water. But the spirit did not devour him. It had no chance to. The man was an evil magician and he had weighed the spirit down with stones so it could not move, and then he whispered the words of his magic spell to it. At that moment, the medicine woman lost her power, and without her guidance the tribe dispersed. Many fish died in the water. Many trees fell, and in place of the trees appeared a labyrinth of buildings nearly identical to the one the magician had built underwater. From then on, the water spirit was no longer wild and free but was enslaved by the magician.'"

To my surprise, the kids and their parents are clapping, and when I look up, the tall girl is showing them the final picture, but just before she closes the book I can see a tuft of paper sticking out from the spine. Extra pages have been torn out from the end. No *wonder* the book didn't have a satisfying ending. Why didn't anyone else notice?

The door opens outward and a young mother slides past me with her toddler son in tow. "Thanks for the story, Carla!" the little boy calls behind him.

Before I can duck out of the doorway, the tall reader turns and waves good-bye to the kid, and her eyes lock on mine. "Leese!" she squeals.

I freeze, caught in the headlights of her searching gaze, then realize I have to go over to her. Obviously this girl and I know each other well. Very well. If I had to guess, I'd say this was my best friend.

Was.

I can't think of one thing to say to her.

"I've been texting you all day." She points to her purse. "Where were you, slacker? Miss school again?"

"Yeah." I shrug. *Again?* So I miss class a lot? A bell goes off in my head, but it's not a lost memory returning. It's the memory of Kerry at the clinic this morning, asking what I'd done to myself this time. Why am I always at the clinic?

Carla grins at me and whispers under her breath, "You were totally hungover from the party, weren't you?"

"Hungover?" I say stupidly, not wanting to commit myself to an answer, but it comes out sounding like, "Yes."

"I knew it. You were pretty sloshed at Dan's. Of course, he was too . . ."

Sloshed, what a gross word. So sloppy and wet, so out of control. I look at Carla's perfectly flat hair and decide she's never been sloshed in her perfect life. Much as it pains me, I need to stay close to her at least for now. She knows so much about me that every sentence out of her mouth gives me new info to process. Like, I went to a party last night.

Hosted by some lush named Dan.

Then again, I'm also a lush. Who misses school a lot, possibly from being drunk-sick. Lovely. I'm afraid to learn more about myself. But I'm even more afraid of staying a blank. Of never being whole again, ending up in the asylum.

"I can't believe you're here." She giggles. "In the *library.*"

Jesus. Am I that well-known for being illiterate? "I got bored, okay?" I say, hoping after the fact that my defensive tone sounds like the old Elyse.

"If you're bored with partying, maybe you should try some volunteering." Carla smiles, a little bit smugly, in my opinion. "Reading to kids is *such* great practice."

"For what?" I ask, before I can stop myself.

Carla throws me a hesitant look, like she thinks I might be making fun of her. "For when we have kids, hello? Ticktock. Graduation's in two weeks, gonna be adults soon."

"I guess." I'm thinking Carla must be one of those obsessive planning types who think ten to twenty years ahead. But as I glance down at the now squirming semi-circle of kids on the carpet, the moms and dads kneeling to zip up sweaters and tie shoelaces don't look much older than we are. They look about the same age as Candace, the college student staying at Preston House. So why haven't any of these people gone off to college themselves? Come to think of it, Liz, my own mother, can't be older than her early thirties. Which means when *she* had *me*—

Before I can complete that scary thought, Carla's purse rings with a tinny R & B riff. She pulls out a sleek silver phone. "Oh, it's Pete!" I can tell from the sudden purr in her tone that Pete is her boyfriend. She thumbs a quick response and flips the keyboard shut. "I was just telling them that I found you," she says earnestly, swinging her purse over her shoulder. Who's them? I can't ask. I'm clearly supposed to know. "And that you weren't answering texts before because you were still hungover. But I only said that part because it seemed like they were getting worried."

"It's okay," I say, thinking that as soon as I get back home I need to find that phone and see who I text and what about. It's probably buried deep in the pink pile carpet.

"Are you sure everything's okay?" She smiles nervously. "I mean, we always text each other back."

I hate lying, but I can't see a way around it this time. "I lost my phone charger," I say, "and the battery's dead. Sorry I didn't get back to you."

"Oh, you don't have to apologize!" Carla throws up her hands, stepping away. "I'm just relieved you're not mad at me."

Inwardly I cringe. Am I a total bully to my friends?

Carla keeps staring at me, like she's expecting me to say or do something. But I'm still overwhelmed by the ugly picture forming in my mind of the person I used to be.

Finally she says, "Um, Elyse? You do remember the plan, right? They're meeting us down by the Ferris wheel."

They again. So it's a group. Well, that works okay, since I was going to catch up with Dark-Eyed Boy at the fair later anyway. He can meet my friends. "Of course." I hate lying, and to make matters worse I'm bad at it.

"Okay, so, I'm ready when you are," she says.

Holy crap. She's waiting for me to tell her it's time to go. This beautiful girl who reads in a rich, hypnotic voice is waiting for me to call the shots. "Let's go to the fair," I say decisively, and she beams and follows me outside to Main Street.

"So, I liked the story you picked," I say as we walk, and again, Carla beams.

"Thanks!"

"But I noticed there were pages torn out from the end."

She blinks at me. "It's a *library book*," she says as if I've said something stupid. "The last few pages are always just ads from the publisher, and the librarian pulls them out."

Really? "But it felt like the story didn't end. I mean what happened to the tribe with no name? Was that part based on a real tribe, by the way?" Because they weren't part of Liz's Welcome to Preston House history lesson, I hadn't even thought of the people who had lived here before.

But, again, she gives me a weird look. "That *is* the end," she says. "And of course it's not real, it's a fairy tale—not like you haven't heard it a million times, same as me. Are you still feeling sick from yesterday?"

I can hear, or imagine I can hear, a hidden accusation in her velvet tones. *Or are you ready for the asylum?* I back off quickly. "Yeah, that's it. I'm still . . . hungover."

Her soft brown eyes stay fixed on me the rest of the way.

By the time Carla and I get over there, the Ferris wheel and the merry-go-round have already started running and there's a carnival excitement in the air. Kids run by with clouds of pink or blue cotton candy bigger than their heads, getting in line for Whack a Mole or the Strong Man. The smell of hot dogs grilling mingles with frying funnel cakes and elephant ears.

Carla makes a beeline for her boyfriend, Pete, a chiseled, auburn-haired hunk wearing an orange and white letterman jacket. I watch them peck chastely at each other's lips, feeling vaguely like I'm watching two dolls make out. They'll make beautiful children together, and if Carla has her way it'll be soon.

Suddenly I'm enveloped by strong arms, held so tight I feel like I'm being choked. *Help!*

"Hey, babe," says an unfamiliar voice. The boy it belongs to spins me around and lunges for me, his lips crashing into mine, his stubble burning my skin, his hot tongue forcing my mouth open. He tastes like cigarette smoke. *Ugh.* I step on his foot, jerk out of his arms.

"Ow!" he yells in surprise. Then he laughs. "What the hell was that about?"

Carla rubs her forehead. "Did you guys have some fight I forgot about?"

The reality of the situation dawns on me. His grabbing and kissing me wasn't a random assault. This guy, whose letterman jacket proudly proclaims him Dan "The Man," felt justified and comfortable putting his hands and tongue on me, and no one else thought it was weird. Which can only mean . . . he's my boyfriend. Or my sort-of boyfriend, at least. Or he *was* my sort-of boyfriend. Is there a proper term for a boy you don't remember but never dumped? Oh, why didn't Liz prepare me? And why do I let him call me *babe*?

"I love how you can be so unpredictable sometimes," Dan says. "My wild girl." He pulls strands of my hair out of my eyes and gazes at me fondly, as if my stepping on him is the most adorable thing any girl's ever done. And the thing is, he's beautiful. Sculpted, tall, sure. Dark-Eyed Boy—well, he's hot, in an intense way. But a picture of Dark-Eyed Boy can't convey his weird charisma, while a picture of Dan would look just as perfect as Dan looks right now, laughing in the sun. He looks golden, like a Greek god.

The kaleidoscope of my world has shifted again. And I have to get away.

CHAPTER 14

DARK-EYED BOY

I FIGURE THAT CROWDS ALWAYS KNOW WHEN something important's about to start, so as the sun's setting I head off in the direction of town square, where a large mob is gathering.

The few picnic tables in the square have multiplied, and spaghetti dinner's being served on checkered tablecloths with fireflies in jars as the centerpieces for each table. At one of the many food booths, I see a woman in pigtails wearing a baker's hat and apron and recognize Hazel, the confused lady who answered the door for us this morning. Other people are preparing plates of cookies and scones and other baked goods, but she just stands there waving at the crowd like a mascot.

As I move toward the front, no one jostles me, with or without an *excuse me*, and no one makes eye contact either. But they do move to let me pass, either silently, if they're alone, or without stopping conversation with their friends.

It's as if when people see me they're aware something's taking up that piece of space—but their minds stop short of noticing that something (me) directly.

Once I realize that, I take advantage of it and weave easily through the mob, checking for Elyse.

I feel her hand on my back before I see her. "Hey," she says. "I ran into some friends."

"Cool, where are they?"

"In line for hot dogs. I don't eat hot dogs," she says. "Plus I sort of had to get away from them."

"Your friends?"

"Just for a few minutes."

"Act normal. You can't let them suspect, Elyse."

"I know, believe me. It's just hard," she says. "Not being able to be honest with people. I mean, I *know* I can't tell them. . . . But it means hanging out with them feels like lying all the time. And lying is exhausting."

I reach over and kiss the top of her head.

"What was that for?"

"For being compulsively honest. It's something I like about you."

A fortyish guy with male-pattern baldness steps up to the statue and speaks into a microphone, and everyone goes quiet. "My dear cit-i-zens," he reads haltingly from his notes. "As your mayor I am proud and pleased to announce the beginning of summer fair." Applause. "Now, before the fun com-men-ces, I have a few public-service messages. It is of utmost importance that you remember to turn off your ovens when you leave your houses." A murmuring in the crowd. "I would also like to announce that Tim's Hardware is running a *great* deal on floor padding. . . . Now, let's all give it up for the Preston Trust, thanks to whose dollars we now enjoy a freshly painted library! Another round of applause. I spot Elyse's parents ahead of us in the crowd, Jeffry's beefy arm hooked around Liz's shoulder.

"All right, folks," the mayor announces. "It's the moment you've all been waiting for, a special Summer Falls tradition. It's time to make the man!"

Elyse and I glance at each other.

"Did he say we're going to 'make a man'?" I ask.

"Weird," she says, shrugging.

"Let him have two feet to stand on," the mayor intones.

A bullhorn sounds, and suddenly Liz is off like a shot, rushing to join a cluster of adult women that quickly splits into two blobs. One on the right, one on the left.

"Let him have legs to carry him forward in the world."

This time when the horn sounds, I hear a squeal, and suddenly girls under twenty-five are running into the fray, arranging themselves in two, thick messy lines above the "feet." This just keeps getting weirder. I turn to catch Elyse's eye, but she's gone too. Disappeared into the mob. I'm relieved, if a little creeped out, to spot her white hoodie somewhere near the man's right knee. Was she just trying to keep from standing out from the other townspeople? No, she moved too fast for that. Some part of her remembers this local tradition from past fairs. But is it muscle memory or brain memory?

The mayor moves on to his next line. "Let him have a strong body to protect what's his."

Most of the men, including Jeffry, peel from the crowd and swagger forward.

"Let him have arms to reach out to the world and make his mark on it."

Boys of all ages race to form two lines.

"Let him have clever hands to work his craft."

This time I recognize Bette, the lady from the antique store, and see several adults in purple Mollie's Milkshakes aprons.

"Let him have a head full of knowledge and a voice to share it with."

I see Kerry from the clinic up at the man's head as well as Joe and other people I assume are teachers. And the doctor too, in his white lab coat and stethoscope.

At this point the only people still in the audience are the mayor and a few hundred people I figure must be tourists. At least there are enough that I don't stand out.

"Let him have blood," the mayor adds triumphantly. "To bring his body nutrients."

With a rustling of excitement, the tourists run into the fray. Haphazardly Candace and Jim walk past me, hand in hand.

I look at the blobby shape on the square in front of me. If you don't think about it too hard, it does look like a person. A person with crooked legs and clown feet, but a person.

The mayor yells into his microphone, "Who is this man in front of me?"

In one voice, each syllable a thunderclap, the townspeople shout, "He's. Our. Town."

"Our town," the mayor intones. "It lives and breathes, like any man. He has a head full of intelligence—our doctors, teachers, and librarians. He stands on a solid foundation of unconditional love and service, our mothers and homemakers. The powerful limbs that move him forward are our youth, our young scholars. He has clever hands like our artisans on Main Street. His body is as strong as our mill—" A strange pause. He must have forgotten the mill closed. Awkward. "As strong as our men who are fathers, husbands, protectors, and providers. Is this man complete?"

"No!" everyone shouts.

"What does this man need to complete him?"

"A heart and a soul." Even some of the tourists yell it out. They've clearly been here before.

"Then let this man have a heart and a soul."

At this, the mayor and priest walk over to the "man" made of people, at about waist level, and are instantly sucked into the crowd. They appear again side by side in the man's chest, carried on the shoulders of the men who make up his trunk.

A photographer snaps a picture.

This is the creepiest thing I've ever seen.

"May he stay healthy, wealthy, and wise till next summer!"

The people making up the "man" all cheer wildly and then disperse.

Elyse comes back, looking sheepish.

"What was that about?"

"I don't know." Her cheeks are growing pink. "I mean, it sounds like it's a yearly tradition. I guess I've just done it so many times, it's automatic. I still feel like an idiot."

"Don't," I say. "At least you have a hometown, stupid traditions and all. I don't even have a name yet."

She gives me a look of sympathy.

"Other than the name you gave me," I add, and she leans closer and smiles, her eyes traveling to mine. In one day we've forged a closeness with each other. We're a two-person team, with our own shared memories, our own language.

Out of the corner of my eye, two guys in green T-shirts slip out of the audience and sneak up behind the photographer. I hear the sickening smack of one of their fists against the back of his head, the choked cry as the photographer crumples. The other guy grabs his camera and they both run. Without thinking, I run after them. I'm not the only one. Before any of us can reach them though, an old beat-up pickup pulls up and they hop into the back.

"Green Vista, bitches!" one of the guys screams as the truck starts speeding off. "That's revenge for the big game." Dude sounds righteously pissed off.

But the Summer Falls folk take it in stride. "Loser!" yells a guy in a letter jacket while the doctor in his white coat checks out the photographer and helps him to his feet.

"They've lost the big game every year since 1963," another letter-jacket guy yells, and high-fives the first. "We're always number one, baby!"

The crowd breaks into a spontaneous chant: "Always number one, always number one!"

I'm beginning to see why the Green Vista ninjas felt the need to even the score when the second letter-jacket guy walks right over to Elyse and puts his arm around her. "Hey, beautiful," he says. "Want to ride the Ferris wheel with me?"

She meets my eyes, and it's hard to communicate with her when all my energy is tied up fighting the urge to physically remove that idiot's thickly muscled arm from her shoulder. After a moment I manage to wave her away, like, *Go, get out of here, have fun, act normal.* And that *is* what I want her to do—that's the smart thing to do. Just because I don't like it doesn't mean I can't see that.

But I turn so I don't watch them walk away together.

CHAPTER 15

ELYSE

OKAY, WHAT DO YOU DO WHEN YOU DON'T LIKE your best friends?

It's not like I *hate* these people's guts, but sitting in the Ferris wheel basket next to Dan, with Pete and Carla in the basket just above us, feels a little like torture. For one thing, Dan keeps leaning over to kiss me and I'm not sure I'm into the way he kisses. He doesn't have bad breath or a tonsil-banging tongue or anything—so maybe it's not fair to imply he's a bad kisser when the real issue is I'd rather be kissing someone else. Someone I actually know and care about instead of pretend to know and care about. Someone with dark, dangerous eyes. But I will say Dan seems to have clear ideas about who is supposed to be the kisser and who is the kissee. I'm guessing that would be the reason he keeps tilting my head back and leaning over me so I have no leverage and can't breathe, so I have to look up at him. The one time I think I might be getting into it and try to kiss him a little more actively, he blocks my tongue with his own. After a while I just pull away and watch the scenery. Kissing may be a sport, but blocking other people's goals doesn't help you win.

Then there's Carla, who's petrified of heights. Every time we get near the top of the Ferris wheel, she lets out a squeal as if we're riding some kind of giant roller coaster instead of the world's dullest ride and grabs Pete's hand, and Dan and Pete yell jokes to each other that basically amount to What a Dumb Girl Carla Is for Being Scared of a Ferris Wheel.

Clearly, this double date is really just an excuse for Dan and Pete to bond.

From the top of the Ferris wheel I can see the fair crowds moving like a giant amoeba.

I can also see a tiny figure. It's the redheaded lady—the one who was asleep on the picnic table earlier—and if I'm not mistaken she's swinging a bat. Into the window of Mollie's Milkshakes.

The next thing I know, the Ferris wheel's gears have ground to a halt.

I let out a "What the hell?" just as Carla in the basket above us cries out, "Oh my goodness!"

Her basket with Pete is near the top.

"I can't take this, I can't take being so high," Carla says over and over. "Who's running this thing?"

"I don't see an operator," Dan yells. "Hey, operator! Get back to work."

"Please make it start again," Carla begs, but it's unclear who she's begging. God, maybe. "Please, please, I have to get down."

"Hell, I can fix this," Pete says. "I can't stand to see my girl cry." He slips under the safety bar and dangles from the footrest over our basket.

Jesus. Is the idiot climbing down?

As he drops into our basket, the seat swings wildly back and forth. In unison Dan and I each grab Pete around the waist, steadying his balance before he can tip over and fall to the ground.

"Steady, man," Dan says, "we got you." He turns to me and winks. "We're pros."

I ignore him. "Pete, why the hell are you doing this?" My heart's pounding, not just with fear for him but with anger. How could he risk his life for something so stupid? I jumped out of a window because I had to, not to impress my date. "Are you crazy?"

"Nah, I'm not crazy, I'm gonna fix this," Pete says brightly, and calls to the couple below, "Heads up!"

They give him a cheer as he nimbly drops one step closer to the bottom of the wheel. Two more hops and he's on the ground. He gives a little bow to the cheering passengers and strides over to the controls by the gearbox.

I breathe a sigh of relief that his stupid stunt didn't get him killed.

He's poking around the fat black power cables. "Aha!" he calls up. "Looks like this one came unplugged."

Gripping the loose end in one hand, he pulls himself on top of the gears and connects the oversize plug into the open socket. "Ta-da," he calls out, as with a mechanical whine the wheel lurches back to life. Our seat jerks forward. The rescued passengers cheer, including Dan.

Suddenly the applause is interrupted by a sickening crunch and Pete's bloodcurdling scream.

Pete falls backward onto the ground, blood gushing from his leg. For a moment he goes silent—the fall must have knocked the wind out of him. Then he lets out another high scream of agony. I stare at the bloody stump of his leg. My god. His right foot is gone. Gone. Crushed between the gears of the machine he restarted.

Dan stares down in shock at his friend's broken body.

Many people are screaming. Some people turn and vomit out of their baskets onto the ground.

Everyone at the fair has now realized something's wrong. A crowd has gathered in horror, but no one seems to know what to do as Pete lies on the ground crying and begging to God, to Jesus, to anyone, for help. A bright, white-coated figure parts the sea of the stupefied onlookers and shoves his way through. The doctor. If he can stop the bleeding in time, Pete has a chance. I breathe out finally, the sound that escapes me halfway between a sob and a sigh of relief.

And that's when I see a small figure perched at the base of the Ferris wheel. It's a little boy with blond hair and faintly shimmering skin. As each pair of panicked riders swings by, he reaches his arms out to touch them and they slump forward in their baskets, unconscious.

The hair on the back of my neck stands up.

Our basket is the next one to swing by the ghost.

"Dan, we have to go!" I climb out of my seat and brace to leap to the ground.

He looks at me blankly. "It's too late. It's too late to save him."

I jump the five feet to the ground and roll to my feet. Looking over my shoulder I see Dan collapse at the ghost boy's touch.

I run away. Away from the crowd. Away from Pete. Away from the ghost.

CHAPTER 16

DARK-EYED BOY

WORD SPREADS FAST THROUGH THE CROWD. Something went wrong on the Ferris wheel. Knowing Elyse was heading for that wheel, I push through, determined to make sure she's okay, trying not to think of the worst.

But long before I get there I can hear the screaming of a guy, can hear the sad, hushed murmuring of the crowd. "Football hero . . . maimed . . . lost his foot . . ." And I know it's not Elyse who's hurt.

Almost as quickly as the rumors fly, mass heatnaps start erupting. People to my left and right just start dropping, and I feel a now familiar zap in my chest and see the blue light for a moment. If Elyse were here, would she have seen a ghost retreating, repelled by my tattoo?

The people on the Ferris wheel are all asleep themselves, and I hope to God none of them fall out and die. Scanning the faces, I don't see Elyse, though I do see the dumb jock who pulled her away earlier.

Even though all the people around him are down though, one person stays up and alert. I see a tiny flash of pink light in front of the doctor as the people around him clatter to the ground. So he's immune to the heatnaps, like I am. The ghosts can't touch him. I look him in the eye, wondering if he has a tattoo like mine and how he got his. He doesn't notice me, of course—I haven't said anything—but he runs to the Ferris wheel and quickly injects the screaming boy with a syringe. The boy screams one more time and goes slack.

Almost instantly a black car pulls up as close to the Ferris wheel as possible, and quickly a crew of gray-uniformed medics descend on the now silent, unmoving boy. Two of them load him onto a stretcher. The other two shut down the Ferris wheel and begin wiping away the blood and bits of bone.

Fuck. If he lives, he's going to wake up without a foot. That's got to be even worse than waking up without a past. He's going to be as confused about his identity as we are. Overnight he'll have gone from football hero to "that guy without a foot." I can't help but notice everyone in Summer Falls is super-healthy-looking and attractive. He'll stick out, even if they fit him with a prosthetic at the hospital. Assuming that black town car is in fact taking him to a hospital. The thought sends a chill of terror up my back. Where else might they be taking him?

As they finish cleaning, one of the medics pulls the lever

and the wheel whirs to life again. The black car pulls away.

Moments later, people start waking up. The people on the Ferris wheel, incredibly, keep riding it. The people on the ground look around with confused expressions, then shuffle into food or game lines. Conversations resume all around me. Casual conversations. Nothing about the boy who just got carted away. They're not wondering what happened to him.

It's like they don't even remember that a guy got his foot caught in the Ferris wheel's gears.

Because they *don't* remember. It hits me suddenly.

Just like the Bishops after they were squared off in the kitchen, fighting their way toward an ugly divorce.

It's not just that they moved on. It's that they lost the ability to look back.

The heatnaps aren't random, like Wikipedia said. They happen after traumatic situations. They erase traumatic memories somehow. But how?

Nearby I hear an old man's plaintive voice and look up to see Hazel, the baker, still down. "Come on, sweetie. Get up."

Sheriff Hank is on the scene within moments. "Come on, get up, old girl."

"Come back to me," the old man pleads.

Hank kneels down to take Hazel's vitals, but it's clear she's alive. Her eyes are even open. But she's not moving, not responding to anything anyone says. The doctor talks quietly to Hank. Then together they lift Hazel onto a gurney and carry her to the sheriff-mobile. Her husband, I notice, has instantly fallen to the ground in a second heatnap.

"Elyse?"

At the sound of her name I whip around and see the jock guy who was asleep on the Ferris wheel. He's searching through the crowd, calling her name.

Without thinking, I walk right up to him. "What happened? She was with you a minute ago."

He blinks at me. "Oh, it's you. Since when has Elyse needed someone like you looking out for her?"

"Apparently she does, since you lost her." While you were passed out like every other idiot in this town.

Letterman jacket grabs me by the arm. "You don't need to worry about my girl. We clear on that?"

Crap. This is not going well. Remembering how the lady in the antique store reacted to being insulted and reminded of bad memories, I say, "You just sat there drooling while your dumb jock friend's foot got pulverized. Elyse doesn't know you anymore and don't tell me you can't tell."

The guy's face gets redder with rage, then his grip on my arm slackens. He crumples to the ground.

As usual when people collapse here, no one around seems to care. They walk around him.

I'm not going to learn anything more tonight in this crowd of zombies and I need to talk to Elyse, so I turn and walk from the fair all the way back to Preston House.

Only thanks to my disguise as a Brazilian tourist, I

can't exactly knock on her bedroom door at night. I hope that if she saw half of what I did at the fair, she'll want to talk as much as I do—and she'll come find me.

Back in the Rustic's Cottage, I take off my shoes and shirt, turn on the bathroom light, and stand in front of the mirror, washing my face and brushing my teeth. The eye tattoo in the center of my chest stares back at me, making me wonder about what the hell possessed me to get a tattoo like that in the first place. It's disheartening that the whole day's passed without my even getting close to figuring out who I am or what happened to me. And now I'm alone, without Elyse. Her absence gnaws at me.

Other than the ink eye, I look pretty normal. I have light brown skin and supershort dark hair. Eyes that aren't too much paler than my pupils. My ancestry clearly isn't European, or not just European. And I didn't grow up in this town, or more people would recognize me. Even though Elyse doesn't feel like she fits in here, she looks like she does. Her clothes, her haircut, her accent, her mannerisms. She was clearly born and raised in this town. But I could be from just about anywhere on earth. How the hell am I supposed to narrow it down?

Through the sliding patio door I can hear crickets chirping. I must be from a big city, because all this quiet is freaking me out.

I have to talk to Elyse about what happened to that boy at the fair. I don't give a damn if I cause a ruckus by heading up to her room.

I pull my baggy shirt back on and slide open the patio door. The night air feels warm through the screen, and the blue-black sky is bright with stars. Endless stars. The breeze smells like flowers and freshly cut grass. I can see Jim and Candace lying next to each other on chaise lounges, talking softly.

Then I see her hurrying across the yard in white pajamas and bunny slippers. She's clutching a large book to her chest. She nods a hello to the tourists without looking at them. I've opened the screen before she can even knock.

"Thank god you're home!" she says.

Thank god you're safe, I think. "Then you saw the accident?"

She nods. "The accident was horrible. His foot . . ." She shudders. "But what was even worse were the ghosts putting everyone to sleep."

"Ghosts?" I think back to the mass heatnaps. "You're telling me ghosts did that?"

"I saw it. I saw it and I ran, all the way home."

I let out a sigh. "I believe you. And I need you to believe this: While everyone else was knocked out, a car with dark windows pulled up and hauled him away. After people woke up from the heatnap, they'd forgotten all about what happened. People at the fair went right back to dancing and playing, like nothing ever happened."

"You're saying heatnaps affect people's memories." She looks at me. "You think that's what happened to us?"

"Maybe. But they all still seemed to remember who

they were. Well, except one person. That old lady whose door we knocked on, she didn't wake up from her heatnap. Her eyes were open, but you could tell there was no one there. The doctor took her as well."

"We have to find out what's going on. We've got to fix our memories before the doctor takes us too."

"Yeah, get our memories and get the hell out of here." Then I think about her mother and her dumb boyfriend. "Or maybe not. You've got family here. You've got friends."

"You're not going to like this." She holds up the book. It's a yearbook. *The Mountain Cat.* "But so do you."

She opens the yearbook to a bookmarked page. It's the portrait of Marshall King. The same picture in the Satanist guy's house, on the bedroom wall. Photo guy. Me. It's like a gut punch.

"Hi, Marshall." Elyse waves at me.

I shake my head, not knowing what to say. "It doesn't feel—"

"Like it's really your name? Welcome to the club."

The room's spinning. If I'm Marshall King, if that room is my room with all my junk in it, then that means . . . the Satanist guy is my father.

"Maybe I should go back and talk to that guy at the house. I mean, you were right, it was my room. He must be . . . my father."

"Who cares if he is?" She sets the yearbook down, her green eyes hard as glass. "He's obviously not a good one."

"Easy for you to say. You've at least found your family."

"They're not my family. They're just people who look like me."

"Well, for now, because you don't remember them."

"It's more than that." She speaks slowly, trying on the words. "I don't know . . . if I like them. It all just feels so *random*."

"Random?"

"Like someone put together this life for me from a box of spare parts. 'Here, you're named Elyse, and you're an innkeeper's daughter in a small town, and you have'"—she grabs a wavy lock of her own hair—"'blond hair.' But it doesn't feel like *me*. It doesn't feel real."

"Right now," I tell her, "you're the only real person I know."

A crashing sound interrupts us, followed by a muffled cry. We look at each other and run outside.

"Sounds like it was coming from the main house," I say.

"Did you hear where that sound came from?" Elyse calls to Candace and Jim. But they don't answer because they're both passed out on their respective chaises under the moonlight. Candace is even snoring. They were awake five minutes ago.

Elyse grabs my arm. "There's someone in the gazebo," she whispers. "A tall man. He's just standing there in the shadows, but I can see the top of his head. He's wearing feathers in his hair."

"I don't see him," I whisper back, trying to remember the ghost-tour brochure. I have no doubt there'll be a description of the guy in the ghost tour. "What do you want me to do? We could make a run for the house." And then I remember she says that woman—the ghost—went after me but couldn't touch me. I'm about to suggest I get closer to investigate when Elyse screams.

"You didn't see, right?" she asks. "He's out in the open, creeping toward the basement window." I look down at the lightly packed garden trail and suddenly under the porch light I can see footprints appearing on the ground, approaching the window. Goose bumps rise on my arms.

"Did he go through?"

She nods. "No wonder I got mad if she left them open," she says as if to herself.

We dash inside after the ghost. It's dark everywhere, except one bedroom at the end of the hall, where a shaft of light shines from under the door. Snoring comes from inside.

Elyse knocks. "Everything okay?" she calls.

No answer. She keeps knocking, over and over. The girl's determined. Finally I hear footsteps walk to the door, and I duck into the hall.

"What's wrong, Elyse?" Liz's voice is groggy.

"Oh, I heard a noise," she says. "It sounded like someone was hurt or something."

"What noise? We didn't hear anything."

"Sorry to bother you, I . . . you really didn't hear anything?"

"Everything's fine, honey," Liz says. "Go back to bed."

"No way in hell am I going back to that tower room alone," she says, so I walk her to her bedroom, praying her father doesn't wake up and see me there. She searches the room until she's satisfied it's ghost free, then closes the window and sinks onto her bed, shoes and all, curling up into a fetal position.

"Don't go giving up on me," I say. "You said it yourself, we're going to get our memories back. We've figured out so much already. Tomorrow we're going to show up at school and see what we can learn from talking to our friends."

Slowly she uncurls. "You're right," she says calmly. "My family's useless, and your dad is crazy. Maybe our friends are the real key to getting our memories back."

"We'll get through this if we stick together," I say. I tuck her into bed, close the door, and tiptoe down the creaky hallway.

Outside, Jim and Candace are awake again and flirting. "You didn't happen to hear a loud noise, did you?" I ask. They shake their heads. "Or see anybody come through the backyard?"

"You mean like the innkeeper's daughter sneaking out to see you?" Jim winks. "Course not, Romeo."

"Your secret love is safe with us," Candace adds. She looks younger in cutoff jeans and a baggy T-shirt, or maybe it's just the relaxed expression on her face. I notice Jim's unbuttoned his top button.

Discreetly I sniff the air, expecting to pick up the hippie-temple reek of pot smoke. But all I smell is fresh-cut lawn and sweet camellias. The tourists grin at me stupidly. Maybe they're just high on love.

In the cottage, I toss and turn in the world's most comfortable king-size bed, surrounded by feather pillows. It's hot so I'm lying on top of the comforter. And since part of me is terrified that I could wake up with no memory again, and this time I'd like to not be naked, I'm wearing all my clothes. But sleep won't come. One by one I throw the feather pillows to the floor, before finally giving up and turning on the lamp again.

Sitting at the desk, I open last year's *The Mountain Cat* to the juniors' section. It opens right on a page with her picture. Elyse Alton. She's radiant in a black-and-white V-neck T-shirt, her hair piled on top of her head, staring straight into the camera with a challenging look.

I spend forty minutes poring over the yearbook, studying it like it's a new school subject: reality 101. Elyse was a cheerleader last year, but she's also everywhere in group shots. Looking down from dark sunglasses; glossy lips parted in a sexy, relaxed smile; tan arm thrown around the jock from the fair. No hint of the wide, startled green eyes, the terrified, trembling girl I wanted to comfort earlier. The Elyse in this book is built of sheer confidence.

Or she pretended to be.

Where am I? I'm not in any of the pictures with her. Did I even know her?

I find myself scanning through every page for pictures of myself. The candids. The theater productions. Clubs. Judging from the amount of space it's given, athletics is obviously the big thing here. There's a Summer Falls high school football team, and I'm not on it. There's also a basketball team, which I'm also not on, and a baseball team, which—guess what? Other than that one lame class picture, I'm nowhere. Not even the science-fiction-and-fantasy club.

According to this yearbook, I am less than a loser. I'm a nobody. Invisible as one of Elyse's ghosts. My chest aches. By the laws of high school, she shouldn't even be talking to me, let alone talking about skipping town with me.

My eyes travel down the signatures scrawled across the end pages. No spot is left blank. People have crowded in their words in corners, in every possible color of ink. But the signatures don't give much information. They're shallow, generic. Not quite "Have a great summer!" generic but close. Joking about shared classes and activities. Too many hearts and exclamation points. I can't find my own signature. Over the varsity football team photo someone's written in grease pen:

HI, BEAUTIFUL. IT FEELS WEIRD TO BE WRITING THIS IN YOUR YEARBOOK WHEN I KNOW I CAN TELL YOU THESE THINGS ANYTIME. YOU KNOW I LOVE YOU. YOU KNOW YOU'RE THE ONE FOR ME. MY PROM QUEEN, THE ONLY

GIRL I'D EVER LET DRIVE MY CAR. TO ME YOU ARE
PERFECT. THIS YEAR HAS BEEN AMAZING BECAUSE I'VE
SPENT SO MANY HOURS WITH YOU, LAUGHING, TALKING,
AND . . . HIKING. ☺ I LIVE FOR OUR HIKES.
LOVE FOREVER, DAN.

Gee, I'm sure no one reading this could ever guess what "hiking" is code for. Why not just write, *I live to fuck you*. ☺

Feeling a sick twisting in my stomach, I flip back through the juniors till I find his photo. But I already know what he's going to look like. Daniel Bellingham. *The Mountain Cat* is crammed with comically impressive photos of him: touchdown, sliding into home plate, in a singlet sitting on top of a cringing, faceless competitor. How could he do both football and wrestling? Two fall sports. I quickly learn to adjust my expectations. Dan can do anything. The captions below his inane grinning mug gush like his mom wrote them: *Dan Saves the Day Again! Dan Leads the Rays to Victory in the Big Game!*

Okay, discovering that Elyse's boyfriend is the school stud shouldn't be a shock. Even if I wasn't so busy desperately trying to figure out what the hell's happened to me, I'd have no right to be jealous. Or would I?

Elyse's bunny slippers are still sitting on the chair; I pick one up and fit it onto my hand. The inside's lined with satin. Who cares if I have a right? I *am* jealous. "I *live for our hikes.*" Bastard. You don't even know her. That's obvious from the generic clichés in his stupid yearbook entry. My face feels hot and my stomach feels so queasy that I have to concentrate on keeping down that blue cotton candy from the fair.

But at the same time, the Dan thing just doesn't feel real to me. I can't reconcile what he's written here with the obvious connection Elyse and I are feeling. Whatever he was in her old life, all Elyse and I have is each other. I fall asleep imagining her blond hair gently drifting up and down with my breathing.

I wake up in a cold sweat in the darkness. I've been dreaming the same dream. Once again, I dive under the cold water and sink down to the eerie calm of the underwater graveyard. Once again I know I'm going to die here. But that, somehow, my death will allow others to live. I'm saving people by sacrificing myself. And so, somehow, again, it feels all right.

CHAPTER 17

ELYSE

I GRAB ON TO MY LIMO DRIVER'S OUTSTRETCHED hand and step out to face the waiting crowd—my crowd. All around me cameras flash as the paparazzi vie for a clear picture of my blue velvet evening gown. They surround me like sharks, begging questions: "Tell us who designed your gown?" "Do you think you'll win this year?" But my personal assistants wave them off, so I can glide past. It all feels so natural, so right for me to be here that I can't stop smiling, and I know my smile is mesmerizing to the crowd.

But a tiny voice in my head wonders, Why does this feel right to me, to be stared at? Why do I deserve to be famous? Why did I even want this?

I turn away from the cameras, hitch up the bottom of my leg-constricting mermaid-style gown, and find that I'm wearing running shoes.

———

Someone's leaning over the side of my bed, smelling like flowery lotion and biscuit batter.

"Rise and sparkle, honey bun." Liz's chirpy voice grates like nails on a chalkboard.

It all comes back to me: I'm in my all-pink bedroom at Preston House. I still have no memory of anything before yesterday. And yesterday was no picnic, between ghosts, window jumps, asylums, squad cars, and relentlessly chipper yet clueless parents. I don't want to be here, but I don't want to be a celeb in a fancy dress having strangers take my photo either. That dream was so shallow and stupid, I actually feel like booing my subconscious.

The unfamiliar smell of Liz's lotion so close to me is making me nauseous. I'm worried she's going to kiss my forehead and am relieved when she pokes at my side instead. "Come on, it's almost breakfast time for the guests."

"Not hungry," I mutter into my pillow, but she just pokes me harder. "Please let me sleep. Maybe it'll help my brain reset or something. . . ."

"There's nothing the matter with your brain, you just have to keep your mouth shut and keep busy," she hisses. "Wash up and dress nice for breakfast. Make the guests feel right at home."

"But it's not their home," I say. She's already scurrying back down the stairs in her scary heels and doesn't hear me. She'd better be careful running around in those, or she'll end up as Summer Falls's latest ghost. And what will her little graphic emblem be, a feather duster?

The guests. It's like the tourists are this mythical beast Liz and Jeffry Alton worship, loathe, and prey upon all at the same time. Without them, I suppose they couldn't afford to keep living in Preston House. But as long as they keep it, they're slaves to them. And so, apparently, am I.

I take a hot shower in the lavender bathroom. Lavender is a sickening color to see first thing in the morning, and the tub floor being padded with three lavender mats is just perplexing. Am I that much of a klutz? The body wash reeks of "white daffodils" so I snap it shut after one sniff and wash with mint shampoo instead.

In the closet I scrounge together the least body-hugging outfit I can: loose cutoffs and a baggy white hoodie. The hoodie feels uncomfortably warm by the time I've finished tying the laces of my worn running shoes, but I'm willing to steam-cook for the sake of modesty.

I spot a light blue backpack in the corner, open it up, and stare at the binder with class notes and doodles. The divider tabs follow my schedule: Red is "Per 1 Math," orange is "Per 2 History," yellow is "Per 3 PE," and it's blank inside except for a handout on nutrition on which I've written, *This is stupid*. I startle at my own handwriting. It's spare, angular, and so hard on the page it leaves a Braille embossment on the other side. I'd expected *i*'s dotted with open circles. Instead my writing is the first thing I've found in this place that feel like it's *mine*.

I feel a tingling in my fingers, a warmth that spreads up my arms to my chest. It's not a memory, exactly, but it's a clear sign of . . . something.

What if the thing that'll finally jog my memory isn't here in Preston House but at school? Maybe school is the key to finding more about myself. The address was in *The Mountain Cat*, 1500 Main Street. I swing the backpack over my right shoulder and lug it downstairs.

The table's half full, with Liz hovering around in her frilly pink apron, refilling coffee mugs and teacups, while Jeffry beams at her from his patriarchal throne at the head of the table. Marshall catches my eye from his seat by the back door.

"Nice of you to join us, princess." Jeffry's voice booms over the din of guests chattering, and everyone chuckles, I guess at his chastising me for being late.

"Hiking clothes?" Liz frowns at me. "That's what you're wearing to school?" She's more worried about my frumpy outfit than my amnesia.

I love being shoehorned into the role of headstrong, surly teen when all I freaking did was get dressed and walk downstairs.

I ignore both my "parents" and sit next to Marshall.

Jeffry rips into one of the three buttered biscuits on his plate and starts methodically loading his fork with scrambled eggs.

Liz, clearly in an attempt to get conversation rolling, addresses the table at large. "So, who's going to the fair again tonight?"

"We are, for sure." Lucia Bishop reaches across the

chalky-looking smoothie in front of her to take her husband's hand.

"I don't know; it's my last night," Candace says, throwing a regretful glance in Jim's direction. "Summer classes at UC Irvine start Monday."

"Ah, college." Frank Bishop swirls his orange juice glass with a nostalgic air. "You think your life's tough now, but when you're out in the real world . . . you'll think of this as the good old days."

"Personally," I say, "I look forward to seeing the real world."

Half the table laughs as if I've said something ridiculous.

"Just wait, honey." Lucia Bishop stirs her smoothie. "You don't know how good you have it growing up in a beautiful, clean, quiet place like this."

"I know, it's like *paradise*," Candace says with a jealous sigh.

"Then you move here," I say, and Liz smiles ferociously at me to shut up. I shrug and scoop a double helping of grapefruit-kiwi fruit salad onto my plate. It's bad enough being forced to hide my memory problem. I'm not going to fake being jolly to make things perfect for the tourists. I'm not scenery.

When Jim and Candace stand and announce they're heading downtown, I grab an apple muffin and my backpack and offer to walk with them. Marshall stands without a word and follows us. My parents look relieved to see me go.

Every step of the walk, the tourists stop to *ooh* and *aah* at something. First the pretty lake, then the pretty trees, then the pretty waterfall.

"I'm hiking the trails this afternoon," Candace vows. "Jim, you in?"

Jim stretches his arms, yawns. "What were we talking about?"

"You sound like a local." Candace shoves him and giggles, then glances at me. "Sorry."

"No, that's fair. He does sound like an idiot." I have no investment in defending the locals, even if I am one.

I'm relieved when Candace spots an "adorable" necklace in the window of the antique store and drags Jim in to look at it with her. Leaving us to walk the rest of the way to school in peace. As we cross the threshold onto campus, Marshall asks, "Ever think about how schools are like prisons for the young?"

I laugh. "You're really not a schoolboy, are you?"

"That should be clear from my report card." He shakes his head at the ivy-covered office wall. "Maybe me coming here was stupid. Fuck, I don't even know my schedule. . . . I'm probably in remedial everything."

"We're here for clues," I remind him. "Not A-pluses. There's something in that building that's going to give us valuable information. I bet just talking to people—"

He freezes. "Promise me something."

"Name it."

"Promise you won't tell anyone else you meet about our memories."

"Who said I would tell people?"

"You're compulsively honest."

I take a step back from him. "You make it sound like a disease."

"I just don't trust these people."

"You think I trust them? The only person I trust is *you*."

He crosses his arms. He's waiting for me to say it.

"Fine, I promise not to tell anyone."

"Okay, good."

"What about you?"

His brow furrows in confusion. "I kind of already know your secret."

"No . . ." God, he's so arrogant sometimes. "I mean, aren't you going to promise me the same thing?"

"Oh, that." He laughs. "Like there was ever any chance of me wanting to open up to someone in this town—other than you . . . but sure, if you want." He mimes signing his name over his heart. "I promise."

The bell rings, and I feel a funny nervousness in my stomach. "I have to go to Language Arts."

"And I have to go to the principal's office." He hugs me good-bye. "See you in the cafeteria."

CHAPTER 18

MARSHALL

MISS NIFFENHAUER—ACCORDING TO HER GOLD nameplate—looks like an aging Tinker Bell, swimming in a dark green suit that might fit a linebacker. When I enter her office, she groans and starts kneading her face rhythmically in a slow circle. I'm mesmerized by her hands, alternately hiding and emerging like turtle heads from within the suit jacket's sleeves.

"Uh, Miss Niffenhauer?" I begin in a respectful tone, but the principal cuts me off.

"Save it." She points to the sign over her desk and recites it like a mantra: "'No excuses. No drama. No bull.'"

Just clichés. Got it. "All I want is a copy of my schedule."

Miss Niffenhauer stops kneading her face and pulls her glasses halfway down her nose. "It's the end of May," she says. "There are nine days left in the school year, Mr. . . . Mr. . . . Hold on, I'm blanking on your name." Stumped, she stands, then sits, then stands again. "Well, son of a gun.

The old memory's not what it used to be."

My stomach feels sick. Why doesn't anyone remember me when I live here, go to school here?

It only gets worse when she finally looks me up in the computer. "Marshall King? How could this even be possible? You've been absent without excuse most of this year!" I have? "You're failing six out of seven courses. You can't graduate, even with summer school. You'll simply have to repeat grade twelve."

While the dot matrix printer takes its sweet dot matrix time over my schedule, I stand there feeling like the loser I am. For crying out loud, how could I flunk senior year? Why didn't I bother to show up to school like a normal person? What was my problem anyway? Then I think about what Elyse said: The point of coming here today is to learn the truth about our pasts, not worry about grades. Something occurs to me. "What about last year?"

"What about it?"

"You said I can't graduate. But I managed to get promoted from junior to senior somehow, right?"

"Barely." She scowls at the screen.

"So my grades were always bad."

"I only have records for one semester. Before that you didn't even go to SF High."

I didn't? My hopes for gaining valuable info suddenly soar. "Where does it, um, say I went?"

"Nowhere. We don't keep copies of grades for home-schoolers."

I was homeschooled? That's not helpful at all. Nor is it comforting. Means I spent all my time at home, probably with that guy we ran away from.

She hands me the printout, and I thank her and turn to go.

"Wait a minute," she says, snapping her fingers. "It's coming back to me now. Your parents are those foreign journalists, aren't they? They still researching . . . what was it again?"

Journalists. My parents are foreign journalists. What would they possibly be researching in some little tourist town?

"Well, I guess you wouldn't be here otherwise," she says, answering her own question.

Elyse was right, I think, walking to my first class—math—with my schedule in hand. I've already learned something in school, even though it's given me more questions than answers.

Unfortunately that's pretty much the only thing I learn for the next few hours. In math, Spanish, and Language Arts I sit in the back and no one calls on me. It's not that people aren't nice to me. They're too nice. With big, happy smiles, they tear out sheets of notepad paper for me and toss me spare pens and pencils, let me look on in their textbooks without complaint. But it's a huge waste of time. The teachers' voices drone, repeating the same lesson points over and over because someone or other still doesn't get it. Or the teacher forgot where she was. Maybe I'm an arrogant jackass for thinking this, but how can a whole roomful of people be that slow, forgetful, and distractible? In some ways it feels more like kindergarten than twelfth grade.

At one point in Spanish a cheerleader bounces up to the teacher's desk and asks if she can go to the bathroom. Asks. To go to the bathroom. Even weirder, the teacher asks her to hold it till break, and she cheerfully agrees, and marches back to her chair. Maybe it's just my own attitude, a holdover from being homeschooled, but I'd never let anyone—teacher or otherwise—tell me when I can and can't take a leak. Over and over I find myself wondering, Am I the odd one, or is it this place? Or both? Either way, I fit in about as well as a wolf at a puppy obedience school. I keep thinking about Elyse, wanting to talk to her and being irritated that something as stupid as a school schedule can stop us from seeing each other. I wonder how she's coping. Is she feeling the same disconnect as I am?

I search for her bright blond hair at break but don't see her anywhere, so I head to the next class on my schedule. American History. Room 209. According to my report card, I aced this class last semester. Somehow. Miraculously. I grab a seat in the back row, the seat closest to the door. The classroom starts to fill up and get noisy fast—break is only ten minutes.

Then the teacher walks in and my pulse quickens. It's the British guy from the antique store, Mr. English.

If I thought he seemed young for a teacher when I met him yesterday, it was nothing compared to how absurdly youthful he looks in his own classroom. Pacing the room in his gray argyle sweater over a blue shirt with its ironed collar and rolled cuffs, he looks as out of place as I feel.

Neither one of us really belongs here.

"All right, settle down, everyone," he says, barely looking our way. "I spent all weekend grading your essay tests, a depressing task, given your underwhelming performance."

Scattered groans from around the room. Two girls exchange notes, not bothering to be subtle about it. Understandable. We're all seniors in the last nine days of school.

"Your ignorance of the American Great Depression is so horrific that I should fail each and every last one of you."

The class looks up. He's got their attention now.

"The only reason I hesitate is your parents. They don't realize how tough it is to find a teacher willing to move to this benighted tourist trap." Why is he being so snarky? I try to catch his eye from the back row. If he keeps talking like this, he's liable to induce a mass heatnap. "If I gave you all the grades you've earned," he goes on, "a mob of hicks with torches and pitchforks would storm my poor little cabin this very night."

Finally I manage to make eye contact, and he stares right at me, clearly confused to see me here. I have to wonder, did I *buy* that A-minus?

"You can relax, folks," he says. "I learned long ago, you can't force people to learn. You can only try to be a good influence. In that spirit, I shall burn these test papers and never speak of them again . . ."

The class issues a collective cheer.

". . . and we're going to do the unit over."

The cheer turns to a groan.

My next class is PE, but I don't have gym clothes, so I just have to sit there while a bunch of people play volleyball. Halfway through I have to pee, but I'm not going to ask anyone's permission, so I just stand up and walk out of the gym. No one notices.

I decide not to go back to the gym at all and head to the library instead. It's tiny, with an unmanned counter, only a few shelves of books. But I spot a row of yearbooks and school directories up front. First thing I do is look up my own address and phone number: King, Marshall. Senior. 863 Finch Street. I tear out the page and stuff it into my pocket with my schedule.

Next I sit at the single computer, pull open a browser, and try Googling my own name. But all I get is unhelpful stuff about kings and marshals. I look up "Marshall King" "Summer Falls" and click on the top link, an obituary. Not from a local newspaper but from a major one.

It's short. Not like you'd write for someone really famous. But it's here, taking up lines in a paper read by tens of thousands.

Journalist Eva Moon passed away August 22 of this year due to complications of hypothermia after taking a midnight swim in a mountain pool. The Ecuadorian-born Moon was in the midst of researching a book about the picturesque town of Summer Falls, Colorado. She is survived by her husband, Bill King, and their son, Marshall King.

A midnight swim in a mountain pool? I shiver, remembering the ice-cold, watery grave from my dreams. I've been dreaming of the place where my mother died. It's been calling me. Had it been calling her too? Everyone who read this obit must have figured she was drunk or even trying to kill herself. I know better.

I stare at the thumbnail photo above the writing. It's the same picture Elyse pointed out on my bedroom wall, the black-haired woman holding hands with the little boy, only he's been cropped out. All you can see is Eva Moon's face, that look of quiet triumph.

My mother, I think, trying to get used to the idea. I had a mother. She took care of me when I was small. She held my hand. I loved her. I'll never see her again.

My mother is dead.

Impossible to grieve over someone you never knew about. Impossible to miss her. And yet I feel something like grief. Anger and sadness and frustration, at finding her only to realize I've lost her forever. Lost her completely. Whoever or whatever wiped my memory obliterated the last piece of her too. I want to smash my fist through the monitor.

Instead I reach toward the screen and touch with my fingertip that tiny, distant, pixilated face. It's silent in the library, and for a moment I feel like I can almost recall the sound of her voice, low and warm and gently accented. But it could just be my imagination, deviously filling in the holes with lies I want to believe in.

CHAPTER 19

ELYSE

NO SURPRISE, I CAN'T CONCENTRATE IN ANY OF my classes. The Language Arts teacher yells at me for not having memorized my poem and makes me copy out a dictionary page as punishment. The PE teacher asks if I'm feeling all right because I don't remember which volleyball team I'm on, even though we've been playing all month.

That's not the weird part though. The weird part is the other students. Like the boys who offer to copy my dictionary page for me. Or, in PE, when I bow out saying I have a headache, the five girls surrounding me with Tylenol and cups of water. It's not like I can just hide under my math book and be invisible. The sheer number of pictures of me in the yearbook suggested I was popular, but I didn't realize what that would feel like. Tiring, is how. Everywhere I go, people won't leave me alone, but it's not like they have anything useful or helpful to *say* either. It's all just noise.

"Love your hair, Elyse."

"Hope you feel better."

"Oh my gosh, is that a new top?"

"Elyse, I have to play you this song at break! It's *so good*."

"What were we talking about?"

That's another thing. People at school are incredibly distractible. Every exchange is quick, vapid, and trivial. If this is what my friendships were like, maybe it's okay I don't remember them. It was probably just wasting space in my brain to remember day after day of "love your hair," especially when more than half the girls in school have my exact hairstyle. Long, wavy, face-framing layers. You don't even have to know someone to say that kind of crap.

When the bell rings for break between second and third period, Carla runs up to me. At the sight of her, memories of Pete bleeding on the ground come rushing back. My pulse speeds up. I'm dying to ask if she's heard from his family or the hospital—then I remember what Marshall said. That after Pete's accident, people forgot what had happened. So I'm careful how I phrase the question. "How's Pete doing?"

Carla looks puzzled. "Pete who?"

"You know . . ." I falter. She truly has no idea who I'm talking about. She hasn't just forgotten about her boyfriend's grisly accident. She's forgotten his entire existence. What's going to happen when he comes back from the hospital?

"Weren't you talking to some guy named Pete yester-day?" I improvise lamely. "At the fair?"

"I wish," Carla says. "I mean, don't get me wrong, being third wheel to you and your guy isn't so bad, but it's been *forever* since I had a boyfriend. Speaking of which, Dan looks hot today," she adds coyly.

Dan. I'd been hoping I'd be able to avoid him all day. It's nothing personal really, I'm just not ready to deal with a boyfriend I don't know.

Too late. Brawny arms grab me from behind and squeeze my shoulders, and this time I don't attack him. "Babe, you look so cute in my old jeans," Dan says. I glance down at my cutoffs. They're *his*? "You took off so fast from the fair last night, we didn't get a chance for a good-night kiss." It hits me then that Dan also probably doesn't remember Pete—his best friend, his teammate. Erased, maybe forever. While I'm reeling from that bomb-shell, he spins me around for a big, sloppy kiss.

"Good to see you too." I'm barely able to choke out the words through his iron grip.

He lets me go. "I even called your house last night, since you weren't answering your cell phone. Your dad told me you weren't home and to stop calling."

"He did?" Why would Jeffry want to keep Dan away from me? Is he so old-fashioned, he doesn't let me date yet?

"I know, right?" He laughs again. "Two years. My brother says Kelly's dad was inviting him on *fishing* trips after two years, and yours is still trying to get rid of me."

I take a step back from him. What does Jeffry know about Dan that I don't?

Then it hits me what Dan just said: He's been calling me for two years. *I've been with Dan for two years.*

"So," Dan says, "you and me, the falls, after work?"

Wait . . . work? Whose work? Do we both work after school? Do we often go up to the falls . . . to do what? Now that I'm finally talking to someone who knows me and things are getting interesting, I'm constantly risking exposing myself as an idiot with no memory.

"I don't know." It's hard enough being separated from Marshall for a morning. He's the only person who knows what I'm going through. But two years . . . don't I at least owe this guy an explanation? Or a chance to make it work as the person I am now? He'd have to quit smoking of course but . . .

"Are you blowing me off?" Dan blinks at me as if he can't believe I just said no to him. "Come on, it's Friday. And we haven't hiked all week because of the fair."

Are we *that* into hiking? "Um, would it be just you and me?" I ask.

His lips part in surprise. "Well . . . yeah. Unless you're into stuff you never told me you were into. If you are, Carla's welcome to join us."

Carla giggles. I feel sick to my stomach. So that's what Dan and I do up at the falls together. I have a boyfriend, a serious boyfriend I hook up with, and yesterday I woke up naked with another guy. It's not hard to do the math: I am a slut.

I can't face him. I can't face anyone.

The girls' bathroom is behind him. "I'll be right back," I say, and duck through the swinging door.

Thank god no one else is in there. I look at the blond girl in the mirror, and I just . . . I hate her. I draw my wrist hard across her sultry pout, rubbing her mouth raw, even though I know for a fact that it's not lipstick coloring those ruby lips. It's just Elyse Alton's face. I'm stuck inside her, but she's not me. How could you do this? I glare at her with her own eyes, green marble irises. How could you cheat on your boyfriend, sleep with another guy, and leave *me* to clean up your mess? She shrugs back at me, shaking her shiny mane. Long hair, pullable, grabbable, yet another sign of weakness.

The hair. I can do something about the hair, if nothing else. I reach into my backpack, hoping for art-class scissors or nail scissors or a Swiss Army knife. There's only a scrunchie. I pile half of my hair on top of my head like a bagel and wind the band around it. I study the effect from different angles. It looks kind of stupid, but at least now you see my face before all that hair. It makes my face look longer, less soft, less appealing. And the first chance I get, all that hair is going right in the trash can.

"You okay, Leese?" Carla pokes her head in. "Dan wants to know if you're ever coming out."

Tears come to my eyes. "Oh, hey. Carla, I—"

"Oh my god!" She points to my bagel-head and squeals, "Love your hair."

And she reaches into her own backpack, pulls out a hair band, and quickly becomes absorbed in the business of creating her very own bagel-head do. I turn away in disgust. Any normal person would have figured out by looking at me that I'm not okay. That I'm broken. I need help. I need a friend. If Carla's my BFF, how come she doesn't seem to notice when I'm upset? How come I felt closer to Marshall two minutes after I met him?

"Love your hair," calls a new female voice.

Behind me in the mirror are three cheerleaders.

"Adorable," the second cheerleader burbles.

There's a mad rush of backpack zippers as they scramble-search for pins and hair bands to tie up their own hair—the weird part is how fast they do it. Like it's a race. A life-or-death struggle. The last cheerleader with her hair down gets her head lopped off. "You don't *all* have to do what I'm doing," I say, feeling like I'm talking to small children or possibly monkeys.

One of them giggles, an obedient giggle. "You're so funny. Of course we have to, you're Elyse."

"And we're your friends," another adds.

It's so ridiculous that I can't help but laugh too. And when I laugh, Elyse Alton's face in the mirror tips back and her laughter rings out to the walls, rich and throaty. Cruel too. Suddenly the point of Elyse's heart-shaped face looks sharper. Her (my) green eyes glow with a mean little power. A smugness. This was her realm, I realize. She wasn't just another cutie-pie cheerleader with more hair than brains. She ruled these girls; she owned this school. I can't imagine what kind of joy it brought her, considering how stupid and zombielike everyone here is, but maybe it was just better than the alternative. At least she wasn't one of them. I feel a twinge of gratitude for that. And then I wonder, Why did she turn out different from the other kids here? What made her special? Her clear green gaze doesn't look so innocent anymore. Her eyes look deep set, misty. Exhausted. Bewildered. That's me, looking out.

I turn to face the new crop of bagel-heads. "All right, who's got scissors?" I demand. "I need to borrow them. Actually." Why not? "I need to keep them."

I'm hardly even surprised when two girls rush to open their backpacks for me with no questions asked.

CHAPTER 20

MARSHALL

THE CAFETERIA'S CROWDED AND BUZZING WITH conversation, laughter, and jeers, each metal table a tribe unto itself, but not a single person looks up as I walk in. When I glide into the middle of the line, the frizzy-haired girl behind me and the bespectacled geek boy ahead of me each silently shuffle aside to let me in, without glancing up or complaining.

I see Elyse at what is clearly the popular table. They're easy to spot, because the guys are all thick-necked hulks in letter jackets, and the girls are all beautiful, their sunburst-orange cheerleader uniforms showing off tan, sexy limbs. In the center, her back to the wall, Elyse stands out in her white hooded sweatshirt, surrounded by guys and girls who lean eagerly toward her. She spots me and jumps to her feet, slipping away from her entourage to stand by me. "Hey. I can't talk right now, but I wanted to tell you not to wait for me after school."

"Hanging with your friends later?" One of them, the tall, dark-haired girl, is still staring after Elyse with a look of concern.

"They're not my friends," she reminds me. "And it's not that anyway. I . . . I seem to have a job of some kind."

"A job?" I can't help chuckling. "What exactly do you do?"

She gives me a desperate smile. "Guess I'll find out soon."

"It's cool, my masculinity's not threatened," I say. "You being the breadwinner. Me being the eye candy." I brush her arm, but she tenses.

"Marsh, wait . . . I have to tell you something else." She lowers her head. "It's about me, my past."

"You remembered something?" My heart beats faster with hope.

But she shakes her head, still looking down. "I just put two and two together and figured something out."

"What?"

"I'm a bad person," she whispers.

"What are you talking about?" But I know what she's talking about. Dan. That she had a longtime boyfriend and woke up naked with another guy. Me.

"God, I'm so ashamed." Her voice is choked with tears. "How could I betray someone like that?"

"Elyse, don't be so hard on yourself. Whatever you did in the past, there's bound to be a good explanation for it. When we get our memories back—"

"That's just it," she says, cutting me off. "There's no

excuse for what I did. It's just gross." She shudders. "It's just sleazy and wrong."

"Listen to me. You're the furthest thing from a bad person. I've seen you under pressure. You have amazing integrity." More integrity than me. I saw this coming after I read his signature in the yearbook and realized they were serious. I should have warned her. I guess I was just hoping their relationship would fade away if I ignored it. And now the tall, dark-haired girl is leaning into the group and saying something, her face animated and conspiratorial, and suddenly all of Elyse's friends are starting to look over at us and whisper. "We'll talk later. You should go back now." Before someone decides she's acting weird, getting up from the table like that all of a sudden.

"I'm going." She takes a deep breath, and I can tell she's battling to compose herself. "Marshall, I need you to do me a favor."

"Anything."

"Stay away from me."

I swallow. The thought of doing what she says makes me feel cold, a coldness that creeps from my fingertips up my arms all the way to my heart. How could I stay away from Elyse? How could we abandon each other to this place? Protecting her has been my purpose, almost from the moment I woke up to this new life. But it's more than that. I need her in order to survive, need her honesty, like a compass, like a knife, like a lit match in the darkness. Need her rare smiles and rich, low laughter like food. Need her trust, her soft arms around me, like water. Parting ways would feel like a death sentence. "No." I look her in the eye. "Wait, I take it back—*hell* no."

Her eyes flash. "You just said you'd do anything."

"So I lied." I throw my hands up. "I'm a liar. I make shit up. You know that. So maybe you lied to someone once in your life too, or maybe not. I don't care, Elyse. I don't care about your stupid boyfriend"—much—"or how we woke up together and what it meant or didn't mean. I just care that you're the only person who really knows me. If we're going to get our memories back and make it out of here alive, I need you and you need me. And when I know beyond a doubt that you're safe, *then* you can get rid of me, if you want to. Not before."

"Thank you." She wipes her eyes. "For the reality check. I've been spinning on this, feeling worse and worse about myself all day . . . but somehow you know what to say to make me feel better. I guess you're the only one who knows me too."

Somewhere in the middle of this she wanders into my arms and then I'm holding her. I can smell the peaches-and-summer-grass scent of her just like yesterday. It's like coming home. And I know it doesn't matter to her if in this high school life she's royalty and I'm invisible.

Someone's poking me in the back of the neck, and when I turn my head my vision explodes and there's laughter all over the cafeteria, and I'm lying in a heap on the ground. I look up to see hairy feet in sandals, muscular calves and thighs like a pair of branches. Dan, riding to his girlfriend's rescue. My head hurts and my ass hurts. What's weird is that my right hand's in my empty pocket, and my left arm's stretched out in front of me in an odd gesture, middle and forefinger bent like a pair of fangs. Why the hell did I do that instead of trying to defend myself?

"Knock it off, Dan." I hear Elyse's strained voice far above my head. "If you want to break up with me, break up with me. You don't have to—"

"Why in the world would I break up with you?" Dan sounds puzzled. "Hey, Computer Lab, stick to your league, okay?" he says to me, not meanly. "No hard feelings."

Blood pounds in my temples. Did jock-boy just call me . . . a computer lab? Is he going to hit me again?

But he's turned to Elyse, who's frozen to the spot, and jokingly says, "It's not nice to give nerds false hope."

A hand reaches out to me, and I grab it, let myself be pulled to my feet by a gangly guy with glasses. "Dude, that was stupid," he says mildly, like *I* did something wrong instead of the guy with iron fists. "Welcome back. I knew you'd get sick of homeschooling. Come on, Ruta's sitting all alone." Still shell-shocked from the attack, I follow Glasses Guy to the very back table, where a slender, small-boned Indian girl sits tugging nervously on one of her electric curls.

"Marsh!" Electric hair—Ruta—greets me with a round-eyed stare of disbelief. "I haven't seen you here in ages."

"What can I say?" Seriously, I'd better think of something. "I missed your nerdy hotness too much to stay away."

Too much? No. She giggles, lighting up her whole face and revealing a mouthful of braces, the silver, old-fashioned kind. "Jeremy and I missed you too," she says. "But why were you talking to *Elyse Alton*?" Enunciating her full name, like she's a pop star. Maybe she's jealous?

I grin. "Relax, we're just friends."

Wrong answer. Ruta's brown eyes are suddenly gazing into mine with infinite compassion, compassion bordering on pity, and too late I realize my error: She wasn't jealous; she was worried about me. Elyse and I are not friends at all. We're so not friends that if I even try to speak to her, her boyfriend punches me. Heat spreads across my face. Humiliation. "I mean, we *could* be friends," I correct myself lamely. "We have friend potential."

"Yeah, and pigs have flying potential." Jeremy chortles. "Forget about her, man, we don't belong with the populars. We're too smart for them."

"She ignores you, Marsh." Ruta's tiny hand flies to her throat, as if my being ignored hurts her physically. "She's one of the mean girls. I thought you'd finally gotten over your crush."

Crush? I crush and she ignores, that's our relationship? I don't think so. That doesn't gel with Elyse being naked in my bed. But if she *was* my friend—or more— then why would she ignore me at school? I steal a glance at the cool table, where Elyse sits surrounded by football players and cheerleaders. Dan's orange letter-jacketed arm fits snugly around her shoulder and I can occasionally hear her throaty laugh. Rationally I know she's trying to act "normal," helping to keep our secret while stealthily gathering information to share with me as soon as we can be alone together. Rationally I get that this cafeteria-table-hierarchy bullshit means nothing to her.

But I guess a punch to the brain stem doesn't bring out my rational side.

I look back at Ruta and Jeremy. At her thick, earnest eyebrows and giant yellow T-shirt. At his horn-rimmed glasses held together with duct tape, the only thing that stands out on his pasty face. The two of them don't look all that similar, yet you can tell they belong together. It's their posture. Shoulders rounded, backs hunched, twitching eyebrows, constantly cringing mouths. If Dan's body language says royalty, theirs says "kick me." Is this my league? Are these my friends? All I want to do is go beat up the football player who broke Jeremy's glasses. I want to shield Ruta from the mean girls. Except that Elyse—my Elyse—is one of those mean girls. How did things ever get so messed up?

"You're just lucky Dan got distracted," Jeremy adds, "before he finished kicking your ass."

"Jer, that's not nice." Ruta frowns.

I blink, disturbed at the thought that even my friends assume Dan could kick my ass. Okay, so he caught me by surprise this time, but we're about the same size and I'm not in worse shape than he is. If I hadn't been so shocked— and I hadn't done that weird thing with my left hand—I could have sprung back up and given him a run for his money. But Dan didn't expect me to hit back. He showed no fear of me at all. Why?

Because I'm nobody at this school.

I'm a loser here.

I'm invisible.

Suddenly I miss Elyse, my friend Elyse, my only actual friend. I miss her with a powerful ache in my chest. Even though I can see her, it feels like she's slipping away from me. The memory of Elyse waking up in my bed—her blond hair shining in the morning sun—feels painfully distant. Untrustworthy, like maybe it was all a dream.

I know it *wasn't* all a dream. At least I'm 99 percent sure. But whatever happened between us in the past, it's over. (And we don't even know for sure what did happen.) The present moment, the one where Elyse is popular and I'm invisible, feels inescapably solid. I sink deeper into my seat at the loser table as the cafeteria noise buzzing between me and Elyse echoes through my head.

"Ruta, eat faster so we can go to the computer lab," Jeremy says.

Ruta gives me a frowny face. "Marsh, did someone throw away your lunch?"

"They'd have to notice him first," Jeremy reassures her. He's drinking a Dr Pepper for lunch. Was *his* food thrown away by bullies?

"I just . . . forgot it," I lie.

Ruta pushes her sandwich forward across the table.

"You can have half my turkey and cheese."

I swallow. I'm not hungry, but I don't want to reject this girl's offer. She looks like too many people have rejected her. I don't want anyone to ever reject her again. "Sure. Thanks," I say, and she beams a mouthful of metal at me. It's still a nice smile.

Hey, at least these two recognized me. Remembered me. That's something, and it makes me feel grateful to them.

The computer lab is a hot, claustrophobic room with a single open window facing the football field, as if designed to constantly remind the school's nerds of their inferior status relative to athletes. Three ancient machines are set up side by side, with dot matrix printers between them. Stone age. But internet access is internet access. I take my place between college web-surfing Ruta and Flash-game addict Jeremy and fire up a browser.

Jeremy glances at my screen. "Are you doing homework?" He says it incredulously. Maybe I'm just stereotyping him, but I would have thought a guy like Jeremy approved of homework. Even the nerds in Summer Falls don't take school seriously.

"Extra credit," I lie.

"Extra credit for what?"

"Jer," Ruta admonishes. "Don't read over people's shoulders. That's considered annoying." She says it so earnestly, like she read it in some self-help book on how to fit in.

To my surprise, Jeremy listens to her. "You're right,

sorry," he says. "I almost forgot, I have a surprise for you." He reaches into his backpack and carefully pulls out a rough wooden box, which he presents to her.

"Oh . . . wow." Ruta touches her cheek, clearly embarrassed. "But you got me a birthday present last week."

I Google "Eva Moon" again but can't find any other books by her. Articles, yes, and in some pretty prominent places like Slate.com. But the subjects are all over the place, with no real pattern: the use of divining rods in central Asia, underground nightclubs in Iran, riding the lava flow inside a volcano, a review of Antarctic cruises. Not that this stuff isn't interesting . . . but I still don't feel like I have much of a sense of who she was. Or why someone like Joe would care about seeing her notes.

The one message that does come through is that she was fearless. She went everywhere. Every byline uses a different photograph of her: on camelback; in a puffy ski jacket with a mountain background; waving from a kayak; grinning under a spelunker's hat. In one she's posing next to a tiger. Really. A *tiger.* After all that danger and travel, I bet it would have pissed her off royally to know she wound up dying in a harmless-looking tourist trap like Summer Falls. In fact, I'm pissed off on her behalf. She deserved better.

"It's a just-because present, a music box." Jeremy opens it, and a miniature baseball player revolves around a platform as "America the Beautiful" plays on a tinny recording. "Because you love going to the baseball games," he explains. "I made the box out of scrap wood from the old mill."

"You snuck in there?" Ruta's jaw drops. "I thought it was boarded up."

"The back door's easy to jimmy open," Jeremy says, obviously proud of himself.

"I can't believe you went to so much trouble to give me a present." She sets the box down on the table next to her mouse pad and leans over to give him a hug. "You're a true friend, Jer."

But Jeremy ducks the hug attempt. "So, I was wondering," he says, and spills out the rest in a rushed whisper. "Would-you-go-out-with-me-sometime."

Oh boy. I stare at my screen, feeling extremely awkward now, wondering if I should leave them alone. But now that I'm online I never want to get offline. The internet's my only lifeline to the real world.

"We just went to Mollie's for sundaes yesterday." She sounds confused, then she cringes. "*Oh.* You mean . . . on a date? Oh, Jer . . . I'm sorry if I gave you the wrong idea somehow. . . ."

Screw my only lifeline, this scene is none of my damn business. I'm halfway out the door when from behind me Jeremy says in a choked voice, "Forget it. I shouldn't have asked. Can we just go back to normal now, please?"

"Normal, of course." Ruta sounds strained.

Man, this *sucks.* Everyone knows you can't go back to being best friends after you ask a girl out, and Jeremy and Ruta can't exactly afford to lose this friendship. They need each other.

I'm hardly even surprised when I hear a gasp for air and turn to see Jeremy crashing to the ground, passed out.

I run over, dive to my knees, and grab Jeremy's wrist, but I already know his pulse will be fine.

"Marsh, relax, it's just a heatnap," Ruta says, sighing. "I feel so awful for hurting his feel—"

And then she does it too. A sharp intake of breath and she falls to the ground.

Zap. The same stinging in my chest, and my vision's glowing with the now familiar blue light.

Moments later, as suddenly as they fell asleep, Ruta and Jeremy are stirring awake again. Jeremy groans and helps Ruta to her feet. She dusts herself off and smiles at him. He leans toward her smile, a man in love. Full of hope.

"Did the bell ring yet?" she asks.

"No," Jeremy says, though he couldn't possibly know any better than she does. I guess he just likes having the answers. He picks up the music box and stares at it. "Huh. What's this?"

"I don't know," she says, sounding intrigued.

"Someone wrote your name on it, Rue."

"What?" She rushes over, picks up the box, and runs her finger across the smooth lid. "For Ruta," she murmurs. "That's so cool . . . I've never had a secret admirer!" She slips the box into her bloated green shell of a backpack. Jeremy looks a little discombobulated, maybe even jealous.

But as our trio treks across campus to the art building, Ruta mentions a science fair she's planning to enter in

Eagle's Point, and Jeremy starts giving her advice on how to present her entry to the judges. The pain and awkwardness between them is gone, as if she never stepped on his heart. And even though I know that every heatnap brings them closer to losing their currently brilliant minds, I'm grateful they don't have to lose each other. In some small way, it feels like a miracle.

CHAPTER 21

ELYSE

AFTER SCHOOL ENDS, I WALK WITH CARLA TO the outdoor locker bay and watch her robotically switch out her textbooks for other ones.

"Don't you need your math book tonight?" she says, gesturing to the locker in front of me.

I stare at the combo, praying for the numbers to magically appear in my mind's eye. Nothing. Did I ever share my combo with her? I can't figure out how to ask in a way that's not suspicious. "I'll be okay," I say.

She gives me a funny look. "All right. Well, I'll be at Mollie's later if you want to hang out."

I'm still staring at the combination and willing my subconscious to remember it when Dan sneaks up behind me, his signature move, wrapping his arms around me. This time I recognize the cherry Chapstick scent of his lips on my hair and don't freak out. Thankfully he doesn't try to tongue-kiss me again either. "Ready to go?" he says. He's as bouncy as a golden retriever.

I hate questions like that. What am I supposed to be ready for? It could be anything: an after-school sport we're both signed up for, the aforementioned nebulous "work" thing . . . or, say, a hiking trip to the waterfall to have sex. I hesitate but feel better when he follows it up with, "Hey, you're the one who hates being late." If lateness is an issue, it's not likely to be something scandalous.

I let him slip his hand in mine and guide me across the street from school. I'm expecting him to talk at me in that vacuous way people have been doing, small talk, surface talk, about a movie plot or a YouTube video I haven't seen. But Dan doesn't do that. He just walks with me. Every once in a while squeezing my hand a little. I'm surprised at how comfortable, how natural, the silence between us feels. Makes sense, I guess, if we've been going out forever.

Suddenly I remember Project California. Was Dan supposed to come with me? After two years, I'd probably built him into all my future plans. But he seems so happy here, I can't imagine him wanting to take off. Is that why I was waiting, to sell him more on my plan? Or had I given up?

I have to know. Was I planning a future with this guy or getting ready to set him adrift? If it's the second one, then, well, it's not like I'd forgive myself for cheating, but at least I'd hate myself less. "Wow, the weather's nice today," I say. Lame start, but I'm going somewhere with this. "Of course it's probably nicer in California."

"Uh . . . no it's not," he says, in a tone that suggests not loyalty but confusion about how I could miss such a basic fact. "Everyone knows we have the world's best weather in Summer Falls. It's that whole glacier effect, or whatever they call it."

"But we don't have surfing. Not like California."

He gives me a funny look. "Why do you keep bringing up California?"

He may be dumb, but he's not an idiot. Dan, my boyfriend of two years, doesn't even know that I'm planning to leave town.

Elyse, Elyse. How could you be so sneaky and two-faced?

Dan and I arrive at the Summer Falls Community Center and Pool. The guy at the registration counter smiles at us as he checks us in. I still have no idea what our jobs are. I keep trying to find a way to subtly ask without asking.

"Meet you after we suit up," Dan says.

"Right." I trudge to the women's locker room, which is packed with moms helping little kids change for swim lessons. Many of the little kids smile at me, the moms too.

Wonder of wonders, at the bottom of my backpack, in a clear plastic bag, is my suit. A black, blue, and red one-piece racing swimsuit—the ugly kind that's made to look athletic instead of sexy and ends up looking even sexier for it. I peel off my clothes and slide into the stretchy suit. Then, facing the three-way mirror, I gather my hair to put it up and that's when I see what my shirt was covering. Ugly greenish-yellow marks bloom all over my shoulders and back. I blink at them in confusion. Some are finger-size. Some fist-size. Bruises. Those are bruises. I feel dizzy and sit down hard on the locker bench.

Someone else did that to me; someone hurt me. Some-one with big hands grabbed me roughly and pinched my skin with enough brutality to leave marks. Who would treat another person like that? Who would treat *me* like that—and why would I let them? The liquid terror swirling through my insides crystallizes into anger. From the color, these bruises are maybe three or four days old. Who could have done this to me in the last four days? Marshall would never hurt me. He didn't even hit Dan back after . . . *Dan.* With sickening clarity I remember how his hairy, tan arm snaked out to clock Marshall in the back of the neck. Just for hugging me. Is that why I didn't tell him I was running away to California? Was I afraid of my own boyfriend?

The locker room is silent, empty. All the 4:00 p.m. swim-lesson kids have gone. If I'm supposedly their instructor, I'd better pull myself together and join them or I'll lose my job. I pull up the back of my suit as high as I can, but that only covers half the bruises. I yank the scrunchie out and let my hair fall loose over my shoulders. So much for giving myself a boy haircut. The long hair I'd thought of as vanity was really armor.

In the pool area, the smell of chlorine threatens to overpower my nose and the echoes of laughing kids over-lap one another and become one song, but all my senses are focused on Dan.

He's perched way up in the lifeguard chair on the right, looking down over his territory like a stern alien overlord in his mirrored sunglasses. The chair on the left is empty.

Oh.

I'm a lifeguard too.

I climb the steps with swift, sure footing—proving I've done this many times—and discover that the view from the lifeguard chair is amazing. There's a beginning swim lesson in the kiddie pool and an intermediate stroke clinic at the shallow end. Lap swimmers share the lanes not being used by the swim team. But one of the best parts is watching the parents watch their kids. The tender expressions on those faces—the parents, not the kids, because the kids are pretty much entirely focused on being terrified or excited. (Sometimes it's hard to tell the difference.) It makes me wish I were one of those kids. To start over, start fresh, not have made so many mistakes. Get another chance. Of course I wouldn't really want to be a kid. Kids get forced to do things by their parents, like take swim lessons. They're powerless against anyone bigger, stronger.

I touch the back of my neck. It's tender, like someone grabbed me and pinched hard. I sneak a glance at Dan. His sun-browned face looks haughty, rigid.

Suddenly Dan blows his whistle and I realize I've been watching him instead of the swimmers. A little girl in the deep end of the pool is floating on her stomach, not moving. What's she even doing over there? My heart's racing as we both dive into the water after her. No air bubbles coming from her nose or mouth. Together we lift her from underneath. But the moment her head's above water, her eyes pop open and she lets out the breath she was holding. She bats her eyes at Dan. "Thanks for rescuing me."

"What, you were pretending to be in danger, for attention?" I realize my voice sounds harsh, but I can't believe this kid. "That's *bad*. Never do that again."

The girl's lower lip trembles, and Dan gives me an incredulous look, like, Cut the kid some slack. "Think about it, Zoe-bird," he says to her in a nicer voice. "What if some other little girl needed our help for real while you were joking around?"

Zoey frowns. "She would have drowneded?"

Dan puts on a sad face on behalf of the imaginary victim. "A lifeguard's time is too important to waste on pranks."

Watching him be so sweet with her, I'm suddenly reminded of the night before, the way Dan yelped and then laughed when I stepped on his foot. Like a big, gentle dog that tolerates ear-pulling from toddlers. Was it possible I rushed to conclusions about my bruises? Maybe some kind of accident caused them. Or maybe I'm just one of those people who bruises super-easily.

By the time Dan and I have deposited her on the shallow end and are through lecturing her together, there are tears in her eyes. I feel bad for yelling, but it'll be good for her to remember this so she doesn't do it again. It's only once we're heading back to the lifeguard stand that I realize what a miracle it is that my body remembers how to swim, how to rescue a distressed swimmer, how to be a lifeguard. The muscle memory is there inside me. It gives me hope.

Two middle school boys break into a splash fight, laughing and shoving each other.

"No horseplay," I hear myself say, but of course they don't stop. Before I can take a step toward them, out of the corner of my eye I see one of the lap swimmers break out of his lone spot in the far lane and start ducking under the lane dividers on his way to the deep area. Bad etiquette. Also—oh, no *way*—he appears to be wearing a full-body swimsuit circa 1900. His white swim cap shimmers lightly as he heads straight toward the girl who faked drowning.

My heart's thumping. I want to run as far away from this pool as possible, but I'm a lifeguard. I steel myself and jump into the pool after her. But I'm never going to make it. He's so fast. He grabs her from behind, his long, ghostly fingers on either side of her small head. I hear her exhale a sigh and then she relaxes, falls back, her head underwater. Where did the ghost go? I pull the girl's body up and swim her over to the side. Zoe's small body is racked with coughs, but her open eyes are wide with shock, not vacant like Hazel's were. She came back. "Just hold on to the side and keep coughing it out," I say, rubbing her back. "You'll be okay." I hope.

A smattering of applause echoes throughout the pool

area. I hadn't realized we had an audience. Why are they applauding? I didn't get to her in time. I didn't save her from the ghost.

Her mother dashes over to me from a chaise on the far side of the pool area. "I can't thank you enough, Elyse. You're a wonder. You jumped in before I could even see she was unconscious." She's grateful, but she doesn't sound really . . . scared. Like she never really thought anything could go too seriously wrong.

No one else saw the ghost swimmer. No one but me.

I had wondered why Marshall couldn't seem to see the ghosts around us, but I'd never stopped to ask myself why I could. I think back to the photo-album pictures of little-girl me, drawing "imaginary friends." The ghosts weren't imaginary, and they definitely weren't my friends. Maybe I was drawing them because it was lonely being the only one who could see them.

When our shift is over at six, we climb down from the chairs and head toward the locker rooms.

"That was pretty light today," Dan says. "Only two heatnap rescues, and one was a fake."

I stare at him. On a normal day we'd have to rescue *multiple* people from drowning? "Huh."

"Got energy for that hike?" he adds slyly, and leans in to peck my lips. I can taste his Chapstick, can smell his chlorinated hair and sunscreen—nice summer smells—and his musky boy scent. I think about it: hiking up to the falls with Dan. Having a real conversation with him. Kissing him more. Seeing if we could have a chance together. But his whole life is hikes and parties and hooking up. My life is invisible ghosts, unexplained bruises, and Marshall at my side—Marshall, who's no less mysterious than our missing memories themselves. Dan and I just don't fit together, if we ever did. It's not fair to keep stringing him along just because I dread telling him the truth.

"I have to talk to you," I say. His eyebrows go up, and then I just bite the bullet. "After graduation . . . I'm moving to California."

"Is that, like, a joke or something?" He smiles, crinkling the skin around his eyes. "I can never tell when you're being crazy and when you're just a step ahead of me. Okay, okay, I'll bite. Why California?"

"To find myself? Break away from here and find my calling?" Things I can't do here.

"Lifeguarding *is* a calling," he says seriously. "When you first tried to talk me into taking the course in Green Vista, I was only doing it to be around you more. Because, let's face it, you're smokin' hot. But now . . . now I know how vigilant you have to be to save lives. It's changed my whole perspective. Like it woke me up."

"Really?" *I* talked him into lifeguarding? I changed his life?

"Absolutely, Elyse." He runs his hand through his messy hair and gives me that golden-retriever grin. "So . . . when do we leave for California?"

We? He's saying he'll come with me—even though he

clearly doesn't want to leave his hometown? My stomach flip-flops, dreading the conflict ahead. "Dan . . . we've been together a long time, and you're obviously a great guy, but I don't even know who I am right now. I can't make a commitment to anyone."

"You already made a commitment."

"I'm *really* sorry, Dan," I tell him. "I'm just not the same person I was, and I don't want the same things. . . ."

"But how could anyone want more than *this*?" He gestures behind him, toward the pool area, the swimming children and doting parents. "What's gotten into you, Elyse? Just a few weeks ago you were showing this off to all your friends." He touches one of the rings on my left hand. A white-gold band with a tiny diamond. Just a chip. I hadn't even noticed it before because it has no sparkle, but now my eyes are glued to it.

Holy shit, that's what that ring is? I'm engaged to him? Maybe it's just a promise ring, please, god?

"You're not listening, I said we're done!" I twist the ring off, thrust it into his hands, and run into the locker room. I did it. I broke up with Dan, which means I'm not a cheater anymore. No. I'm still a cheater; nothing will change what I did. But I made it as close to right as I could.

Only, Dan doesn't seem like the type of guy to just let a girl—the girl who changed his life—walk out on him. Anxiety chills my limbs as I wonder what kind of ex-boyfriend Dan will be. What if he clings to denial, like Liz about my amnesia? He's liable to blow his savings on a truckful of roses and show up at Preston House pleading with me to take him back. If guilting me into being his girlfriend again doesn't work, what would he try next? Stalking me? And then there's his loyal football buddies. They could gang up on Marshall and really hurt him. The ring may be off my finger, but I know this isn't over yet.

CHAPTER 22

MARSHALL

TO KILL TIME BEFORE MEETING MR. ENGLISH AT Mollie's, I zigzag down Main Street and wander down side streets, checking out smaller storefronts. Trying to get a feel for this place that Elyse grew up in.

The downtown sidewalks are crowded; first Friday night of the season. I bump into Jim and Candace holding hands on Main Street, dreamy looks in their eyes. Jim's traded his button-down shirt for an orange "I ♥ Summer Falls" T-shirt, and Candace is feeding him some kind of pastry from a pink waxy paper bag that smells like cinnamon. They're too besotted to notice me.

Across the street in the town square, the young homeless woman's busy balling up tiny pieces of bread and arranging them artfully on the statue of W. P. Preston. Pigeons and sparrows and crows surround her, adding to her aura of insanity as they peck at the morsels of bread left on Preston's austere bronze face, his giant boots, and the crotch of his trousers. When one pigeon poops right in the statue's lap, she cackles, revealing a mouthful of crooked teeth. What keeps her out of the asylum?

I turn the corner onto a tiny side street just in time to see a familiar figure step in front of me. It's Elyse's mom.

"Hey, Liz!" I wave—and that's when I see the sign on the door of the building she just exited. "Pleasant Nights Motel."

"Oh god." Liz looks mortified. "Please don't tell anyone I was here." My face must look pretty shocked—Elyse's mom's having an affair?—because she quickly adds, "It's not what you think. I just . . . well, sometimes I get real tired, I guess. I don't even remember booking the room."

I look down at the duffel bag over her shoulder and feel a tightening in my gut. "You just woke up in a hotel room . . . and don't know how you got there?" Not a sign of stellar mental health.

"We all have moments," she says as if trying to reassure herself. "Especially at my age." Right, thirty-three is the onset of senility.

She glances down at her watch and bites her lip. "Shoot, dinner's going to be late. . . ."

"Don't worry, Jeffry can figure something out." Actually, that guy didn't seem tech-savvy enough to nuke a plate of leftovers. But I had to say something. To reassure her that things would be all right, even if I'm not sure they will be.

As she walks away, her shoulders look sadly uneven, the left one dragged down by her heavy duffel strap. The bag's neon red vinyl, a screaming clash with her faded pink sundress. Liz packed a bag and checked into a motel, but now she can't remember why? And from the sound of it it's not the first time. I *have* to share this with Elyse. We have to help her mother—somehow—before it's too late.

———

I arrive at Mollie's Milkshakes at the same time as Mr. English. It's packed to the gills, mostly with high school kids. Couples especially. It's a hot day, but the ice cream's cooling them down, as well as the huge fans hanging from the rafters. Sunglasses rest on top of sun-bleached heads. Spaghetti-strap tank tops and sundresses show off tan arms.

A few people look up to see us, and from one of the group tables two girls call out simultaneously in flirtatious voices, "Hi, Mr. E!"

"Emma. Bryn." Joe nods at them stiffly, his smooth cheeks turning pink. His silver-tongued classroom act is gone—here, he's just an awkward young guy in owlish glasses. Really young, I realize. In the bright sunlight, his unlined face looks not a day older than any of ours. Despite his stodgy teacher costume of khakis, shined loafers, and blue button-down shirt, he could be our peer.

He catches me watching him. "So," he prompts, eyebrows raised, "you brought her notes, I take it?"

My mother's notes. I remember the book Miss Niffenhauer was talking about. "Are you a journalist too?"

"Journalist?" His head jerks back as if I've insulted

him. "Marshall, are you messing with me?" His thick lenses seem to magnify the worry and eagerness in his blue eyes. "My god. You don't even know who I am, do you? It's me, Joe. Joe Clifton. From the Institute?"

What Institute? "You're . . . not Mr. English?"

"Mr. English is just my cover story. I'm the occultist assigned to investigate your mother's . . . well, your mother's death."

I can't feel my arms and legs. It feels like I'm floating an inch to the left of my body.

"Good gracious, this is bad." Joe is so taken aback, he pulls off his Coke-bottle glasses and sticks both temple tips in his mouth. His eyes look normal-size now, but his face looks even younger and smoother. His eagerness to please reminds me of Ruta, his nerdiness of Jeremy. No wonder we were friends. "But Eva's defense spell should have protected you!"

"Spell?" My heart pounds. "You're talking about a *magic* spell?"

Joe looks overwhelmed. "What other kind of spell is worth talking about? Marshall, what's happened to you? This is worse than a few heatnaps. It's like you've been erased from the ground up."

My stomach sinks. He knows. He knows I'm broken. I made Elyse promise not to tell a soul and then I gave it away just by acting stupid. Okay, damage control: At least I didn't tell him about her. I'll keep her secret to the end.

"Wh-who could have done this to you?" Joe's eyes

have gone round with fear. "Because if they could get to you, I'm cooked. Let's just say there's a reason my father pushed me toward investigation and not spell casting."

"Dude, calm down." I'm not sure if I'm telling him or myself. "What do you mean, someone did this to me? Someone wiped my memory using . . . magic?" It still sounds ridiculous.

He gives me a pitying, patient sigh. "Of course with magic, Marshall. And magic is how you'll cure it too. But first things first. Let me fill you in on the history you're missing."

My head's already spinning, but he had me at "cure."

A cute pixie redhead appears with a notepad, and Joe orders a strawberry phosphate while I stare at the menu, unable to concentrate or make a decision. She pops her gum.

"He'll have a chocolate shake," Joe says with confidence.

"Is that what I usually get?"

"No. I just figured you were never going to order, and besides it doesn't matter. She'll get confused and bring us the wrong thing. They always do."

I laugh, relieved. "How many times have we come here together?"

Joe hesitates. Then he breaks into a geeky smile. "I could tell you anything right now and you'd believe it, wouldn't you?"

It's not a reassuring thought.

"What do you want to know first?" he asks.

"I want to know about me, what kind of person I am.

What I was like. I'm tired of connecting the dots to try to figure it out."

"You're not alone." His owlish eyes turn suddenly serious. "All human history's full of holes. As a species we've forgotten almost everything about ourselves, and still we move forward. Well, except here in Summer Falls. I think evolution's stopped for a little nap here, if you will."

I feel relieved. "So, other towns aren't like this then?"

He laughs. "Other towns and cities are *very* different from Summer Falls. This place is enchanted, like Sleeping Beauty's castle. Only people here aren't quite asleep, they're just pleasantly drowsy."

"You mean like the heatnaps." And Liz's moments. "How does anything keep running in this town if people are so scattered?"

Joe glances around, then lowers his voice. "Something's holding this town together, but it's not the townspeople."

"Something? What could possibly do this to everyone?"

"The answer to that's above my pay grade," Joe says. "But they don't seem to mind. It keeps them happy before it burns them out."

Pixie Waitress ambles over to us with an order of fries and three Cokes carefully balanced between her arms. Not what we ordered. At all.

"Thanks, love." Joe pats her on the head like she's a puppy. She smiles shyly and wanders back toward the kitchen. "You can tell that one's had a lot of bad memories wiped, for her age," he says grimly. "Childhood trauma, most likely. I give her another five years, tops."

His tone is casual, but his meaning sinks in like a cold knife in my chest. "Wait. Are you saying in five years that girl will be catatonic, like the lady at the fair last night?" The openmouthed stare. Dead inside. A void.

"Oh, but she doesn't know what's coming," he assures me. "They live in the moment. Probably better that way."

I shake my head. If he's trying to comfort me, he's failing miserably. Her not knowing that she's losing her mind makes it worse. If she knew, she could do something about it. Like leave town. If people knew what was going on here, they'd all leave and never come back. No one would ever set foot in the city limits if they knew . . . except that Joe did. And maybe my mother too. I take a deep breath, bracing myself for the answer to a question I'm almost scared to ask. "Why exactly did my mother come to Summer Falls? What was she mixed up in here?"

Joe sighs. "I think Eva was trying to change this place. To end the cycle, redirect the magic somehow. Her notes would give us more information, but we know that her body was found near the—" He stops, hangs his head. "Sorry, Marshall. How insensitive I've become, living alone in this place . . ."

"No, go ahead. Where was she found?"

He nods. "In a small cavern. Just behind the waterfall, next to a natural pool. I believe—and we at the Institute believe—she was trying to perform a ritual of restoration, returning strength to the townspeople. After living here nine months and three days, I've been tempted to try it myself . . . but I'm not the genius that she was."

I'm starting to get the feeling my mother was some kind of rock star in the world of occultists. Strange as it all is, I can't help being a little proud of that.

Our waitress is crossing over to us with a check when an orange flare leaps into the edge of my vision. Fire. A grease fire's just broken out in the fryer, and the fry cook's staring at it with a puzzled expression.

I bolt from my chair and start scanning the walls for a fire extinguisher. "Joe, can't you put it out with magic?"

Joe's already jumped out of his own chair. "Pains me to say it, but I'm crap at magic. This is where we run."

"We have to evacuate them!" I spot a red extinguisher behind glass in the far corner, but no one's moving toward it. Nor are they mobbing the door. Everyone's just gaping as if mesmerized by the bright flame. I don't know how I remember this fact, but if you don't put a grease fire out in the first few seconds, it's too late. And water makes it worse.

I smash the glass and lug the heavy canister behind the counter. "Out of the way!" I yell to the fry cook.

"Okay, everybody, line up behind me and start moving outside!" Joe calls halfheartedly from the door. "They're just staring. I've seen zombies smarter than these people. Really."

I aim the extinguisher at the blaze, but only a thin dribble of foam spews out. And the second it makes contact with the fryer, a tower of flames shoots up. I hear screams from the tables behind me. What now? Keep spraying or run? If I give up, the fire will spread for sure. Take the risk or take the loss. I can't afford the loss. I hold my finger on the can. Instantly, the column of flames dies down to silence. The fire's out.

I let myself exhale.

Behind me I hear a *splat* and a *thump*, then another and another. I turn to see the whole restaurant full of people passing out into their ice-cream bowls and French fry baskets. Collective heatnap.

"Very impressive." From across the sea of unconscious townspeople, owlish blue eyes meet mine. "Heroic, even."

With my T-shirt I wipe beads of sweat from my forehead. No one got hurt. Everyone's safe—*everyone*.

"Sleepers." Joe leans toward me conspiratorially. "That's what my father used to call nonoccultists. I called him an insufferable snob at the time, but now . . ." He pushes up his glasses and sighs. "Now I rather see his point."

"Yeah, well, I don't." Since we're the only ones not drooling on our plates, I'm guessing all occultists must have some kind of defense against heatnaps. I don't see how that makes us better though. Just luckier.

"You're clearly your mother's son," he says with a broad smile, and it occurs to me again that he seems to view my mother as some kind of deity among occultists. I can't help but feel proud on two levels. He pulls a business card from his pocket. "Call my mobile anytime. Or just stop by. I'm renting a cabin just off the main trail near the waterfall. You can't miss it . . . looks like it's a hundred years old, but that's what a teacher's salary gets you out in the sticks. And it's well-kept, like everything is here. Stop by for a cup of tea. I wouldn't mind the company."

His airy tone sounds strained, and it occurs to me why. He's trying to hide how desperately lonely he is. This is probably his first assignment as an investigator. "You miss home, don't you?" I ask. "It's nothing to be embarrassed about. I miss my home, and I don't even remember it."

"Sure, I miss London." He smiles sadly. "But I wouldn't fit in there anymore. Sometimes I wish I'd never taken this post, but even magic can't change the past."

He hunches his shoulders and walks out the door. As usual without paying.

All around me, Mollie's is waking up noisily. The kitchen's completely covered with white powder. The smell of smoke and chemicals is overpowering. Feeling sorry for whoever has to clean up this mess, I shrug, grab a moist towel, and start wiping powder off the grill.

The pixie redhead, who'd passed out on the ground, stretches and saunters over to me with the same peaceful smile as before. "Are you, like, the new guy or something?" she asks.

"Marshall." I stick out my hand. "Yeah, I'm brand-new."

CHAPTER 23

ELYSE

I LINGER IN THE WOMEN'S LOCKER ROOM, SHOW-ering off each and every molecule of chlorine, then slowly dressing. In front of the mirror I blow-dry every section of hair till my waves smooth out into a glossy curtain that blankets my shoulders and covers my bruises.

When I step outside, the guy and girl who work the front desk are flirting. Smacking each other on the head with their name tags and giggling. I let out a heavy breath. Dan's nowhere to be seen. He gave up on me. For now.

By the time I reach downtown Main Street, the after-noon light's slipping to pink and purple around me. The sidewalk's bustling with tourists and local teenagers alike, mostly couples. At one of the metal sidewalk tables outside Mollie's Milkshakes, I spot Carla in a group of couples snuggled up with a guy in a letterman jacket. Auburn hair.

"Pete!" He's out of the hospital already. He's all right. Thank god.

But as I rush toward them, Carla and the guy turn, and I see it's not him. It's some guy I've never seen before. Carla's already moved on.

"Leese?" Carla says in a worried voice. "Who's this Pete guy you keep talking about?"

"Never mind." I shake my head. "Just someone I used to know."

Carla's brow creases, and too late I realize how nuts I sound. "We know all the same people," she says. "I'm worried about you. You've been having a lot of weird . . . moments."

Suddenly demon butterflies are attacking my stomach. People think *I'm* going crazy, because I'm the only one who remembers Carla's maimed boyfriend? "I'm fine, really."

"If you say so." Carla looks around expectantly. "Where's Dan? Still at the pool?"

Announcing that I broke up with Dan is just going to cause more problems. "Dan and I just had separate plans tonight."

Another cheerleader laughs. "I thought you guys took your 'nature hikes' on Fridays."

"Yeah, well, maybe I felt like doing something else for a change," I say.

Carla glances around the table, and her new boyfriend nods encouragement.

"You're not acting like yourself," Carla says finally. "I'm going to call Dan and have him pick you up." She pulls out her phone. "I think we'd all feel better knowing you're not alone."

That's the last thing I want. "I need to get home and help my mom," I say. "I won't be alone, don't worry." And I hurry past before anyone can stop me.

Near the quiet end of Main Street, the homeless lady's bouncing up and down on the pavement, red ringlets hopping around her head like snakes, a spray-paint can clutched in her dirty fingers. She's already sprayed an obscenity on the sidewalk.

"What's going on, girl?" she calls to me, like we're old friends. "We haven't heard from you in days." *We?* Is that her and her multiple personalities? I turn away from her crazy eyes and wait for the stoplight to let me walk.

On the other side of the street, facing me, a thin woman digs frantically through her purse. She's in her fifties and the purse is worn and brown and something about her looks, I don't know, motherly, and the next thing I know I'm smiling at her, like it's okay, you'll find it, whatever it is. As she hoists the purse over her shoulder and crosses toward me though, her mouse-colored bob starts to shimmer, and then her complexion does too. She's one of them. Her grin has frozen into a hunger-trance, and she's bounding straight for me. My heartbeat's shaking my whole body.

"'Samatter, girl, you forget how to run?" the homeless woman shouts at me.

I take off, her laughter bouncing behind me. I duck behind the library, dash down the dirt path, halfway to the falls before I meet the main road again and risk spinning to check behind me. No one's there. Yay for running track. Is this why I became a sprinter? I pause to catch my breath, panting frantically.

It's not till I'm halfway up the driveway of Preston House that it hits me: I'm not the only one in Summer Falls who can see ghosts. The homeless lady can see them too. But then why didn't she run? Why did she just stand there laughing? The answer is because she's crazy. But how did she get to be crazy, anyway? She's hardly the only one, either—there's an asylum right outside town. I'm working on a glimmer of a theory, but I need to talk to Marshall before I can get further. It always helps to talk to him.

I have so much to talk to him about that I decide to walk around the house, through the yard, and straight to the cottage rather than going upstairs.

When I knock on the cottage door though, Jeffry opens it and pulls me in. For once he's not smiling.

"I came to install the new shower rod," he says calmly, "and what do I find in here?"

He's pointing to my goofy old bunny slippers, on the chair where I left them.

Shit. My heart's pounding as if I just sprinted up a hill. "We were just talking—"

"You're *lying*." The slap almost knocks me down. "He can't even speak English. What were you doing in there at night with that grubby foreigner?"

"Nothing." Grubby foreigner? I back away from him, panic rising. Tasting blood from where he split my lip. "Where's Liz?"

"You tell me." He hurls the slippers across the room. "She disappeared again, without making dinner. I can't seem to keep track of all the things the two of you do while my back's turned." He sounds so paranoid and angry, I suddenly get why she felt she had to lie to him. "Slut," he says grimly.

Even though I was calling myself the same bad word earlier, his saying it feels like a knife tip slashing my belly. It feels like my insides are coming out for him to see and poke at with disgust. Shame leaks out of me, the shame I'd been carrying since I met Dan and realized I'd (probably) cheated on him.

"My own daughter's a slut." Jeffry's voice is thick with disgust. His dark blond mustache twitches above his squeamish grimace, as if he's manning up to crush a giant cockroach. The roach is me, and also sex itself. The whole idea of it horrifies him: sex and bodies and dirt.

I dodge the next slap, but now I'm trapped in a corner. Jeffry lunges for me, pins me against the wall, his hands clamping down on my shoulders. Jerking them so I have no choice but to shake with his will. Every gasping breath I take reeks of his medicinal pimple cream. The back of my head smacks the wall, and somewhere deep inside me a dark flower blooms. Rage. Rage, but I can't use it to move, to fight back. It's far away from what powers my limbs, wrapped up in a spiderweb of mental fuzz. Then Jeffry shifts one huge hand to my throat and squeezes, not quite hard enough to choke me. Just hard enough for me to seize up in terror.

Suddenly it feels like there are two Elyses. There's the conscious me that's livid, shocked. How could he? Why am I not fighting back? Why am I just waiting for it? *He could kill me.* Then there's the deeper me, my body, and it's not shocked at all. Of course he can do this, *he's done it before.* This me has no ego, no will but the will to survive. And this is the me that takes over.

As if drugged, I go limp, and Jeffry nods and kind of grunts in approval, like this is what he expected from me all along. Ashamed but even more scared, I sit still and let him move his right-hand grip to my upper arm, big fingers digging into my flesh till it feels like they'll pierce through and meet his thumbs. A groan of pain escapes me, and I hate myself for crying out, even though it hurts so bad.

Jeffry fixes me with a cool, stern gaze. "Let's see, now," he says calmly. "You live in my house. I let you have my name. Is it too much to ask that you not pollute yourself while you're under my roof?"

I don't want to answer him. But I'm in trouble here. Marshall's not coming back; Liz is nowhere; no one's going to rescue me. "No." I whisper it. Not me. My body. It's made its calculation: I'll be safer not fighting. It won't *let* me fight.

"Is it too much to ask that you don't shame me by acting like a filthy whore?"

"No, sir," I breathe, hating myself for my own fear, my own weakness. My mind's still foggy, but my body's twitching, pulsing, shaking, sweating in anticipation of more pain. And I'm starting to understand that I need to trust my body, because whatever else it may be, it is always, always right.

My body knew it was him who gave me the bruises, right from the start.

He reaches back one arm and cuffs my left ear, hard enough to make it ring. He doesn't care how much he's hurting me. I'm not a person to him, I'm just a malfunctioning machine. "Tell me where your whore mother went." His voice so calm, despite the crazy things he's saying. "She should be here making dinner. What's she out doing that's more important? Or *who*."

I'm ashamed to admit this even to myself, but the fearful part of my brain is spinning, trying to think of something to say that will make him stop hurting me. To divert his wrath. I think of Liz, tiny harmless Liz who runs this place with hardly any help and never complains. Whose happiest moment was painting her daughter's bedroom pink. No way am I sacrificing her to feed this monster's paranoia.

Fight back.

I force myself to raise my knee, but he blocks it with his own.

A knock on the door startles us both.

Jeffry's voice hot in my ear. "Keep quiet." He's leaning over me, so close I can smell the acrid, angry sweat mingling with his acne cream. My throat opens to gag. His mustache tickles the back of my neck, and the dark flower of rage deep inside me bursts open. Instead of retching, I scream as loud as I can in Jeffry's face.

The glass door slides open, and I see Jim and Candace standing there, wearing twin somber looks of horror.

Jeffry drops his arms and I slip away from him, feeling numb.

He clasps his hands together and smiles at them, all warm and jovial again. "Oh, hello, folks! Anything I can help you with? Fresh towels?"

Jim swallows. "We came out to watch the sunset and heard yelling."

"We were just having a discussion. Right, Elyse?"

My scalp is tingling, like an alarm. Not danger, but urgency nonetheless. There's something I have to do *right now*. I have to get to my room. Without saying a word, I grab my backpack by its plastic top handle—it feels featherlight—and turn toward the door.

That's when I see the ghost slide in behind Candace and Jim, laying a hand on each of their backs. She's an older lady with a beehive, wearing an old-fashioned suit. Candace and Jim gasp and topple to the floor, and the ghost grabs on to Jeffry next.

I make a beeline for the door and run through the

balmy backyard, sucking down hungry breaths, not stopping till I reach the kitchen.

Liz is humming cheerfully at the counter as she chops carrots into evenly spaced little orange coins. On the counter a loaf of crusty bread peeks out from the top of a grocery bag. "Hey, you're home." She leans over to peck my cheek, and I don't even feel her lips. "Can I get some help with dinner?"

"I need to talk to you." I barely recognize my own voice, it's so quiet and serious, but Liz doesn't even look up, just slides her chopped carrot from the cutting board into a roasting pan and starts chopping a second one.

"I got a late start, hon, so why don't you peel potatoes while we talk?" She grins and with her free hand passes me a peeler.

I inspect its loose steel blade and rusted handle. It looks a hundred years old, like maybe Mrs. Preston left it in a drawer somewhere before she died, and then when Liz and Jeffry bought this place it was just one more thing that didn't have to be changed because it still technically worked.

"I'm not cooking for him," I say.

Did she not hear me? Of course she heard me, she's just pretending she didn't. Pretending everything's okay. Like she must do every day. But I can't do that. What happened to me today can never happen again.

My fingers are tingling again. Have to get in my room, *now*. Lock the door. Shove the dresser in front of it too. I drop the peeler in the sink and back out of the kitchen.

All the way upstairs my fingers are on fire. As soon as I've barricaded the entrance, I march over to my sock drawer. I pull out my stash, stack the bills, and wrap them in a rubber band, and dump it in my backpack. I can't stay here tonight; I'd rather sleep on a park bench in the town square like that crazy redhead. Sooner or later I'll find Marshall and we'll figure out a plan—together. I crumple up all the Hollywood crap into one ball and slam-dunk it into the pink-and-white-striped wastepaper basket.

Something's still not right, though, still feels left undone.

My pulsing fingertips reach for my backpack again, but this time they lift out my binder. Experimentally I tear out a piece of loose-leaf and stare at it. Why'd I just do that? It's not like I'm going to solve math problems at a time like this. My head turns to face the desk, my eyes focusing in on a blue gel pen. Before I know it the pen's in my hand and I'm scribbling, filling the page with what just happened. The horrible names he called me. The horrible things he did. At first I write it cold and clinically, then I add in my fear. My helplessness and shame. Angry tears sting my eyes as I write it, but when I get to the end, all I feel is exhaustion. Drained, I sigh a deep breath.

And that's when I smell it, Jeffry's acne-cream-and-sweat scent. A knot of fear rises in my stomach again, but he's not here. Couldn't be.

To reassure myself, I move the dresser and press my ear

to the door. I can hear Liz and Jeffry laughing over a TV show together, scraping silverware on plates.

It's me. His harsh antiseptic smell is all over me, in my clothes, in my hair. Whatever I do *I have to get that stink off me, now.* To wash off his aura of judgment.

My pink clock says 7:03. The show they're watching just started. My stomach's still queasy with fear, but I try to reason with it. I'll take the fastest shower in the world, then I'm out of here. Forever.

I stumble into my bathroom. My face is red and blotchy in the mirror; so's the skin on my neck and shoulders. I peel off my clothes and step into the shower. Under the hot water I hug myself and let out a sob that leads to another sob. My belly muscles are contracting, my spine curling forward, as if my body itself is telling me it's okay to cry, to let go of this awful feeling—till a soft *thump* behind me makes me freeze.

What was that?

Peeking out from one end of the lavender shower curtain, I can see that the bottle of vanilla body lotion on the sink is still teetering back and forth. Something jostled it.

My heart's pounding in my throat. I'm trapped.

On the other side of the curtain a handprint and the outline of a face appear; I let out a piercing scream. A long, shimmering arm reaches toward me. I feel a strange liquid pressure to open my mouth, and my knees feel weak, and I hear the thud on the padded floor, but I don't even feel my body drop.

—

I wake up sputtering rainwater. No, not rain, it's hot. I'm in the shower, the lavender bathroom. What happened?

I stand, feeling soreness all over my right side, where I fell. I turn the water off and tie on the white fluffy bathrobe on the door hook, willing myself to put the pieces together. I was at the pool; I jumped in after that little girl who passed out. Then I somehow got home and fell asleep in the shower? My whole body's aching.

No, I didn't fall asleep.

With a shiver I run to my bedroom. I'm dressing when I see the letter on my desk. I stare at the familiar angular writing. *Dear Elyse,* it says at the top, and underlined, *Remember this happened to you.*

CHAPTER 24

MARSHALL

I PACE THE BLOCK FOUR TIMES BEFORE I CAN bring myself to climb the steps to Bill King's front porch. I rap on the knocker, fighting my irrational urge to run away. Or maybe not so irrational. After all, I did jump out a second-story window to escape from him yesterday. But he's my father. Maybe the only family I have left. And there's a lot we need to talk about.

There's no answer. Well, fair enough. After the whole baseball bat incident, I don't blame him.

I jiggle the knob. Locked. What now, find a way to climb back *in* the window?

A dried-out flowerpot catches my eye. Of course I didn't notice it yesterday, but this house is the most neglected property on the street by far. The lawn's two feet high. I lift up the heavy ceramic bowl, where some poor houseplant died ages ago, and hear the clink and scraping on the concrete before the key comes into view. I hesitate.

This is your house, dumbass, I remind myself. Probably your own spare key.

Feeling like a criminal nonetheless, I turn the key in the lock and push the door in. "Hello?"

The living room is dim and stuffy, the only furniture a pair of scuffed IKEA couches. One is covered in piled-up mail. The place smells like tomato soup.

"Hello?" I nearly bump into a wall of cardboard boxes. Moving boxes. "Bill? Dad?"

"Marsh?" I can see the bald man in the kitchen, in his bathrobe, shivering on the floor against the closed back door. "Thank god you're back." He jumps up and hugs me. It's weird to have a stranger—or someone who seems like a stranger—hug you, but I feel bad for not knowing him, so I pat his back. "I thought I'd lost you," he says.

"Sorry about the window," I say. "And I'm sorry I don't remember you or anything else."

"It's not your fault." His finger tugs down the stretchy collar of my T-shirt, revealing the ink eye. His brow furrows. "I don't understand. It's still there."

I glance down. "Why wouldn't it be?" It's a tattoo. You can't erase them.

"Because your memories are gone."

"Wait, the tattoo is what protects me . . . from losing my memories?"

"You and your mother both had personal defense spells. But in the end something must have gone wrong with hers."

"That must be what Joe was talking about," I say, putting it together.

Bill's head snaps up. "Who's Joe?"

"You know, from the Institute." I stand and turn on the light. Tired of sitting here in the dark. "The guy investigating her death."

"An investigator?" He lets out a groan of annoyance. "Freakin' typical. Those assholes at the Institute did nothing but look down on your mom while she was alive. Now that she's gone, they finally realize what they had in her."

"Why would they look down on her?"

"Oh, they never understood her work. They're very traditional, conservative stuffed shirts. . . ." He pauses. "You know, I don't exactly know the details. Wasn't my world."

"You mean, you're not an occultist yourself?"

He shakes his head. "Magic tends to run in families, and it didn't run in mine. That's why your mother warded this house. For me. As long as I stay inside, I'm safe; ghosts can't get in."

I feel an ache. "Does that mean you've been in this house for over a year?" No wonder he's a little batty and short-tempered. I have to get him out.

"It was fine as long as Eva was alive."

"Tell me about her," I say. "Then it'll be like I remember her too, sort of."

He points to a leather-framed photo on the counter. "That's her." It's Eva and a younger Bill together in a Parisian café, croissants and giant coffee cups in front of them.

He's gazing at her adoringly. She's gazing at the camera straight on. "Eva Moon," he says. "She was one of those people everybody thinks of by their whole name. Even though she was physically small—I could carry her—she was somehow a big person. She just had that something."

I look at the Eiffel Tower behind them. "You traveled a lot."

"No, *we* traveled a lot, Marsh. You're the one who took that picture. You were always a trooper, you just fit right into our lives."

Did I have any choice?

"I wasn't sure I wanted kids," Bill says. "Eva and I had lived such an exciting, amazing life together before we had you, and I was scared of losing that. But we just kept right on traveling. This whole trip to Summer Falls, it was supposed to be a one-time gig to get money that would take us to our next big adventure, a set of New Zealand caves with—"

"Wait, what do you mean, gig?"

"Just that. She was hired. Fifty grand to do a fairly simple ritual for an occultist who needed fresh blood."

"Blood?" I pull my head back, away from him.

"Not literal blood," Bill says patiently. "Fresh blood just means fresh talent. Magical talent, in this case. According to Eva, nothing in the world is permanent. Once a spell—even a powerful spell—has been in place for a hundred years, it starts wearing off. It's like the elements themselves become immune to the spell worker's signature. So he or she hires other, younger magicians to refresh it, give it a new spin."

"Wait a second. If it takes a hundred years, wouldn't the original . . . um . . . person be dead?"

"Normally, yes. But occultists aren't normal people, as you've probably guessed, being one. Often the more talented they are, the more twisted they are. According to Eva, the man who founded this town was downright warped."

"Wait, Preston? Shouldn't he be dead?"

"After a hundred and fifty years, you'd think, right?" Bill barks a laugh. "I'm not even sure if he still looks human. She did a job once for a spirit that talked to her through Tibetan crystals."

I shudder. "How did Preston talk to her?"

"As far as I know, they communicated by text and email only—anyone could be writing those words. At any rate the gig was simple. She had to walk through his underwater labyrinth. The sacred geometry in her movements would renew the strength of the spell performed more than a hundred years ago. The spell that tied all the local spirits to him, made them his servants. Including the big one, the elemental spirit of the waterfall."

Underwater. "That's how she got hypothermia and died."

"No, not then; she did the spell and she was fine. The bastard cheated us though, never paid us a cent, but it wasn't the first occult scam we ran into. The whole story wasn't a big deal, in the greater scheme of our lives. Except, when it was over . . . she couldn't stop thinking about that place." This is obviously hard for him to talk about. "She said she's never seen such beauty in the world, felt such power. And then she confessed to me in tears that the founder of Summer Falls was exploiting this beautiful place, using it for evil. She felt so bad that she'd agreed to work for him."

"So everything that's screwed up about this town is because of the founder's spell?"

"Hell, this entire town *is* the founder's spell. He's the man, everyone here works for him even if they don't know it. Anyway, after she did this for him, she started hatching these ideas of how to reset things here and restore the balance. She talked me into renting a house for a month and staying longer so she could investigate. She didn't even tell me she was planning to go under a second time. I didn't find out until . . . until some hikers found her body. I couldn't even go and identify her. I had to send you. That was one of the hardest things, making you be the adult because I couldn't go out there. But your mother's spells still worked, even after she was gone. The wards around this house, for example. Elyse can attest to that—she was over here enough."

"Really, she was here a lot?" I lean forward, hope quickening my pulse. Had Elyse been a friend of mine after all? I explain about how we woke up and that I stayed at Preston House last night. "Were we close?"

"Honestly, Marsh, you haven't been cluing me in that much on your personal life. After your mom passed . . .

things haven't been great between us." He sounds so morose. "Which is rough when you're practically the only person I ever see. After she died, I was a mess at first. Then I wanted to get us out, but you wouldn't help me. First you kept putting off renting a moving truck or even a car, then you flat-out said you didn't want to leave. Said we'd dragged you all over the world against your will, and now that you finally had a choice, you didn't feel like moving."

I shake my head, feeling my eyebrows knit in confusion . . . not just confusion. Anger. At the guy who left his grieving father to rot in Summer Falls. "Dad . . ." I can't even say I'm sorry. I don't feel sorry, because I can't connect that Marshall to me. "You should have gone without me."

"You think I haven't thought about it?" he says. "Marsh, I built my life around this family. I've got nothing left but you and my memories of her. Now I'm the only one left who remembers her. When I lose it, when they catch me, then she'll really be gone."

I can't stand to see someone so sad. Especially knowing it's partly my fault. I need to fix this, but how? It seems so much bigger than me. Then I remember that the heatnaps only seem to erase bad memories, not good ones. "Hey, no matter what, you'd still remember the good times," I say, but it comes out hollow.

He scowls at me. "I don't want to just remember the good times," he says. "What we had was real, and I want to remember it that way."

"I get it," I say, because I wouldn't want to remember

just the happy moments with Elyse. We've had hardly any happy moments, in fact, but I wouldn't want to forget her. "So that's why you're stuck here."

"It's not just that," he says. "I'm worried about you, the types of spells you're doing lately. It's hard to get you to come out of your room."

"Spells?" I ignored my grieving father because I was practicing magic? But if magic works . . . "What I need is a spell to get my memory back."

Bill points to the dusty bookcase. "Magic books are all up there," he says, gesturing vaguely. "Oh, and you left your kit in your room the other day." Bill picks up a velvet drawstring bag from the shelf and tosses it to me. "First time I've seen you without this in your pocket in five years."

I tip the contents into my hands. It's a pile of elliptical gold coins and a handful of crystals. Gingerly I pick up the clear crystal. Its smooth weight feels just right in my hand. I realize I'm unconsciously sticking out my bent fingers in the same fanglike gesture I made when Dan hit me. I hold the crystal out toward Bill. "Do you know what this is for?"

"Whoa." Instantly he ducks away. "Careful with that thing. You never aim those at people."

"Got it, sorry." I put the velvet bag in my pocket. The instinct had felt so natural when I was attacked. Even if Bill was squeamish, I was going to need to figure out how to use these.

I walk back to the bookcase and open a dozen thick volumes before I find one called *Returnings* that's got the right theme. The spell on page 689 is called "Unseal." It involves doing an unpronounceable incantation over a "charged labor." Huh? Hard to magic your memory back when you don't remember how to understand occultist jargon.

I have to leaf through several more books before I figure out that a "labor" is an object made purely for reasons of love and to "charge" an item is to anoint it with an element from a place of power. Okay, then. That part's actually pretty simple. Water from the falls, though it'll involve a hike in the morning.

As for the labor of love . . . I look around the room, but I don't know what motive people had for making anything in here. The books were probably made by bored bookbinders. Our clothes could have been made in sweatshops. The IKEA couches were probably made by robots.

Liz's meals? But that's at least as much obligation as love.

I could make something for Elyse . . .

Except I'd really be making it for my spell, so it wouldn't count. Also, you can't love someone after a day and a half. Can you? Especially not someone with a boyfriend.

Then I remember Jeremy and Ruta in the computer lab, the awkward music-box gift. There's a school directory buried under a 10-inch pile of unopened mail in the kitchen. The only Ruta is Ruta Paulraj on Finch Street. Two blocks away from me.

When Ruta sees me at the door, she grins and claps her hands once and sort of bounces up and down on her tiny feet. "Come on in! I saved the last piece for you."

Of what? I must come over here all the time if she saved food for me. I follow her into the kitchen and watch her open the fridge and pull out an old-fashioned crystal cake pedestal with a fitted glass cover. She transfers the single slice of cheesecake onto a plate. It's topped with a yellow-orange glaze that I'm not so sure I'll like. "Want to split it?"

"No, I want to watch you love every bite."

I take a tiny bite. Creamy filling, moist graham cracker, and tart tangy mango. "Oh my god, I do love it." I load up a second, bigger forkful and savor it on my tongue. "This is the best thing I've eaten in my life."

She giggles, then covers her mouth shyly. "That's what you said when you had it on my birthday. Orange zest," she adds, "in the crust. Brings out the mango flavor."

"If you made this, you are a goddess."

"You said that on my birthday too." She beams, flashing silver metal with no trace of self-consciousness, then—as if catching herself—shuts her mouth and blinks down at the white linoleum. My mind flashes back to Joe, the condescending way he patted that waitress's head, like she was a cocker spaniel. He wrote off the Summer Falls folks as zombies, but it's amazing how Ruta remembers minute details of conversations between us. She must have spent hours making this cake and she's getting a bigger kick out of watching me feed my face with it than having some herself. Joe was wrong. People here aren't zombies or pets—they're just people.

She grabs two water bottles from the fridge and

motions me to follow her. "Come on."

I follow her down the hall, lagging behind to cover the fact that I don't know which room is hers. Her bedroom is as spare as the rest of the house: a twin bed, a pine desk, a single framed print on the wall. A Hubble telescope–slice of the universe, galaxy upon tiny galaxy. The rest of the walls are decorated with straight-A report cards and honor-roll certificates. Trophies from regional science fairs.

"So." She throws herself on the bed, barely mussing the sheets, and takes a deep breath. "I think I'm finally over it."

Over what? From her expectant look, I'm obviously supposed to know. "Good," I say, nodding. "I mean, finally."

She pouts. "That's it? A three-year crush and all you can say is *good*?"

Crush . . . she had a crush on someone . . . was it me, or someone else? If it was me, that's kind of insulting for me to say *good*. "How did you get over it?"

"Actually." She brightens. "It's mostly because of you."

Oh no.

"Well, indirectly. Okay, so you know how it drives me crazy the way people ignore you."

"Right." So it's *not* just me thinking that people ignore me?

"I mean, you're the coolest guy I know, and no one realizes it because you sit all slouched in the back row and don't exactly draw attention to yourself. But still. You don't let being ignored get you down, you just accept it. You even take advantage of it—like how Ms. Niffenhauer never busts you for cutting class because she can't remember you're a student or how . . ."

I don't catch her second example. I'm still mulling over a single word she said: *advantage*. Is it possible people aren't ignoring me because I'm a loser but because I'm somehow making them ignore me? I glance from my cheesecake down to my tattoo. My mother put it there to protect me, but maybe some of the ways it protects me aren't 100 percent great.

"Anyway, I got to thinking," Ruta goes on. "There must be some advantage to being me too. Being, you know, the kind of girl guys don't ask out."

"Ruta—" I start to tell her that a guy asked her out just today, but she doesn't remember that. "Of course there's an advantage to being you. You're pretty and you're nice, not to mention smart as a whip." Looking at her, I realize I'm not just saying that. Ruta *is* pretty, nice, and smart. The trifecta of long-term-girlfriend material. At least in a normal world.

"Guys don't want smart," she informs me glumly.

"Bullshit we don't." I think of Elyse, her sharp intellect peering through those big green eyes. "Smart girls are the hottest, trust me."

She looks down. "Not to guys like Dan."

"Dan?" I blurt out. "You had a crush on *that* moron?"

"He's not that dumb," she says. Too quickly, like she's

used to defending him. We've probably had this conversation a hundred times. "All right, fine. He's as dumb as a box of hair. But that's part of his charm, right? He's so . . . unexamined."

I look around at Ruta's bedroom walls, at the neatly arrayed awards, and feel sadness well up in my throat. If she wasn't living here in Summer Falls, being stymied by constant heatnaps and memory wipes, she'd probably be a genius. But she is here. Which means instead of helping to find a cure for cancer, she'll lose more and more ground until she finally winds up in the asylum. "Ruta," I say slowly, "have you ever thought about going away to college?"

"Don't try to sell me on that again," she says. "You know my parents would be lost without me. Who would turn the oven off when they forget? Anyway, I think there might be something wonderful waiting for me here after all. Someone, I mean." She jumps up and bounds over to her dresser, points to the small box displayed on top. "See? I have a secret admirer."

It's Jeremy's music box, the lid open, revealing the pewter baseball player in all his tackiness.

"Wow, um . . . who do you think it is?" I feel like a jerk for asking a question I know the answer to.

"It's a mystery." She picks up the box and holds it close to her chest. "It might be Tom Bradley. Or Evan Watson. But what matters is whoever it is made it just for me. It probably took hours, maybe days. Someone likes me that much."

It occurs to me how easily I could manipulate her and steal the box from her. I could make her forget all this, just by telling her the truth about Jeremy asking her out. While she was out cold I could tuck the box under my arm like a football and run. An act that would hasten the demise of her sharp mind. "Ruta," I say instead, "could I borrow your music box? Just for a day or two."

She glances from the box to my face and takes a deep breath, and I know that even though she'll miss it, she's going to hand over her new most prized possession, no questions asked. Because she's that good a friend. "Oh sure." She smiles and shrugs. "It's not like I *need* it for anything. It's just nice to know someone was thinking about me, you know?"

"I do know, Ruta." I put it in my knapsack with the crystal, the coins, and the book *Returnings*. "Thank you."

"No problem. Wait . . . what were we talking about?"

———

Hiking to Preston House in the starlight, the music box in my knapsack, I feel guilty and small, exactly the opposite of how I felt after killing the grease fire at Mollie's. I took something from a girl who doesn't have much. As the roaring of the falls gets closer and drowns out the crickets, a dull throbbing rings out in my chest. It's probably just guilt, but I glance down at my tattoo anyway, half expecting to see a blue light. Not that I could see it last time anyway.

Preston House is quiet and dark. Before I can open the

front door, Elyse bursts through it. Seeing me, she nearly crashes into my arms. "Oh thank god."

"Whoa, where were you going?"

"I don't know, I just have to get out of here." She looks rattled, her hair wet, her backpack on one shoulder. "I fell asleep in the shower." She bites her lip like she's trying not to cry. "I'm missing time."

Even though I've seen and heard about how people here fall asleep and lose little bits of their minds, I never pictured it happening to Elyse. She's different, she's not of this place, even if she was born here. "Elyse, it's going to be okay. I think I found a way—"

"How could it ever be okay?" She pulls a piece of paper from her pocket, unfolds it, pushes it in my face. "Look."

The black scrawl is inches from my eyeball. Angry flourishes of ink transform into words and phrases before my eyes. Ugly ones. *So scared. Jeffry's dead eyes. Against the wall. Dirty slut.* "What is this?" I say, feeling coldness spread through my limbs.

"It's my handwriting. I even wrote the date at the top, see?" She flicks the page, making it jump even closer to my face. "It's my memory of today, unabridged."

CHAPTER 25

ELYSE

MARSHALL STARES AT THE PAPER, HIS DARK EYES burning through it. "That son of a bitch."

"It's not like it's the first time." I lift up my hair and turn to the side. His sharp intake of breath reenergizes my own outrage. Just seeing the evidence of what happened to me is tearing him up. "The worst part is, Liz has no clue what's going on," I say. "Though if he's doing this to me, what's to stop him from doing it to her too?" I remember the noises in their bedroom last night, the crash and what sounded like muffled crying. "Do you think what we heard last night was—"

"Of course. He's abusing her too." His fingers are gripping the paper tight enough to crumple the edges. "*That's* why she's been waking up in a motel room with a packed duffel bag. She's trying to leave him . . . but she keeps falling into a heatnap and forgetting her plan."

So Liz was a victim too? But she didn't know it—at

least most of the time? "This is . . . bigger and more complicated than I thought."

"It's very simple, actually." He looks up at me. "He hurt you. I will end him."

"Get in line."

"I'm serious." His soft voice chills me. "I learned some things today about myself, my past. Let's just say it wouldn't be hard for me to . . . neutralize him."

"Neutralize?" My own voice comes out strained, an octave too high. "Neutralize as in kill?"

"Elyse, I *have* to make sure he could never hurt you again."

"*You* have to make sure— Oh, great, let's make this all about you and your macho heroism."

From his wounded eyes I know it was a mean thing to say, and I feel a little bad, but at the same time, it's true. His rage on my behalf isn't making me feel better anymore. It's just making me feel more helpless, more *stuck*. Stuck in my own anger and frustration. Stuck in this life I can't remember. Stuck in my pink-and-white frilly dollhouse prison. "I don't care how disgusting Jeffry is"—and just saying his name makes me twitch as if a tarantula were creeping up my arm—"if you attack him in cold blood, you're no better."

"Okay, you're right," he says. "This isn't about me. I have a lot to tell you that *is* about me, but I'll wait. What can I do to help you?"

I reach for his hand and squeeze it. "Get me out of

here. I'm tired of being scared. And being judged." At least if I'm outside I can run from the ghosts.

He nods. "You stay here. I'll sneak up to your room and get the quilt off your bed. I have an idea where we could go."

———

From the outside, the abandoned mill looks like any other warehouse. We slip in through a back door and Marshall lights a candle. Cautiously we explore the factory floor till we find a clear spot against the back wall to spread our quilt.

I'm dazed from all he's told me on the way. "I still can't believe all that magic crap *was* yours," I say.

"Why? Why is magic harder to believe in than ghosts?"

"Because ghosts are, you know, just spirits of the dead." I shrug, unable to think of a logical reason. The word *spirit* reminds me of the story Carla read at the library. I tell him about it, including the unsatisfying nonending.

"Interesting," he says, "though the symbolism's way too obvious."

"What symbolism?"

"The magician's the town's founder, the guy I was telling you about. The one my mother worked for."

"I didn't see that. I thought the symbolism was about pitting spirit-seeing people against occultists."

"I didn't even see that, but good point. Only the occultist's a straw man, he's totally evil." He settles down on the quilt beside me and pulls a dusty volume from his bag. "Let me prove to you that not all of us are." He's close enough that I can smell his soap and sandalwood scent. Or maybe I'm just imagining it. A lingering olfactory memory.

"Here's what I was looking for. Lie down." Marshall stalks the floor around me, leaving a circle of coins around the edges of my quilt. He touches each one, warming it in his hand, and muttering some incantation.

Finally he looks down at me. "It's temporary, but it should last the night. I wish I was strong enough to do a larger area. You might as well get some sleep though."

I lie back, but I'm so cold and creepy and dank in here, I know I won't be able to sleep.

I'm in California again. This time I'm lying on my own private beach, watching the purple and pink sunset behind the water. Frothy waves break on the hot sand, teasing my bare toes before retreating to the ocean.

"You look good in red." I glance down at my red bikini and turn to see Marshall lying next to me. His eye tattoo glows blue from his bare chest. I'm so happy he's here, so happy we both made it out of that place. I lean toward him to give him a hug that turns into a kiss, but the moment our lips touch he turns into Dan.

"Hey, babe."

I jerk my head back.

"You forget about me already?"

This is wrong. We broke up. Dan's orange-and-white letterman jacket doesn't belong on this beach. He belongs in Summer

Falls, in my past. My fingers scratch letters into the sand: I'm dreaming.

——

I open my eyes. In the cold, dark warehouse, a furious candle flame burns yellow, its bouncy reflection flickering on the ceiling. A tall figure's hunched over a chair in front of the candle, muttering some incantation that doesn't sound like English. I barely recognize the low voice as Marshall's. The words shoot out of him harsh, cold, fast. Even when I pick out my name from the jumble of harsh sounds—*Elyse*—it sounds like a growling command. Quietly I sit up and flip on the light switch. "Jesus, are you still trying to do a magic trick?"

He whirls around. "Did it work?" His eyes have that cold, determined focus, looking into the distance at something that isn't there. "Did you dream about me like I willed you to?"

"Willed me to?" I feel a blush spread over my face. Only problem with light, it makes you visible too. Exposed. "Yes. Yes, I dreamed about you, okay? When did I ever give you permission to go inside my head like that?"

"Relax," he says, which makes me want to do the opposite. "I didn't actually enter your dreams; that's way more advanced. I just . . . induced a theme." His superior tone still doesn't sound like the Marshall I know. "If I'd asked your permission, you would have discounted the results. Understandably. That's the only reason I didn't tell you. Do you believe me now that magic works?"

"I believe that it's turning you into a jer—" I stop. Silently crawling out from one of the giant metal ceiling pipes is the figure of a little girl. Only I know it's not a little girl. Little girls can't appear out of nowhere. Can't float overhead, staring down at us with mournful eyes. Can't shimmer.

"What's wrong?"

I try to sound composed, but my heart sounds like a galloping horse in my ears. "Time to test your coin-circle spell."

"Where is he?" He looks around, like that's going to help.

"She, and it's a kid." Wearing an old-fashioned white cotton nightgown. "I want to run *so bad*," I whisper, instantly embarrassed that I said it out loud.

"Hold my hand," he says, reaching for my palm. "You're safe here, I promise."

Agile as a spider, the ghost child drops to the ground and clambers right up to my quilt. I shrink back toward the wall.

"How close is she to the coin circle?"

"Too close," I breathe.

"Okay, here's what's probably going to happen," he says, squeezing my hand. "When she comes to the edge of the circle she's going to stop like she hit a brick wall. Then she'll fade away."

I keep my eyes on her as she inches closer. "Where will she go?"

"According to my mother's notes, back to the place

of power. Which I presume is the waterfall. Spirits of the dead can be tethered to it, with the right spell, so they'll always return there."

But instead the ghost child turns to Marshall. Her curious finger reaches out to tag his thigh, and suddenly a blue light flares out of his chest. Just like the stroller lady, the ghost child goes flying backward. This time I feel a tiny bit sorry for her. It's not her fault she's stuck here as a ghost, just like it's not my fault I'm stuck here as a living person.

"Do you think it hurt her?"

He starts to shake his head, then says, "I don't know."

We snuggle together under the quilt for warmth, and he's so quiet I wonder if he's falling asleep while I quietly go insane from how good his arms feel around me and how good he smells.

It's okay, I tell myself. I broke up with Dan. It's not wrong to want Marshall.

Experimentally I run my hand along the back of his neck. His whole body tenses with anticipation. He's definitely not asleep. I stop to gently tug on the short hair there, and he shivers. And kisses me hard.

His lips taste so good. I kiss back hungrily, never wanting it to end, never wanting to think about our problems again, all the things we have to worry about, how alone we are in this place with only each other to trust. Not caring if we've done this before or if it's our first kiss. Just wanting our mouths to keep finding each other, biting and sucking and exploring and never wanting the sun to come up and force a new day of worries and fears to start.

Suddenly the blue light is back, but instead of being a faint flash, it's lighting up the whole warehouse. Splitting off into ten or twelve separate branches that crackle and zing and sizzle upward toward the ceiling.

"What the hell?" Marshall says, opening his eyes.

The ceiling's now lit up, and I can clearly see a giant mechanical wheel hanging from the center of it. I watch in awe as the separate branches of blue light begin moving together like hands, slowly turning the giant wheel. As it begins to whir, the whole factory floor lights up in orange, so bright I can actually see the machines. They're not ordinary pulping machines, as I expected. They're futuristic engines—oversize, brightly colored—whose purposes I couldn't begin to guess.

I breathe out. "Okay. *Now* I believe in magic."

"That wasn't me." The blue light, his light, has gone out, but the orange one remains. He looks around the room. "I think it was my mother," he says in a strange voice. "I mean, her magic. Bill said she was trying to do something else with the place of power, something better. My dad said the founder blamed her for the mill's closing. Whatever she was planning, she never got to finish it. I wonder if I study her notes enough, maybe I can finish it for her."

———

In the morning the coin circle around me is still intact. Marshall gathers the coins into a velvet drawstring bag and stuffs it into my backpack, along with his magic book and the music box he says we're going to use in the spell. We've decided he should carry the backpack, since I might have to run from a ghost at any moment during our walk. In fact what happens is that we run into Tomoko—she must hang out in this neighborhood a lot—and I'm able to verbally pinpoint her location to Marshall, who blue-lights her away before she can get to me. We're both actually laughing by the time it's over, from the tension of it and the challenge of communicating precisely under pressure. But together we make a great ghost-shooing team.

When we get to his house, I feel dread in my stomach at the thought of being introduced to his father—the man I ran away from—but he turns out to be a sweetheart, taking my hand in his and telling me how sorry he is about my amnesia.

While his father cooks us eggs, Marshall explains that he wants me to stay home with his dad while he hikes to the falls to bring back water, but I veto that plan. First, even though I hate to say it in front of his dad, I don't feel safe inside the house. Its protections may not work anymore, and I don't think I could sit trapped inside a five-foot coin circle all morning. Second, I'm the one who grew up here. My feet and eyes probably know these trails by heart. There's another reason I want to go with him. We'll be hiking to the place where his mother died. What if her ghost is there? Would Marshall's protective tattoo work on her, considering she's the one who created it? At least I'd be able to see her.

We pack a messenger bag with an empty thermos, two bottles of spring water, and peanut butter sandwiches. His father ducks into a room and comes back out with a pair of tan hiking boots. "These should fit you," is all he'll say, setting them on the floor in front of me. I hesitate. They're way too small for him or Marshall. It doesn't take a genius to figure out they were his wife's. "The trail's dangerous in sneakers," he says. I start unlacing my sneakers, once again feeling guilty for running away from him the other day.

Near the trailhead, in a shady cedar grove, we pass an old cabin with smoke coming from the chimney. "That's where Mr. English lives, right?" I ask. "I mean Joe. You said he was lonely and really wanted to help. Maybe we should ask him for advice on this spell thing."

"Spells are kind of about the spell caster," he says, frowning. "You can't just ask other people for help and advice."

"So that's why you hate asking people for help."

"That, and I'm a guy," he agrees.

I glance back at the cabin. It looks like it's a hundred years old. "Do you think Joe even has electricity?" I ask. "I don't understand anyone who would come to this town *knowingly*."

"Occultists know how to set up their own defenses," he says, with a touch of that cold voice I remember from the dream-spell. Too late I realize it sounded like I was criticizing his parents. His dead mother. Whose hiking boots I'm wearing. I let the subject drop.

The wide, paved trail leads us toward the roaring sound of the falls. We cross a footbridge over a sparkling brook and the trail narrows some. Then after a quarter mile or so, it starts to climb at a steady grade up rocky slopes. Here the trees are smaller but packed more densely. The scents of earth, bark, pine, and dead leaves mingle; twigs crunch under our feet and several times we have to brush branches out of our way. Scrambling upward through the green canopy of moss and brilliant red rocks, I feel like an ant. Every time I glance at the sheer drop on my left, I think of Tomoko hurtling to her death. I'm grateful to be wearing shoes with traction.

The falls come into view, majestic, tumbling down a craggy red wall of mudstone. Beyond the chasm, on the opposite side of the falls, the Kiowa glacier towers above it all, a giant river of ice stretching up the mountain. Glare from the midday sun makes it shimmer with a blinding purity. I shield my eyes and look lower, at the rushing water falling and falling, emptying into a lake far below us. From here I can see a panoramic perspective of town—Main Street, the school. Marshall's neighborhood. The grounds are all verdant, the colors of the buildings and houses bright and new. The sky above them a brilliant blue. But just beyond Summer Falls, everything looks different. Maybe it's a trick of perspective or light, but the towns around it look poor and barren in comparison, the ground, the sky, and the buildings all painted similar dull shades of gray. It must be my imagination, I tell myself. Landscapes don't shift that abruptly.

I'm uncapping the thermos when I realize Marshall's not next to me. I panic, thinking of Tomoko slipping and then falling off the cliff. But he's on my left, only a few steps away, staring. Staring behind the falls, beyond the trail, at a rock overhang, like a shallow, wide-mouthed cave carved into the mountainside. Inside it is a still and silent natural pool.

"It's so serene here," I say, though even that word can't convey the pool's secret beauty.

"I know this place." Marshall's voice is odd. "This is where my mother . . . where she died."

"How do you know this is the place?"

"Because I've been here before. In dreams."

I stand beside him, close enough to touch. "Tell me about them."

"I'm always dying in the dreams." He swallows. "But somehow it's okay, because I'm doing something good. I'm sacrificing. My future. And it's worth it."

"No, Marshall." I shake my head, terrified for him. I'm about to tell him no cause is worth losing him for when we run smack into a figure coming down the trail from the other side of the falls. An orange-and-white letterman jacket. Oh shit. Marshall slips his arm around me protectively.

"Elyse!" Dan beams his golden-retriever smile at me, but it fades instantly. "What are you doing here with him?"

"Dan." Dread in the pit of my stomach. "It's none

of your business who I'm with. We broke up; it's over. Remember?" But of course he doesn't.

"How could it be over?" Dan takes a step toward me, shaking his head as if he couldn't have heard right. "You're my girlfriend."

"*Ex*-girlfriend. I told you, I don't want to be with you anymore." I feel cruel spelling it out again, but what else can I do? Suddenly I wonder how many times he and I have broken up and slipped back into each other's arms with no memory of the pain. How does anyone ever break up in Summer Falls? If I don't give up, it'll have to stick eventually. "We're not right for each other," I say firmly.

"You're right for me," he says. "You're perfect for me, you're the one, Elyse . . . I love you." His voice is choking up, and it's hard for me to go on, knowing how much I'm hurting him. After all, he really does think our relationship was perfect. He doesn't remember all the parts that weren't, and that's not his fault. But I'm telling the *truth*, so I keep going.

"Well, you're not right for me, and I'm sorry, but I don't love you anymore. I need you to leave me alone."

"But I've never felt like this before." Dan's trembling. "I can't stand it." He grabs my shoulders, not that hard, but I gasp because they're so sore.

"Please let go of me."

"No. You said you loved me forever!"

"Let her go." Marsh is at my side. Dan lets go of my shoulders, then suddenly shoves him hard. I gasp as Marshall stumbles on a rock, sliding two feet away from the cliff side.

He rises to his feet quickly, ignoring the bloody scrapes on his leg. "Chill out, man," he says. "This isn't the place."

Dan's answer is to take a running jump at Marshall, who throws an elbow in his ribs.

"Stop it!" I scream. They're both too close to the cliff. I launch myself between them, praying it'll bring an end to the fight, but the next thing I know Marshall's pulled a crystal out of his pocket and when Dan takes a swing again he dodges, grabs his arm, and pulls him along, throwing him with his own momentum into the pool.

From below, a deep throbbing tremor rings upward through the air. Like the buzzing of an angry beehive, only so low it's more vibration than sound.

I look at Marshall. "Can you hear that?"

He nods, unable to take his eyes off the clear water. "I don't just hear it," he whispers. "I feel it."

I nod. "Me too." It's almost like there's something alive down there. . . . Not a person, exactly. A force. Some kind of wild, ancient consciousness. Lonely, ravenous, but clinging to its life nonetheless. Like the spirit from that children's story Carla read in the library.

"The spirit's still down there," Marshall says suddenly, as if reading my mind. "It's not the waterfall that's the place of power, it's *here*."

Dan's blond head bobs back up to the surface, glaring and spitting water, just as Marshall grabs the thermos out of my hand and dips it in the pool. The buzzing grows ominously louder, sending a chill up my spine. Now the spirit sounds livid.

"Dan, get out of the water," I say, trying to sound calm. I hold out my hand to him. "Please."

He only snarls at me, but his chattering teeth steal from the effect, making him look like a little kid distressed in the water. The suddenly dark water. Looking down, I can see that the pool's dark because it's completely full of ghosts. Dozens of them, rising fast to the surface.

"Dan!" I scream.

Marshall's eyes narrow, his body freezing to hyperalert. "Where's the ghost, Elyse?"

Before I can manage more words, the surface of the pool breaks as the ghosts start to emerge, surrounding Dan from all sides. Men and women ghosts, young and old. A teenage guy with hippie dreads, a woman with a fifties beehive, a man with a top hat and monocle. I can only imagine what he sees, water dripping down bodies that aren't there. The right side of Dan's mouth twists up in alarm; he probably thinks there's been an earthquake. Then a circle of ghostly arms reaches inward toward Dan, pushing him onto his back. His head is like the center of a flower, and their arms are the petals. He kicks once, then his eyes close and his body goes slack, spinning slightly in his float as they feed.

The lifeguard in me knows we have to fish Dan out of the water or he could easily drown. But I've never seen that many ghosts all at once. My cowardly feet are frozen to the spot.

Luckily Marshall's already kneeling on the mossy rocks next to the pool. He reaches as far as he can to grab hold of Dan's ankle in mid-spin. I watch in terror as, one by one, the ghosts clutch at Marshall, their long arms outstretched, but with a flash of blue his magic sends each one flying backward, disappearing under the surface. Patiently he reels Dan in closer, pulling him by his legs back onto solid ground.

"All right, he's safe. Let's go before he wakes up." Marshall backs away, and we both run down the trail, not stopping till we hit the main road. He collapses into a sitting position on the ground, leaning forward, and clutching his knee to his chest. "I swear, if I'd known the pool was full of ghosts, I never would have thrown Dan there."

I crouch down to take his hand. "It's not like he hasn't had a heatnap before," I say, trying to reassure both of us.

"But there were so many of them."

"I've never seen anything like that," I admit. "Why were there so many of them in there?"

"Spirits are always drawn to a place of power," he says. "Even living people are, to some extent. Like the founder was, and my mom. And me too, I guess. But ghosts are even more susceptible." He looks at me expectantly. "You think he'll be okay?"

"Sure." I pull him to his feet. "He might even forget he wanted to kill you. On the downside, he's going to still think I'm his girlfriend."

———

Marshall's dad is asleep in front of the TV when we get home. There are Chinese lanterns on either side of the couch, a pipe and lighter on the coffee table. The whole room smells like pot, giving me a hint of how he makes it through the day.

We head back into Marshall's room, where he lights the yellow candle. To save time, I open the thermos and start pouring water into the box.

"What are you doing?" He grabs it out of my hands, sounding panicked. "I have to do this myself or it won't work."

"Oh. Sorry." Trying not to feel hurt, I sit back on the bed as he lights more candles. "So your dad didn't help your mom?"

"Not with actual spells—the talent didn't run in his family. You're born with it or you aren't."

"Got it." And god knows Liz and Jeffry are no occult-ists. I sit on my hands, hoping I haven't already ruined the spell.

He pours water from our flask into the box, sub-merging the tiny baseball player up to his belt. Then he shuts the box and winds it up. Holding the dusty black book open, he recites the incantation in his new, brutal alien language. Then he opens the box and starts saying it again. As the miniature baseball player starts revolving around his little platform, "America the Beau-tiful" begins playing, each note tinny but deliberate, as if there's a tiny harp inside the platform.

The top of one candle flame undulates gently, and after I stare awhile I can see a faint blue aura shaped like a heart around each one. I can't hear Marshall's voice anymore, but it takes effort to tear my gaze away to check on him, and when I do I see he's sinking to his knees. I reach out my hand to him but feel myself pulled to the ground by force. The music slows till it feels like there's a full second between each note. Now all the candles have blue auras around their flames, and when I look back at the baseball player he has an aura too. My eyelids feel heavy. And then the space between the notes widens to a field. I'm pulled into the sunny, soft warmth of the flame.

———

Phew! *I blow out all six candles on a square snow-white bakery cake decorated with swans.*

"Happy birthday, Ell-bell!" An olive-skinned man with warm green eyes behind glasses bends down to kiss my cheek. He smells like soap and cotton. His face is a little scratchy with stubble, but I don't mind.

"I hope you wished for a bike." Liz winks at me just as my eyes treat me to a close-up of a shiny red one-speed with a banana seat.

Suddenly the scene changes. The man—my father—is outside on the street with me in front of our house. I'm sitting on the bike but not moving. He's holding the bike and me up. "You move the pedals now," he tells me, "and I'll hold on as long as you need me to."

I sit on the bike, feeling a tiny bit nervous when my feet leave the safety of the ground. But I can see my father's shadow behind me, running along the concrete. I can feel his strong hands holding the bike steady, keeping it vertical. I'm not scared, even as we pick up speed. And then we're really racing, flying, my feet turning the pedals and his shadow is farther behind me, no longer touching my bike's shadow. "You don't need me anymore, sweetheart!"

"Dad!" I yell, because I didn't know he would let me go. Not yet. My feet forget their job and the pavement swims toward me, but before I can hit the ground the scene changes again.

I roam through the house, searching each room, but Dad's not there and Mom isn't either. Finally I can see her in the garden, kneeling over the bed of purple camellias, her head slumped over into the dirt. Heatnap. I run to her side, wait for her to wake up, then ask the question that's been on my mind. "Where's Dad?"

She smiles. "He's down in the basement watching the football game."

I run downstairs . . . but I never get there.

I'm racing on a track, the pack of slower runners at my heels. Faster, faster, got to finish first. I'm number one.

I'm in a candy shop.

"Look at those strong legs—you're running faster every year." The young woman in the white Frieda's Sweets apron smiles and passes me a chocolate truffle from over the counter. "On the house." She tucks a stray red curl back under her hairnet. "Keep running like the wind, girl."

Then I'm sitting next to Mom on a bus-stop bench, short legs swinging in front of me. "It's our big day, baby." She smiles at me, but her eyes are shiny. "We're finally going to get out and see the world." She strokes my hair, which hurts a bit. I have stitches behind my ear, six, the doctor said, but I don't know why. And it doesn't matter, because I got a chocolate shake afterward; I'm still drinking it. Then Mom slumps over asleep toward me, her beautiful hair splayed over the duffel bag between us.

I'm lying on top of my quilt in bed, writing in a book, scribbling furiously.

Then I'm doing it again, only at my desk under the lamp.

It's not a book, it's one of those blank journals. The cover is blue and green, iridescent like an oil slick, the colors bleeding into each other. I open it.

I open it again.

Applause mixes with chlorine bouncing off the walls of the indoor pool as a young boy coughs out his lungs against my shoulder. "You'll be okay," I tell him, "it's going to be okay . . ."

"H-E-L-L-O, Hello!" The crowd roars as we cheerleaders shake and shimmy behind a swirl of orange pom-poms. Next to me Carla wipes her glistening forehead. The punishing sun is making me feel light-headed, but it beats getting packed like cattle into the bleachers. The fate of Summer Falls High's rank and file. I have to be the best. I have to stand out. Or I'm nothing. "Explode! Ignite! The Rays are dynamite!"

In his tuxedo jacket, Dan leans over me and ties a snow-white rose corsage to my arm. "Perfect rose for a perfect girl." I beam up at him, basking in the glow of his love for me. And all I have to do to keep him is stay perfect. . . .

Then I'm breathless, lying on my side in a dark bedroom, lips *locked bruisingly hard with someone else's, our open mouths kissing hungrily. A soft blue light shines all around us. It's Marshall's light, his magic. I relax and lean into his warm sandalwood scent. I know I'm safe here. Desperate to be even closer to him I press my body against his and feel his response. I grab his hand and guide it under my tank top.*

"Mmmmmm." He pauses kissing me and murmurs into my neck. "What about jock-boy?"

"I don't care. Please don't talk about him, please just keep touching me." I moan as his firm, warm hands cup my breasts over my bra, his fingers lightly squeezing the nipples. "Don't stop, keep doing that."

"Whatever you say." His mouth claims mine again, tongue slowly licking my lower lip, then probing between them.

Then I'm opening the silver-blue-green journal again.

I'm staring at the inside cover. A blurry photo. Underneath with Sharpie someone's written, Elyse, Remember this happened to you. *And underlined that word,* Remember.

Again, over and over, *Remember this.* The same shadow of a recollection, repeating, but it's just a sliver. A tease. It always ends before I read the damn book; then it restarts. Brain torture, like a fever dream.

I can feel my hot, bare legs underneath me now, feel the scratchy carpet of Marshall's bedroom and smell the burning wax. The baseball player's still spinning his pointless rotations to a high-pitched robotic accompaniment. But I've slipped out of the trance.

Marshall's curled in a fetal ball on the carpet, staring

up at the flames. Even though his eyes are open, every once in a while he gasps, like he's having a nightmare.

I come over and rub his back. Maybe he's stuck having the same memory over and over too. Or maybe he's just remembering something sad.

Huh.

All *my* memories were joyful. Pleasant. No flus, no breakups, not even one bad hair day. How could that be? No one's happy every second.

Have I really had *everything* unhappy . . . wiped?

My fingertips survey the spot behind my ear, where the stitches were in my bus-stop memory. There's a long scar.

My father in the memories, the olive-skinned man running behind me on the bike. He wasn't Jeffry. Jeffry is not my father.

Where is that journal? If it was so damn important to me, why wouldn't it be hidden in my stash with the money and California maps?

Because it's *more* important. So important I take it with me everywhere. It's not in my backpack. That leaves one place, and I don't want to go alone.

I nudge his arm. "Wake up, Marsh." But he doesn't hear me.

CHAPTER 26

MARSHALL

EVA PUSHES HER TORTOISESHELL GLASSES ON top of her long black hair and spins the hotel swivel chair to face me. "I think you're finally ready."

"Mom, I've been ready for years."

"You've been impatient for years. Not the same." She sounds amused. "Doing spellwork is not like reading about it. It's serious. Sometimes dangerous." I like those words: serious, dangerous. "We'll start with a simple dream spell." She pulls open the bottom desk drawer and snaps up three pillar candles, which she holds up to me.

I gasp at the sight of the black candle underneath. "Holy crap, Eva!"

She sighs. "Never been lit, I swear." She fishes it out and shows me the unused wick.

"Why do you even have one? You said black magic trashes your soul."

"It does. But there are scarier things than me in this world,

Marshmallow, and if this was the only way to protect you and your father from them . . . I wouldn't blink." Gingerly, she sets it back in the drawer, then scoops up three brightly colored pillar candles. "You'll start with these. Blue for healing. White for blessing—"

"Red for strength," I finish, opening my hands eagerly, but my eyes linger on that sleek, shiny black candle. I want to reach for it, crush it around my fingers, light the wick and speak the unspeakable. I want to be like her, protecting, not like my father and me, being protected. "If you had to do black magic someday," I say, "wouldn't it be a stronger spell if I helped? If we both put energy into it?"

Eva's mouth drops open and she laughs. "Such devious ambition. You take after me too much." But she glances down at the drawer, suddenly thoughtful. "It's true that together, we could—"

The hotel-room door swings open and Bill's triumphant smile fills the doorway. "I found a tea shop with internet!"

Shaken from her trance, Eva launches herself from the chair, black hair flying, silver bangles jingling. "Perfect timing, my love!" She wraps her arms around Bill. "Sometimes I think you are the magician."

"Wake up, Marsh." Elyse's voice is far away. "I need to talk to you. There's something really wrong with my memories."

What? I try to say the word, but I'm only thinking it.

The wrought-iron patio chair creaks beneath me as I shift my weight on the overstuffed, flowery cushion. I'm reading the X-Men comic I slipped inside my physics book, which isn't really a physics book at all but a spell crafter with a book cover reading

"First-Year Physics" and some cheesy clip art of an atom.

It's annoying to read with sunglasses on, but it's better than staying in my airless bedroom inside Preston House. The brown-haired lady who served Bill and Eva and me French toast that morning had claimed there'd be a "nice breeze" on the porch. I'd nodded, though I couldn't understand why they didn't just have AC like any normal hotel on the planet. Bill and Eva had told me Summer Falls would be weird.

From the corner of my vision I see a feather duster and turn to meet a pair of clear green eyes.

"Hey." It's the innkeeper's daughter. I remember her from breakfast, though she came downstairs late and her father gave her crap about it. I figure I'll remember her, or certain parts of her at least, all my life. Light blond hair swings down to the top of her tight cutoffs, highlighting the curve of her ass above her smooth, tan legs. "Good book?" she asks.

"It's just for school," I say automatically.

Her nose wrinkles. "Homeschool sounds so weird." Yep, that's more or less what I've come to expect from townies, people who stay in one place. But this girl doesn't sound judging, just intrigued. She leans closer, so close I can smell her hair. Peaches and cut grass. Despite the heat, there's an energy to her. "Your mom seems nice," she says, sounding confused, surprised. "She was asking me all these bizarre questions about the waterfall."

"She's doing research." I reach for the handy, worn-out line. "My parents are journalists, writing an article about . . ." Fill-in-the-blank. "Tiny little towns," I finish, pleased with myself for coming up with something that's both plausible and *a subtle dig. You're insignificant, just a small-town girl, I don't care what you think of me.*

"That's a new one." She snorts. "Usually you wizard people just pretend to be tourists."

My heartbeat speeds up. How does she know what we are? And what does she mean "usually"? How many occultists have stayed here—Eva always likes to know if there are other occultists around her; she doesn't trust them. She doesn't even trust the one she came here to do the job for. What would she think if she knew there were more in town?

"Don't be so shocked," the girl says. "Look, I need you to do something for me, something from that book that you're pretending is a physics book."

"You looked in it?"

"My mom had me make your bed," she explains, "and straighten up all your stuff."

"Oh!" *I'm still stunned that she looked in my book.* "Wow, that was you? Um, thanks for making my bed."

"My parents made me," she repeats.

If her goal was to embarrass me, it worked. My cheeks are scorching. There's something intimate about making someone's bed, touching their pillow, their sheets . . . It has never occurred to me that a hotel bed-maker would open up my book and see it wasn't what it pretended to be. Partly because it's disguised with the most boring cover in the world. But also partly because, well, it never occurred to me that any hotel bed-maker would have enough intellectual curiosity to open a book, period. And now I feel like an ass for that assumption.

"Usually the magic people don't show up till June or July," she explains. "I'm glad. Most of them aren't as nice as your mom." She looks away. "Can you do me a favor and not tell your parents or anyone I asked you?"

I nod, though it's annoyingly hard to keep a secret from Eva and Bill; they're my parents, but since we travel together they're also my best friends by default. Pretty much my only friends.

"Can you do the protection spell on me from that book, make me safe from the ghosts? Like you are."

I tilt my head from side to side as if considering. What she's asking for is impossible—even my mother couldn't do it for my father. But the sight of this girl asking me for help is so intoxicating I can't make myself say no.

She groans. "Forget it, I mean if it's beyond your level—"

"It's not that," I say with a derisive snort and shrug. "Actually the problem is you. A protection spell like that would only work if you were an occultist yourself, so . . . ."

"Maybe I could learn magic." She still sounds hopeful.

"It runs in families. You're born to it or you're not. Sorry," I add.

"Got it." Her face has closed up somehow. The pleading look has been replaced by barely concealed anger. Anger, at me? "Cute teddy bear, by the way," she says, meanly. "Does he have a name?"

"Um, Doctor Bear." My comic slips out of my book, and I can feel myself shrinking under her glare of judgment. She lives in a haunted town; I'm just an arrogant ass whose mother thought it would be interesting to see the hauntings. She asked me for help, and I basically told her it was her fault I couldn't do anything.

Eva steps out onto the patio. "How's the homework going?" She leans in to whisper in my ear, "Family meeting in our suite."

I leap to my feet, eager to put some distance between me and my shame. Still, as we walk away Eva's small hand feels oppressively heavy on my shoulder, and I can feel the girl's curious eyes follow us into the house.

My parents sit together on the overstuffed chair, Eva on Bill's lap. Just in case I'd forgotten that in this family it's always two against one.

"So," Eva prompts me, "what do you think is wrong with this town, Marsh?"

I shrug. "There are ghosts." Homeschool sucks because no matter where on the globe you are, you're still at school.

"Tell me more." She's leaning forward, raising her eyebrows a little. She expects me to say something smart, to follow in her footsteps so she can beam with pride, but I'm pissed that she's quizzing me instead of telling me what the hell's going on around me.

"People seem kind of whacked-out and spacey," I say. "But I kind of like it here. At least it's better than Paris."

Both my parents seem to find this hilarious. They laugh so hard they snort and clutch each other's arms as if for support. "Better than Paris!" Great, I just know it's going to be a catchphrase between them from now on. They have a lot of catchphrases, a whole language built for two.

"I know you can do better," Eva says, and sighs.

"It's this damn heat." Bill fans himself with the magic book. "Melts your brain."

"Bill, even you can tell it's more than that." Eva sighs indulgently and takes the book out of his hand. "I should think it would be obvious. Some occultist has rigged up a brilliant loop here. The town is tied to the place of power. Specifically, by souls tethered to the place of power who suck the life force of the townspeople and feed the energy back into the town itself."

"But the townspeople are still alive," I point out.

"But are they, really, fully alive?" For the first time ever her soft voice strikes me as condescending. "Life force comes in many flavors. You've heard of undead souls who eat blood or brains. Others eat sheer energy or light or even—as in this case—certain thoughts."

"Thoughts?" The idea terrifies me, of someone rummaging around in my head for a snack. Unconsciously my hand has drifted to the top of my chest, to the ink eye. I'm safe, I remind myself.

I swallow. "So how do you fix a place like this?"

Eva's small forehead wrinkles, and I can tell she's already given the question a lot of thought. Obsessive thought, knowing her. "If only I could figure out how to claim the place of power for myself," she says. "I'd retrain the ghosts to eat greenhouse gases. Or garbage. And instead of putting that energy toward a town, I'd turn it into clean power. Think how we could change the world."

"Your mom is brilliant," Bill says, stroking her hair.

"But wait, how would that help the people in this town?" Don't you give a shit about them? "They'd never get their memories back."

Eva gives a rueful chuckle. "I'm sorry, Marsh, but look around you."

"Zombieville," Bill agrees, grimacing. "It's too late for these poor people."

I think about the innkeeper's daughter, Elyse, the angry spark in her eyes. The way she shocked me by knowing things she shouldn't have known. And it's the first time I can remember my parents being wrong.

———

"Wow, you were really far gone," Elyse says. I'm back in the room with her. She's blown out the candle and closed the music box.

"Why did you stop it?"

"Because it wasn't working right."

"It worked perfectly for me. I already remembered my parents, meeting you . . . all kinds of stuff."

"Really?" She leans closer, her expression turning wistful. "I'm happy for you, Marsh. But for me . . . there was a glitch or something."

"How could there be a glitch for you and not me?"

"I don't know. It felt like I was watching a movie—"

"Right." I nod. It was like that for me too.

"—only some scenes had bits cut out of them, like someone fast forwarded parts of my life. And other scenes would repeat, like they were badly edited. After a while it felt like I was seeing the same thing over and over, from different angles and with different backgrounds. It was all just a jumble."

"Huh." My heart's sinking at her words, but I don't

want to give away the depth of my concern for her. I knew her mind had been messed with, like everyone's in Summer Falls, but I'd been hoping against hope that the spell would work on her anyway. But it didn't; her memory's still Swiss cheese. What's Plan B?

"We have to go to school. Now." Her voice is intense, certain. "I need to get something out of my locker."

———

On the way to school we pass downtown, bustling with people. The red-haired homeless woman's sitting on the library steps today, barefoot as usual, her patched brown dress draping between her knees.

"I've been meaning to talk to her ever since she told me to run from the ghost yesterday," Elyse says. "I think she used to work at Frieda's, at the candy counter. Gave me free candy when I was little."

I shake my head. "She doesn't look old enough for that. Maybe it was someone else who looked like her."

"No. She called me 'girl.' I know it was her."

We quickly walk the rest of the way to school. She stands in front of her locker, takes a deep breath, puts her fingers on the combo lock, and twists right, left, right. It opens.

Inside the locker door, a magnetized mirror with a pink plastic frame catches my sleepless face. On the shelves textbooks are neatly arranged, spines aligned. And on the metal bottom, behind a cosmetics bag, behind a box of tampons, is a journal with a green and blue cover. Elyse dives for it, grabs it, opens it.

Someone's taped a photo to the inside cover. A little girl with a gap-toothed smile and lion-colored braids all the way to her elbows. Gripping her right hand is Liz, younger, without crow's-feet. On the left is an olive-skinned young guy not much taller than Liz, with green eyes behind horn-rimmed glasses. In red Sharpie it says, *Dear Elyse. Remember this happened to you.*

The first few pages are crayon drawings, clearly made by a child: a monster with jagged teeth, a rain cloud with spindly arms reaching out. But the Sharpie hand has crossed these out and written in large letters across the fold, *Read this book from cover to cover, every time you see it.* And, *You're not crazy. The ghosts are real.*

"What is this?"

"Don't you get it?" She looks at me sadly. "They're my memories."

"In *there*?"

"Where they can't be wiped."

My eyes dart back to the crude crayon drawings. It hits me like a punch in the stomach. What she's saying. What she's been doing, all these years. She cracked the system.

Even when she was a little girl, Elyse could see ghosts. Frustrated at the people around her not believing her, she must have started drawing what she saw and then, when she could, writing about it. Over time, she would have amassed a pile of pages she didn't remember writing. Pages that, experience taught her, contained vital knowledge. So she trained herself to record every bad thing that happened to her as soon as possible, before it got wiped away.

I remember her look of anger and defiant triumph as she held up the notebook page on which she'd documented Jeffry's assault. She couldn't remember scribbling those terrible words, but she never doubted they were true. She was that used to trusting her handwriting.

It was how she tried to preserve herself.

We flip through the pages together. Ugly words pressed into the paper jump out at me. It's all ugly, or else just sad, or awkward. Arguments. Breakups. The Sunday her real father went to the bakery for bread and never came back. The afternoon two days later when her mother was weeding the backyard in a daze of tears and a Salvation Army man pushed his way past Elyse into the house and carried away all her father's things. Even his socks. Even *pictures* of him. And when her mother drifted back inside, her jeans and peasant blouse caked in garden dirt, she was in a chipper mood and seemed to have forgotten Elyse's father ever existed.

"I didn't question it when I was seven," she says, frowning, "but why would the Salvation Army want photos of some random guy?"

"Because whoever that was in your house," I say, "he wasn't from the Salvation Army."

She shivers. "I know. But then who was he?"

"Maybe someone who knew how the ghosts worked, like you. Who wanted to ease your family's pain."

She chortles. "If they really wanted to ease our pain,

why not just take *us* out of there?"

I think back to my parents, how they'd felt bad about the locals' plight but never even entertained the thought of rescuing them. "Not everyone's a hero."

We turn back to the book and read about Elyse's mother remarrying a man with strange habits and a temper. Her husky puppy, Silver, getting run over by a drunk tourist's rental car. Her waking up at twelve to find a male guest in her bed kissing her breasts.

"God." Elyse exhales sharply. She hands me the open book. Silently I read:

Dear Elyse, I'm still shaking. Sorry if the handwriting's hard to understand. Mom was waiting in my room when I got back from school. Her makeup was a mess. Mascara all over her face. She held up this book—said she was cleaning the baseboards and she found it. She started crying hard and calling me a liar. I just stood there. "I know none of this is true," she said. "Your father loves you and would never lay a hand on you." She asked me why, what would make a girl tell such terrible lies about her own loving family. Did I do it for attention? To hurt my parents? To feel sorry for myself? "I know you're a liar," she screamed at me. "Admit that these are lies."

She never hit me, but her words cut me to pieces. Of all the things to call me, liar hurts the most. I try to tell the truth, but deep down I've always been afraid that maybe nothing I've written in this book really happened the way I wrote it. What if I do exaggerate or make things up? How can I be completely sure I'm not crazy? But those doubts live in my mind. Not my body. And no matter how much I wanted for her to stop screaming at me, I couldn't do what she told me. Couldn't say it was lies. My mouth wouldn't let the words come out.

In the end she fell down on her knees and begged me. "Please say it's not true, please say it's a lie."

Looking down at her—my own mother, crying on the floor—I felt overwhelmed with loneliness. Like she had magically transformed into a little kid and I was supposed to be the parent. Only I didn't know what to do, how to comfort and calm her. I still couldn't bring myself to say what she wanted to hear. Then I saw it appear behind her, the ghost in the window. A white-haired lady in a long black dress and reading glasses.

I made a grab for the book and pushed Mom as hard as I could toward the ghost, then ran out the door.

I take my hand off the book. "Do you want me to stop reading this? I feel like I'm inside your head or something."

"I don't want to be the only one who knows this stuff happened. It helps that you're here."

We keep reading, but it's so grim, I want to stop. If Elyse weren't turning the pages, telling me she didn't want to be alone with these memories, I would shut the book and throw it away. Especially when Jeffry enters the picture. Half the entries are about Jeffry. Jeffry breaking Elyse's pinkie finger, kicking her down the stairs, calling her names. *Worthless. Disgusting.* Her mother's miscarriages. Grandma Bets dying of a stroke. Pain. Physical pain and emotional pain. And she doesn't just write the bare facts, she tells the stories, including how she felt. That's part of why it's so hard to read.

Halfway through, she lets the book snap shut and sinks down to the bottom of the lockers. She sits with her head in her hands and weeps, and none of my magic spells can help her feel better. All I can do is watch while the girl I love hurts.

CHAPTER 27

ELYSE

AFTER A FEW MOMENTS, HE SINKS DOWN TO HIS knees beside me.

"You did something amazing with that book," he says. "You outsmarted the system of Summer Falls."

"Ha. Not really." I sniff and wipe my eyes with the back of my hands. "Don't get me wrong . . . I'm grateful to have this record of my past. It must have been hard to keep it up, all these years. But there's nothing amazing about doing what you have to do to survive. It just makes me sad, reading all these awful pages. What a waste. I mean, I started out as this healthy, happy little girl—you can see it in that picture—and then I spent so much time being scared. And running away from ghosts. And feeling alone. And feeling ashamed. I didn't outsmart the system, it shredded me. Like it shreds everyone. The only difference is I chose to remember. Maybe I'd be happier if I hadn't."

He shakes his head. "You wouldn't have been you." He pulls me close and holds me tight in his arms. "I wish I could go back in time and rescue that little girl," he says. "I'd do anything to stop those things from happening to you. But as bad as it was, you *did* survive. You grew up to be strong, and fierce, and in control . . . and the best person I know."

"Then you need to leave this town and meet some better people." I pull back from his hug. "You don't get it, Marsh. I'm not upset because bad things happened to me. I'm upset because they infected me with their badness, and now I'm bad too."

He fixes me with a dark, questioning gaze. "So let me ask you this: You think *I'm* a bad person?"

"I don't want to talk about—"

"No, for once we're actually going to talk about this." Gently he turns my chin toward him, forcing me to look him in the eye. "Yes, we slept together," he says. "Last I checked that's a two-player game. So, how come it makes you a bad person but not me?"

"It's not the same."

"Why, because I'm a guy? Or because I don't have to be perfect, like you?"

I stand, slam the locker shut, and turn away, toward the classrooms. "Because you weren't cheating on anyone. You weren't lying. You just . . . trusted the wrong person."

"Still, I'm not exactly a paragon of ethics if we slept together while you were with someone else. Plus I'm a known liar with a huge ego. Nobody's perfect. Everyone makes mistakes." He picks up the book. "And anyone who's been through what—"

"*Don't* make excuses for me. Just because I have reasons for being broken doesn't mean it's okay."

"I'm not saying it's okay. I'm saying there's such a thing as forgiveness. Ever heard of it? It's this fucking brilliant invention that lets you learn from your mistakes and move on, instead of just repeating them and saying you can't help being bad."

"Maybe *you* can learn," I say, "because your whole brain is in your head instead of part of it being in some book. When you finish getting all your memories back, you'll be whole. Well, I won't be. Ever. If this is all there is to me, I'm damaged goods, so don't make me try to celebrate that. I have a right to be pissed about it."

"Don't call yourself damaged. And you do have a right to be angry, but please don't take it out on me."

His saying *please*—not a word that often comes out of his mouth—almost stops me. I know he's right: I *am* taking it out on him, and maybe it isn't fair, but I'm jealous of him. For having a mother who protected him from ghosts, protected him forever. For having a father who loves him even though he isn't perfect. For having a chance. A chance to grow up and be okay someday, when it's too late for me. When no matter how hard I work to glue the shards of myself back together, I'll always be broken. Shattered.

"I never even had a chance," I whisper.

Marshall reaches out to touch me, his gaze liquid with compassion. His gentle hand strokes my cheek, then rests soft and warm against my collarbone, on my heartbeat, as if to say, I know how you feel. But he doesn't. Can't. And I just want to push him away as hard as I can.

I step back, away from the warmth of his touch. "If I were you I'd give up on the broken girl," I tell him. "And get your father the hell out of town, before it's too late for him too."

With that I drop the book on the ground at his feet, turn my back, and walk away from him.

Nothing's quite as surreal as reading your depressing autobiography, then walking through a town square still abuzz with carnival lights and games. The Ferris wheel's running, packed, and tourists wearing childlike smiles roam like lost buffalo. A barker calls out to me, "Get your cotton candy. Fifty cents for blue, fifty cents for pink!"

Down the street I see a familiar figure, hands full of grocery bags, entering the antiques-and-secondhand shop.

"Mr. English!" I call.

"Elyse." He looks as guilty as a thief caught red-handed, but what's in his bags is mostly boring sports equipment: a catcher's mitt, jerseys. Then I see the letterman jacket.

"Are these . . . Dan's?" I pull out the jacket. His half-empty pack of cigarettes spills out.

"I'm so sorry you had to find out like this," he says. "Hikers found Dan near the waterfall. Catatonic."

"Oh my god." The ghosts surrounding him. They ate

into his mind until it was picked clean. Guilt washes over me. Could I have saved him, if I'd been thinking of helping him instead of just being anxious to break up with him? Even though I don't smoke, I put the half-empty pack of cigarettes in my backpack's front pocket.

"They used my cabin's phone to call the sheriff. Hank just drove him up to the asylum. Look, it happens," he says. "I've seen how crazy the families can get when they keep seeing the person's things. So I took the liberty of dismantling Dan's bedroom while his parents were out."

Just like the Salvation Army man, I think. I'm almost certain he was an occultist too, although that couldn't have been Joe since Joe would have still been in England at the time (and about twelve years old). Funny how occultists seem to have this caring, sensitive side they're careful to keep hidden, so it doesn't mess up their tough, spooky mystique.

"So when will you be quitting the charms of this picturesque hamlet?" Joe's voice drips sarcasm. "Bet you'll miss the . . . oh, no, wait. You won't miss anything."

I know I was just saying how much I hate this place and can't wait to be out of here ASAP, but something about his mocking it that way bugs me. It's like, *I* can say that, I'm *from* here. You're not, you can't. "No disrespect," I say, "but this is still my hometown, the only place I've ever known. Sure, I'm saving up to move away, but even then, it'll be *my* hometown. Not yours."

I stumble numb through downtown, images of Dan

floating in the water surrounded by ghosts stuck in my head.

The redheaded homeless woman is dancing a jig (or possibly a reel?) on the library steps. Should I talk to her? I don't know if I can talk to anyone right now.

She sees me and stops dancing. "You don't have much of a poker face, girl," she says with a cackle. "Everybody knows what you're thinking before you do. You want to talk about ghosts, don't you?"

I blink, stunned that she could be so lucid. "So we *have* met before."

"I've met you once, you've met me a hundred times. I'm Elizabeth, since you forgot again." She thrusts out a dirty, sticky paw. I hope she didn't notice my hesitation before I took it. "Hundred and one," she says, winking.

"I do want to talk about the ghosts," I whisper. "If you can see them too, why don't you run away?"

"Ghosts don't bother me anymore." Sharp eyes, like a bird's. "Not the same way. Now they give me the poison that flows in my veins."

Oh-kay . . . so she's clearly gone back to crazy mode.

Sheriff Hank's squad car pulls over beside us. He hops out and strides over to us. "Time to move along," he tells Elizabeth. "I'm getting reports of you scaring off tourists."

"Good," she snaps, "maybe they won't come back."

Quick as a wink Hank's handcuffs come off his belt. "Going to have to move you myself, ma'am," he says, ducking his head apologetically. "For your own good, and everyone else's."

It's finally happening. He's taking her off to the asylum. Where people go in but don't come out. And that's when it occurs to me that there *is* one place I can go where I could never make another stupid, thoughtless decision. Where my brokenness could never cause anyone else pain again.

"Sheriff. Put me in the asylum too, please."

Sheriff Hank half turns, sees me, and groans, and several tourists turn to look at me too. "I'm not locking anybody up. Just taking her to Green Vista, where the church provides extra beds."

Oh. "Fine, so just lock *me* up then. I'm about to go crazy. I might qualify as crazy already. Seriously, I'm begging you here. . . . I'm a danger to myself and others."

"She sure *sounds* crazy," Elizabeth speaks up in my defense. "Only a crazy person wants to be locked up." But she gives me a look as if to say, What are you playing at, girl?

"Run along, Elyse. You're not crazy, you're just a pain in my backside."

It's now or never. In full view of dozens of tourists, I let my knees buckle and, my arms flailing, crumple to the ground. Gasps of anticipation fill the air, and even with my eyes closed I can feel the tourists watching me. I don't stand up.

"Oh, good gracious," the sheriff says, and I can almost see him roll his eyes, even though my gaze is fixed on a spot on the sidewalk where someone spilled a chocolate milk shake. "Come off it."

I keep doing my best imitation of Hazel while Sheriff Hank gets Elizabeth into handcuffs. She seems to offer no resistance.

"Is that girl okay?" says an unfamiliar voice of concern. A tourist.

"She's just fine, ma'am," Sheriff Hank says. "Elyse, get *up*."

"She doesn't look fine," says another voice.

Hank waffles. You can just tell he wants to do the right thing, but just like when Kerry talked him into giving me a ride home instead of reporting me to the doctor, he lets other people change his mind about what the right thing is. It takes about ten minutes for the tourists to wear him down. From being sure I'm pretending . . . to being equally sure I should be the state mental institution's next guest. I stay deadweight, my eyes focused straight ahead of me on a stray lock of my hair, as he carries me to his car and deposits me into the backseat next to the uncomplaining Elizabeth.

The car rolls along, lightly bumping my head a few times, but I don't mind. I guess Hank doesn't mind either, since he figures my brain's useless now anyway. The radio clicks on with plenty of static, and Hank whistles along to an old-time country song. I let my eyes dart toward Elizabeth just for a moment, and she winks at me.

A second song starts, and Hank sings along instead of whistling. Then, abruptly, he stops singing and yells, "Holy shit!" He slams on the brakes.

What could have happened? Our car doesn't appear to have hit anything. I would have felt a bump. So what could make the squeaky clean sheriff cuss like that? I'm dying to know what's up, but since I'm pretending to be catatonic, I can't exactly turn my head to check it out.

Still, it doesn't take long for me to get a chance to figure it out though. He kills the engine, throws open the door, and runs out.

"Hey, Elizabeth," I whisper. "Where's he going?"

No answer.

I steal a glance to my right and see the handcuffs hanging empty from their hook.

Her seat belt's still buckled. But she's not in it.

Holy shit indeed.

Where the hell did she go?

As my confusion edges toward fear, I feel my senses growing more acute. My eyes zero in on the key ring, jangling like a wind chime, still in the ignition. I catapult myself into the front seat. Wait, do I know how to drive? Dan said I was the only girl he'd ever let drive his car, so I must. What if I don't remember how? Then I feel my fingertips tingle. And I see her in the rearview mirror. Ten feet back, standing by the side of the road, next to Hank, who's yelling and pointing his finger at her. He's so much bigger than she is. I can't just leave her there.

I step outside . . . and instantly a wave of dry heat surrounds me. I seem to have entered a rocky desert. Beside the potholed road only a few scrubby plants peek out of the pale reddish dirt. But as I run toward Hank and Elizabeth, the climate seems to change before my eyes. About five feet behind the car, I see the "Welcome to Summer Falls" sign and suddenly I'm walking on vibrant green grass. The road from here on looks smooth, new. When I'd looked down at the valley from the falls, I'd told myself that regions don't shift that abruptly and, up close, the change in landscape would be subtle, gradual, not a clear line where green meets gray.

Yet here in front of me is a clear line between Summer Falls and the world outside it.

As if Summer Falls were somehow *exempt* from the surrounding drought. Free from the punishing dry wind and barren soil. Saved from the grayness and poverty they lead to. I stare at the line, remembering the angry faces of those three young men from Green Vista who crashed our fair and kidnapped our yearly town photo. No wonder the areas around our town feel such a bitter rivalry toward us. We seem to be immune to Mother Nature.

"How the hell did you get out?" Hank grabs her arm and tries to pull her along with him back toward the car.

"Take your hands off her!" I yell, though Elizabeth is doing great on her own. She won't cross the line into gray land. It's as if she's got superstrength.

Hank's breathing heavy, and finally he gives up. "What are you, some kind of witch?"

Of course. She must be an occultist. That must be why she doesn't have to run from the ghosts.

"I answer to a higher law than you, baby boy," she says, as if by way of explanation. "Don't take it personally." Then she pats him on the head. He really does look as lost as a child. "You'll forget. Soon."

Those words send a warning chill to my bones. Wandering toward the highway from a nearby thicket of aspen trees is a familiar pigtailed figure, still in her peach frilly apron and baker's hat from the fair. Hazel. Confusion roots my feet to the ground. Did she escape from the asylum? Do people get let out after all?

Then Hazel stretches her skinny arms toward Sheriff Hank. His mouth forms an O just before he crumples onto the spongy, forgiving Summer Falls grass. Hazel grins at me next, her apron fluttering in the breeze, her pale, papery skin shimmering. My heart jumps in my throat. Poor Hazel never left the asylum. She must have died there. Her body's probably still frozen in a morgue locker, but her spirit's back in Summer Falls. Her hungry eyes focus on me.

I don't have to wait for Elizabeth to yell, "Run like the wind, girl!"

I race for the car, tumble into the driver's seat, and slam the door.

Even as I turn the ignition and hear the engine come to life, Ghost Hazel's still chasing me in the rearview mirror, and then—*bam*. Just as she reaches the town limits, it's like she hit an invisible wall. She turns around and wanders off, away from me. Once again, Elizabeth doesn't bother to run from her.

So a ghost can't get past the edge of town. Weirder, neither can Elizabeth. That's why she wasn't worried about going to the asylum. Well, either that or because she's crazy. But Sheriff Hank was right: She must be doing magic. What other explanation is there? If Marshall were here—then I remember I'm driving to the asylum and might never see Marshall again. For the best.

I drive along the empty highway and follow the signs toward the state mental hospital. I'm expecting the asylum to be some creepy old castle at the top of a hill. But the hospital complex is extremely modern-looking, surrounded by a gate, not a moat.

I drive up to the gate, hoping that if there's no free visitor parking I can maybe try to charm whoever's manning the entrance into letting me through. Instead of an attendant though, there's just an electronic card reader. Crap.

I reach into the glove compartment, pull out a white card, and swipe it. The gate parts, letting the sheriff's car through. Once in the indoor garage, I make my way to the elevator—keeping my eyes peeled for nosy personnel—where I swipe the card again. I hit level four, the top floor, "Catatonia." That's where the Summer Falls people will be. Maybe where Grandma Bets will be.

The elevator drops me off at a landing with double doors.

There's no glass window on the door, so I can't peek. I have no choice but to walk through and take the chance of being instantly caught and removed . . . or worse. I take a deep breath and walk through the double doors.

Instead of a waiting room or nurse's station, I find myself in a giant dorm room with octagonal black-and-white floor tiles and equally ancient-looking, lumpy single mattresses with faded puke-green sheets. Some people are lying in bed, staring at the wall pensively. Some are even *tied* to their beds, staring at the ceiling. Most are older, like Kerry said they would be, but not all. I nearly trip on a pale, small-boned young woman sitting cross-legged near the doorway. "Sorry," I say, leaning over to make sure she's okay. She just keeps gaping at the far wall.

I follow her gaze . . . and my eyes lock on the very familiar young face of the guy leaning up against that wall. He's wearing a green gown instead of the orange jacket I know him by, his luxurious golden hair has been shaved, and his cheerful swagger has been replaced by a slump, but I know that face. Only days ago, I was kissing that face.

"Dan, are you okay?" I rush to his side, kneel down, and wave my hands in front of his face, but he doesn't acknowledge my existence. Is this my fault too?

In the corner sits an olive-skinned man with glasses and shaggy hair graying at the temples. His legs are straight ahead of him, his green eyes focused on the far wall, his brow furrowed, as if deep in thought.

I can't look away from his eyes. So much like mine.

Oh my god.

"Dad?" My voice is tiny. "It's me. Elyse."

The man's expression stays somber, carved, implacable as a mountain.

"You don't remember me," I say, wondering if he can even understand me. "I remember you, a little bit," I say. "You pushed me on the swing set. You and Mom held my hand on either side so I could jump—it felt like flying, but I knew you were holding me tight and you'd never let me fall."

He blinks once, twice.

Heartened by even this tiny response, I go on. "I remember learning to ride a bike, when you ran behind me. My journal says you disappeared that year, and Mom cried in the garden, but then—"

Suddenly the man who was once my father lunges for me, his eyes wide, his flat hand heading fast for my face. But strangely my body doesn't flinch. I go still and silent as his hand covers my mouth.

Half a second later, I hear the elevator buzz and foot-steps in the hallway. Voices. No, one voice. The doctor's on his cell phone. Shit shit shit. What now?

Just as the double doors open, I dive into the bottom shelf of the supply closet and the man who was once my father covers me with a thick, scratchy blanket. Darkness envelops me.

My heart's pounding so hard, I can barely hear what the doctor's saying on his cell phone as he enters the ward.

". . . and we are so close to a cure for this tragic illness," a friendly male voice says. "Our researchers have narrowed its cause down to a metallic toxin, the makeup of the local soil, or just the air itself. . . . Ten mill would go far, yes.

Fifteen would get us further. Thank you. I look forward to hosting the grant committee in Summer Falls again." *Click.* The doctor sighs, then hits a button on his phone.

"Preston," he says in a decidedly quieter tone. Preston? Is the doctor really on the phone with the evil town founder himself? "There's nothing I can do without more staff. Problems keep increasing. Oh, really?" His pitch rises. "Well, if you have such a problem with my stewardship, why not come out here and run the asylum all by yourself? Oh, wait . . ." He snaps his finger. "I plumb forgot. You can't leave town! Ha-ha-ha."

Preston can't leave town? Is he just too busy or . . . suddenly my mind flashes back to the sheriff struggling to get Elizabeth back into the car, but her body just wouldn't budge across that line. She literally could not leave the town. *"I answer to a higher power than you, baby boy."* My mind is racing. All this time I'd been thinking of the founder as a man, William Phillips Preston. But if someone can magically own a town *and* live forever, what's to stop him from changing his gender at will too? There's probably a spell for it, even. What if Elizabeth is the founder of Summer Falls? But then . . . why would she be constantly vandalizing her own creation? But if it's not her, who else *could* it be? The answer is: it could be anyone. Or no one. Terrifying thought: the founder is probably powerful enough to take any form.

"I'm going to tell it to you like it is," the doctor goes on, "because I have no reason to kiss your ass. Your spell's fading. As they do, after a hundred years. What's the matter, having trouble finding overambitious suckers to hire these days?" He gives a hearty laugh. "You're kidding, right? Boy, you must be desperate to even ask. No thanks, boss. You know I like my body intact and my pocketbook comfortably full."

Desperate. The founder—who he, she, or it was—was desperate for fresh blood, for occultists to refresh the ritual. Occultists who were "overambitious suckers"; in other words, Marshall's mother, who'd dreamed of claiming the place of power for herself but had died there instead. And Marshall seems determined to follow in her footsteps.

I have to go back. Have to warn Marshall. If I can make it out of here alive.

CHAPTER 28

MARSHALL

I SEARCH THE CROWD OF FAIRGOERS ON MAIN Street but can't see Elyse, and I get tired quickly of drunk and dropped tourists constantly bumping into me because they didn't notice I was there. So I shuffle back home, half expecting her to be there already. But no, the only person there is my dad, snoring on the couch while ESPN drones in the background. Where the hell's Elyse? Don't be another Dan, I tell myself. Back off, give her some space. She has a right to be upset. She needs time to regroup, then she'll come back. In the meantime I wind up the music box, light my candle, and wait for the movie of my past to start playing a scene.

———

Ding-ding.

For an unsure moment, Bill and Eva and I sit speechless at the kitchen table, forks frozen over our bowls of stew. We've never heard that sound before.

Then I spring up, excited. "It's the doorbell! I'll go see who it is."

My best-case scenario is a special delivery of some spell books Eva ordered from Peru. Instead, standing on the rain-soaked doorstep is Elyse.

Her hair's soaked straight, stuck to her neck in wet clumps. Cheeks pink, like she's been sprinting. White puffy jacket and jeans drenched. I've never seen anything more beautiful than the sight of her.

She squints at me but can't quite see me through the protection spell.

"Hey." I wave at her.

Immediately her eyes focus on mine. "Hey," she says. Then, "You said I could come by anytime."

"Yeah, I meant that," I say. "Come on in. I'll set another place for dinner," I add, like this happens all the time. Like my heart isn't thrashing around in my chest.

She deposits her sneakers by the door between my work boots and Eva's ballet flats, unpeels her wet socks and stuffs them inside each shoe. I catch her staring at Bill's giant Doc Marten boots (size 17). In fact, she stares at everything in our living room. Dad's set of dumbbells. The IKEA bookcases overflowing with ancient clothbound volumes.

"You guys have more books than the library!" I can't tell from her tone whether that's a compliment, an insult, or sheer disbelief.

I reintroduce Elyse to my parents ("Her parents run the bed-and-breakfast, remember?") and move some books and papers from the end of the kitchen table so she can join us for dinner.

"Nice to see you again," says Eva, though I know she's forgotten Elyse.

"I was exploring a root-vegetable theme tonight." Bill eases a steaming pot onto the centerpiece trivet and ladles out a bowlful for Elyse. "Petite carrots, yams, parsnips, and celeriac."

"Wait . . . you *cooked* this?" Elyse glances from him to Eva and back, then blinks over and over, as if her brain is still trying to process that. My parents keep eating, ignoring her as deftly as they ignore me.

"This stew reminds me of winter," Eva says after a while. "Real winter."

"Well, it is winter," Elyse says, looking confused.

"She means actual, freezing-cold winter," I say, again with the nervousness that comes out smug. "Like we had back in Vermont, or Bern. Or Siberia."

Elyse sets down her fork. "I get it." She holds my gaze. "You've been everywhere, and I've been nowhere."

I can feel a hot blush spread across my face. I hadn't meant to come across as a show-offy asshole, but I can see why she thought I was being one. Suddenly, instead of wanting to impress her, I want to win her approval, but I don't know how. I sit there, tongue-tied.

"I love your ballet flats, Eva," Elyse says politely, changing the subject. "Where'd you buy those?"

Eva smiles. "Hong Kong," she says, glancing at Bill.

He cracks up. "God, was that a crazy trip . . ."

"Year of the Monkey!" they both squeal, grinning and nudging each other.

"Just ignore them," I mutter. "They kind of live in their own world."

After dinner Elyse lingers at the table until Eva excuses herself to go back to her desk to work, and Bill starts washing the dishes. Elyse offers to dry them, but Bill says, "Why don't you go start your homework?"

"Sure. I mean, I guess I could stay longer, if you don't mind."

She wants to stay here longer, despite my being such an ass and my parents being weirdos? I toss her a soda and try to play down my nervous excitement. Elyse, hanging out in my room.

Must pretend I don't care about the mess, that's the only way to play it.

"So, you want to start with our math homework?" she says, sitting on the floor and opening her backpack.

I'm about to reach for my Trig book when it occurs to me that I may never, ever have this opportunity again. Elyse is in my room. I have to make it count. "What's the point of doing math homework, really?" I say.

Her eyebrows go up. "Grades, graduating?"

"One day won't make a difference. You're going to California to be in movies, so wouldn't it be more educational to spend the evening watching an Oscar-winning performance?"

She grins. "Okay . . . just this once."

Wisely avoiding the bed, we sit side by side on the floor in front of my laptop, browsing descriptions of recent Oscar winners for Best Actress. She finally picks Erin Brockovich and we both sit there, riveted. She's riveted by the story of one heroic woman fighting for the truth against powerful forces of corruption. I'm riveted by her, the one girl in Summer Falls who knows what's going on.

When it's over she says, "I've never gotten so into a movie before. I don't want to go home. I feel so relaxed here."

"Even with my crazy parents and their passive-aggressive weirdness?"

She snorts. "That's nothing. You have no idea what it's like to be running scared all the time. I don't think I even knew until I walked in here. I feel almost . . . safe?"

I touch her arm, just for a moment. "You are safe."

She takes a deep breath when I say that and lets it out. Her eyes look shiny. I hit some kind of nerve. Found her weak spot. A good person would back off of this train of thought, suggest another movie. A PG comedy.

I'm an evil person. I want to see the real Elyse, under all that armor. I want to know how it feels to have the queen of Summer Falls High School crying in my arms.

I push a lock of hair out of her eyes and say it again. "You're safe here, Elyse. Nothing bad can get you here."

Her eyes flutter, like she's blinking back tears. But she doesn't cry. Instead she leans in and kisses me, hard, grinding her lips against mine. My mind is numb with shock, but I feel my body respond instantly. Before I know it my hands are in her hair, grabbing it, pulling her close to me, and my tongue's parted her lips. She's softly moaning.

I pause. "Hey, um, what about jock-boy?"

"I don't care." She grabs my shoulders and looks into my eyes. "I don't care about him, I don't care about anything, just don't stop."

"Whatever you say."

Her lips brush the side of my neck, then she bites it. A growl escapes me and I yank the back of her hair. I roll on top of her, covering her mouth with mine, her low happy moans melting into the lower, softer sounds coming from me. She guides my hand under her top, to her smooth warm stomach. Suddenly the darkness is interrupted by a blue light.

She pulls her mouth from mine. "What's that?"

"Nothing." I climb off her, embarrassed. "This just happens to me sometimes." When I'm really happy or excited. Rarely. Almost never. "It's a surge of magic."

"Oh, okay. That's kinda cool." She reaches for me again.

"Wait, you're not weirded out by it?"

"Not really weirded out by anything." Her hands are behind her back now, undoing her bra. "Remember, you've seen the world. But I've seen Summer Falls."

———

Afterward, she puts her clothes back on, silently, mechanically, under the covers so I can't even see. It's like she's a different person now. The aloof ice queen she used to be, the girl who could hardly believe I'd have the gall to approach her in school. It's hard to believe we were as close as it's possible for two people to get only a minute ago.

"Hey, I just want you to know that I've been tested," I say, because now that I'm back to my senses too, bullshit is back to flowing from my mouth. Lies to make myself seem more suave, less vulnerable. I've never been tested for STIs, for the excellent reason that I never needed to be. The whole V thing.

She nods. "I figured you had experience. I mean, you had condoms and everything." Because my Dad gave me a pack along with the safer-sex talk last year. "I wouldn't even know how to put one on a guy."

I feel my eyebrows go up. "Sorry to pry but, um, don't you and Dan use condoms?"

She says nothing but turns red.

"I guess if you're on the pill," I say aloud, "and you were both each other's first . . ."

Her flashing eyes sting, almost like a slap. "You were my first, you idiot."

"Oh," I say, sitting down again. "Oh." And you were mine. Just say it. Now would be a good time to say it. "I just don't get it—you've been with the guy forever!"

She hugs herself. "I don't want to talk about Dan."

"Is he secretly gay?"

"No. He wants to. I just . . . wanted to wait."

"So you're not that into him." Triumph of the occultist over the jock.

"Of course I'm into him, he's my boyfriend. Forget it. I have to go home." She walks to the door, and then she turns to me and says the words that smash my small, evil heart to smithereens. "This never happened."

CHAPTER 29

ELYSE

FOR WHAT FEELS LIKE AN HOUR, I WAIT FOR MY biological father to give me a sign that it's okay to leave the supply closet. I wait so long that I have to pee and get a cramp in my side from being folded into a pretzel shape, but I still don't want to move and reveal myself, in case the doctor is still prowling around.

Finally I take the silence as a sign and make my move. I hurry into the elevator and from there to the garage. Back in Summer Falls, I decide to abandon Sheriff Hank's car behind some trees a few blocks from Main Street.

As I start walking toward Marshall's, a voice calls from behind me. "Elyse, wait up." It's Joe, looking contrite.

"You were right," he says. "Your hometown is your hometown, and I have no right to put down your home, scary as it might seem to me. That said . . . you mentioned you were saving up to leave." He reaches into his pocket and hands me a square of card stock. "This is an Amtrak pass. Takes you anywhere you want on the train, but you have to use it in the next five days."

"Oh my god." Anywhere. I think about California, escaping. Then I think about his secondhand clothes, the tiny cabin he lives in. "This must have cost you a fortune."

"Please, it's worth every penny." He adjusts his owlish glasses on his smooth, young face. "How often does a guy like me get to be the hero and rescue the girl?"

"I'll pay you back. As soon as I can."

"My dear, you don't owe me anything. I just want you to be free."

Tears fill my eyes. "Thank you." I slip the ticket into the back pocket of my jeans. And that's when I notice there's already something in there, something exactly the same size and shape as the train ticket.

I have two train tickets. And no memory of buying one—no note of it in my journal either. Which means someone likely gave me the first ticket too. Someone had wanted to help me before. Or someone just wanted me out of town. Was it him? Have we had this conversation before?

"Joe." Pulse racing, I step back from him. "Are you the one sending me the dreams of California?"

"Oh boy." He blinks twice and coughs, looks away from me. "How did you—? Never mind, not my business. None of it was my business, I know I crossed a line."

I fold my arms. "Why did you?"

"Because you stood out," he says. "In my classes, you

were practically the only student with a spark. I knew you'd never be happy here. I wanted to help you, encourage you to get out of this benighted place and see the world. But the Institute has rules. You see, I'm only an observer. We're not supposed to get involved with subjects." He cringes. "Locals. I could lose my post for this . . ."

I think it over. I'm not really angry at him. There's a lump in my throat, but it's not anger. It's—I'm touched that someone was thinking about my future. "Relax," I say. "I'm not going to report you to some snooty Institute that thinks my life isn't worth saving."

He breathes a sigh, looks skyward. "Oh, geez, thank you!"

"But stay out of my dreams from now on. My head's messed up enough already."

"You seem all right to me."

"All right?" I laugh. "I'm a total and complete mess. I don't know who I am, and I hate who I was."

He waves me away. "You're just human."

"Thanks, Joe." I put my arm around him in a quick hug. "For the tickets and for caring."

"My phone number's on the back of the ticket," he says into my shoulder. "Call me when you want a ride to the bus station. I want you to get out and see the world, kid."

Get out and see the world. Why do those words sound familiar?

All the way back to Marsh's house, I clutch the

tickets in my hand, reassured by their smooth feel, the bold blue ink, the date unexpired, the promise of a glimmering possible future outside this town. But Joe's final words to me keep reverberating in my mind. They're still nagging at my subconscious as I open the gate and slip into the side yard overgrown with rosebushes, scarlet blooms pushing through the rotting wood fence posts. My sneakers bounce up the back porch steps and I reach for the doorknob.

And nearly trip over a sad, person-size crescent hugging the doorframe.

Gasping, I jump backward.

A woman's form curled on the mat. She's beautiful, small, and dark, with slender limbs and wild black curls. She turns to me, her warm, dark eyes gazing up at me.

When I look at her again, she's shimmering in that way that they do.

"I know you from the pictures," I say. "So this is where you've been hanging out." As close to her family as she can get. "Can you hear me, Eva?"

Marshall's mother nods sadly. Her magic that always protected them is now protecting them from her. Keeping her memory alive. Then she gives me an apologetic look and suddenly she's on her feet, those melted chocolate eyes inches from mine and her hungry ghostly hands grabbing for my face. I run all the way around to the front yard and bang on the door.

Marshall answers, and I collapse in his arms. I pour out

my whole story: Elizabeth, Hazel, the asylum, my father, tickets, seeing his mom, and Dan.

"What if we could have saved him?" It's the first time the thought occurred to me. "I mean, what if we'd opened up to Dan? He wasn't the brightest bulb, but he was open-minded. He had possibilities. Now they're gone. What if we'd brought him in, told him the truth, put a coin circle around him . . . why didn't we?"

He says nothing.

"Because you were jealous? And I felt guilty? Is that why we left him to rot?"

"You can't blame yourself for this one, Elyse."

On some level I know he's right. But nothing will ever be the same.

In front of the bathroom mirror I smoke Dan's last few cigarettes and with the borrowed scissors that had been in my backpack I begin to cut my hair. Idly, absently. Trapping a clump of it between the scissor blades, my other hand sucking in nicotine. Shorter and shorter, in unceremonious rounds, till all the smokes are gone. Till my head's surrounded with bouncy waves less than an inch long. Small, round ears with tiny gold studs in them. I was wearing earrings all this time and I didn't even notice. No smoke alarm goes off. I've changed into one of Marshall's T-shirts and like the way it hides my shape. The girl in the mirror looks sad, looks tired, looks like a mess, but she no longer looks like a stranger.

When I come out of the bathroom, Marshall's sitting

on his bed with a book across his lap and a look of intense concentration as he waves a red crystal at the plastic trash can. Remembering how Marshall knocked Dan around with another crystal before, I start to say something to let him know I'm here, when suddenly the trash can explodes, showering the air with plastic confetti.

"Whoa, what was that?" I ask.

He looks as startled as I am. "Just trying to figure out what I can do."

"You know, just because you can do something, doesn't mean you should," I say.

He stares at the pile of rubble in front of him. "Yeah, why don't we keep that one in reserve?" Finally he looks at my hair. "Holy shit. You look fierce. You realize every girl in school is going to copy you."

"Actually, they won't." I decide now's as good a time as any to blurt it out. "I'm not going back to school," I say. "I'm leaving town, today. And I want you to come with me. We can buy a ticket for your father too." I want him to say yes so much that my heart's pounding as I say it.

But he shakes his head. "What if I'm not ready to leave? And what about your mom? You're going to leave her behind, with Jeffry?"

I remember how Jeffry talked about Liz, the bruises telling the same story mine do, that he must have shaken her. My stomach drops—I can almost smell Jeffry's pimple cream. But what could I possibly do to help her? She won't listen to me. We can't even have a real conversation. "She's already a zombie," I say. "A pod person."

"Don't say that. She's just a person who needs help, like my father."

"She's *nothing* like your father!" The forcefulness in my tone surprises me. "All your dad needs is a goddamn moving truck. Liz needs a new brain."

"Okay." He says the word in a supercalm voice, like coaxing a crazy person off a ledge.

"It's not okay. You think our problems are the same, but you don't know how lucky you are. Your father is begging you for help, you just won't give it to him. Why didn't you, all this time?"

He exhales hard, his eyes searching his own mirrored reflection as if for an answer. "Maybe because I knew I could do more," he says finally. "I can help more people than just my dad. I'm not leaving till I've done whatever I can to help *all* these people."

"Marsh, I know you're a hero at heart and it's tough for you to hear this. But how can we save everyone?"

"I've been studying my mom's notes, her plan to reclaim the place of power." He starts rewinding the music box. "I bet I'll find out more the next time I go back under."

I sigh. As much as I fear I don't deserve someone like him, I don't want to leave without him. If he really believes there's a chance we could heal Summer Falls, I want to help. But is he just kidding himself?

Am I kidding myself thinking I could leave without him?

He lights the candles. I've gotten used to the smell of beeswax. "I'll stay for one more night." I lie on the green-and-blue plaid comforter. "Let me see those notes."

CHAPTER 30

MARSHALL

TWILIGHT AND THE THUNDER CRACK OF BAT HIT-
ting ball. A wave of cheering erupts through the bleachers as a
light-footed figure rounds the bases. When he dives into home
plate, the band floods the field. Raucous trumpets and saxophones
blaring the Summer Falls High School song, the cheering turning
into a chant, "Dan! Dan! Dan!" and people are rising to their
feet. In the next to last row, Ruta jumps to her feet beside me.
Jeremy shrugs and joins her, and I stand so I won't be the only
person in the crowd sitting on my ass.

The Sunrays have won the big game—as they always, always
do. The kids from Green Vista look dejected. They huddle close
together in their dark green jerseys and worn out cleats, a sweaty
forest of shame and disappointment.

Dan, hoisted on his teammates' shoulders, dives into the
stands. He surfs on his back, bobbing over a sea of orange jerseys.
"This is the best night of my life!" he yells. "I could die right now.
Tonight all my dreams came true."

"Douche," I mutter under my breath, covering it with a fake cough.

"Incoming!" Jeremy yells.

Along with everyone around us we lift our arms, even tiny Ruta, to accept Dan. He passes over us, hairy, sun-browned limbs and a rock-hard trunk reeking of alpha-male sweat.

"Very firm butt," Ruta reports when Dan has been handed off to the row behind us.

"Yeah, 'cause his entire head's jammed in there." Jeremy laughs bitterly.

"Jer." She slaps his arm playfully. "Why don't you like him?"

I watch, feeling a twinge as Jeremy stuffs his hands in the pockets of his dorky Bermuda shorts. "Just don't trust him, I guess," he says cheerfully. "Eyes are too close together." Right, nothing to do with the dozens of swirlies he's given you. The times he's slammed you against the lockers. That's all forgotten, but not forgiven. "I could have played baseball too," he says. "If I wasn't working at the mill on weekends."

And if you hadn't been cut from the team. "I know, man," I say.

Dan's finished his crowd-surfing and has been reunited with Elyse up front. Members of the baseball team hoist each of them into the air so they can kiss in front of the crowd. He devours her lips, holding her so close that all I can see is the back of her skirt and a pair of giant paws grasping her windblown hair.

"So, you guys want to come over?" Ruta asks finally. "There's still three slices of cheesecake."

"Yeah, sure," Jeremy says, a little too eagerly.

I shake my head. "Got a project to work on, sorry."

"It's the mango cheesecake," Ruta says, as if that detail could clear up a terrible misunderstanding, could change my plans. "You said you liked it at my birthday. Did I remember that wrong?" She frowns.

"Dude, you'd rather do homework than go to a girl's house?" Jeremy puts his arm around Ruta, who doesn't protest. "Forget about that geek, Rue."

"Yeah, forget me," I say, though it's the last thing I mean. If everything goes well tonight and tomorrow, no one in this town will ever forget me.

———

Five hours later, the full moon is shining through my bedroom window. Inside the air smells like rosemary and hawthorn leaves, and wax from the three fat candles forming a triangle on my desk. White, red, and black. Slowly, carefully, I set my mother's gold chalice in the triangle's center. Peer down at the thick red liquid that's making it so heavy. The potion. The seal. It's by far the most advanced thing I've ever done. Unless you count the antidote now cooling in a shot glass on top of my dresser. That was even harder.

I flip around on the web for an hour, checking the window for her face a thousand times before I finally see her outside, a fast-moving figure in white against the navy blue sky.

Downstairs in the living room I pass my father snoring in his easy chair, robe falling open to his chest. The TV's playing static again.

I let her in, reaching over to kiss her lips as she stands in the entryway, but she pushes me away, grinning, her hands cool with the night air. "Your dad's right there."

"So?" I smile back. "He's out cold." For the millionth time I can't help staring at Dan's promise ring on her finger, the world's tiniest diamond.

"And he's probably getting cold." She shoots me a reproving look and covers my dad with a crochet blanket from the couch. We tiptoe past him up the stairs.

"So how's the spell casting, Harry Potter?"

"All systems go. How was the after-party?"

She groans. "Parties, they all blend together. The keg, the red plastic cups, the mating call of the drunk cheerleader . . ."

I wouldn't know. "I'm surprised jock-boy actually let you out of his sight tonight."

"Let me?" She rolls her eyes. "Dan doesn't own me. Come on, let's make the video." It's the way she smiles and shrugs that tells me it's bravado. Has to be. No one, not even Elyse, could be this cool about drinking a memory seal.

"Elyse . . . I just want to say, it's okay to change your mind. I mean, I know this is asking a lot—"

"Marsh. I'm not wussing out. This is the most important thing I'll ever do." She's looking right at me, her clear green eyes serious, sincere. "When this is all over, assuming I don't die, I'm going to California and never looking back. But I don't want to leave Summer Falls like this. I have to try, even if it kills me."

I just nod again. I've been trying hard not to think of that possibility, of her dying underwater. I've also been trying not to think

270

of the almost-certainty that she will leave town forever the second I hand her the antidote and say, "Congratulations, you saved Summer Falls." That I'll never see her again. I want to tell her all these things, but they're too sincere. Too raw. I'd sound like a dork. It doesn't help that no matter how many times I've crushed my lips against Elyse's, kissed her so hard it hurt us both, no matter how many times I've held her close in this dark secret room away from her real life, when she is this close to me I'm always a little starstruck by her beauty. Not cover-model beauty. Not old-fashioned-painting beauty either. Just some strange power I can't name but that makes her impossible to turn away from.

She perches on the edge of my bed and whips her phone out of her pocket. I sit next to her, careful not to touch her.

"Hi, Elyse!" She waves at the phone screen. "I know you don't remember this, but I'm you. I recorded this just last night. First, don't worry, you will get all your memories back. I promise. Second, trust this guy." She turns the camera toward me briefly. "Because I trust him with my life." Her voice breaks. "I know nothing makes sense right now, but this is all going to be worth it in the end. You're doing this for Mom and Marshall's mom and all the other people out there who deserve a better life. Or, afterlife."

"I'm deleting that part." I grab the phone from her. "Too specific. Anything you know, Preston could find out if a ghost catches you. Just say you trust me and nothing else. It's not like I won't be there to explain things."

"Good point," she says. "Better hide your spell notes from me too."

I nod. I've actually memorized the labyrinth, having studied the notes I took after going under two months ago. A part of me is worried that she doesn't have the power to pull this off, that she's only barely adept as an occultist. She was just joking around with one of my books the other day when she managed to pull off a simple regrow spell, shocking us both and hatching this plan in my twisted mind. But there's no other way to do it. I can't go down there twice. The place has got my signature in its memory now. It would stamp me out like a virus. Like it did to my mother.

"Okay, enough chatting. Let's do it."

I can't help smiling as I hand over the chalice. "I love it when you talk dirty."

"Shut up." She raises the chalice in a toast, her voice turning serious. "To my hometown."

"To Summer Falls," I say, because it's not mine. No place is.

She takes a long, deep drink. Then explodes in a fit of coughing. "Oh my god." Her voice raspy. "When I swallowed it felt like a burning hot pinwheel spinning down my throat. And now my fingers feel numb."

"Don't worry." I'm reassuring myself more than her. "It's all part of the process."

"Don't leave me alone for a second while this is happening," Elyse says, grabbing my shoulders and pulling me in for a kiss. "Stay with me. You know what, Marshall? You're, like, the only person I know . . ." I wait for her to finish but she can't get the rest of the words out. She's run out of words and switched over to communicating in kisses, hungry, passionate kisses. Loss of inhibitions, also part of the process. A part of me I'm not so proud of has been curious about what Elyse without any inhibitions would be like.

Even in the height of passion, she never stops being herself. Even in the middle of a make-out session she's likely to laugh, or get pissed off, or think of something interesting to say and say it. Our time together is always a mixture of conversation, touch, and argument. But not now.

Every minute that goes by without her speaking I know there's less of her there.

It's a painful thought, almost like I'm erasing the girl I love.

Did I say love?

It doesn't matter. I'd never say it to her face.

"What's happening to me?" Her voice sounds softer, younger. "Everything's so hot, I can't stand this heat anymore." She peels off her top, then struggles with the hook of her lacy pink bra. Finally she pulls her hair out of the way and manages to undo the bra, and then I can't help staring, and it's not in a good way.

Even though my hands know her body by heart, she's always insisted we keep the lights off in my bedroom. I've imagined—over and over—what she would look like naked. But my imagination has failed me. Finger-size bruises bloom on her shoulders under her hair. Some are purple and fresh, some greenish-yellow. Angry blood pumps through my body, but I don't know who to attack. Who did this? Who did this to you? And how come I never knew, never imagined? The shameful memory of all the times I'd tried to impress her with some black magic spell. She could never understand the dark depths of my soul. Christ. As if she didn't know darkness.

She fans her cheeks. "Marshall? Why do I feel so empty?"

Because your memories are disappearing, fast.

But that was the plan we agreed on, and now the plan's set

273

in motion. She'll wake up an amnesiac. She'll follow my step-by-step instructions, dive underneath the waterfall pool, and reverse the hundred-and-ten-year-old ritual that bound the town to its founders . . . freeing the ghosts and leaving the place of power ready for a new occultist's claim. Then we'll unseal her memory and she'll leave town for California. Either that or we'll fail and Preston will learn from the ghost's memory snacks what Elyse and I were up to. He's ruthless enough to shoot us both in the town square, to pump up the number of shocked witnesses.

"Stay with me," she murmurs. "Don't leave. Don't ever leave."

"A guy would have to be really stupid to leave you," I say, being honest for once because she won't remember. But she's the one who's leaving, not me. Disappearing now, maybe dying later, and even the best-case scenario involves her leaving town without me. There's no way around it. I finally found someone I care about, and she's going away.

Unless . . . my eyes dart toward the chalice, still a quarter full. It's a really sneaky, unethical idea—even more so than my usual ones—and Elyse would never forgive me for going back on our plan. Then again, if Elyse never got her memories back she'd never even know what I'd done. And the best part? Neither would I. Because I wouldn't be me anymore. I would get to ditch my old self, the self I'm sick of, like a snake's skin. I wouldn't remember my mother's death and ghostly enslavement to the Prestons, my father's breakdown, the fact that Elyse wears another guy's ring. We could leave town together. Start over.

Elyse is lying on the bed with her eyes closed, so I walk over to the dresser, pick up a sweater, and then turn and behind my back

pour the shot glass containing the antidote over the sweater. I grab her
phone and stuff it under my mattress, the side Elyse isn't lying on.

My heart's pounding. Before I can change my mind again, I
pick up the chalice, drink down to the dregs, savoring the way it
burns from my nostrils down to my stomach. I collapse into bed.

Elyse wraps her arms around me, sighing happily. "I'm so
glad you're here." She sounds more like she's seven than eighteen.

I wait for unconsciousness to wash away my aching sense of
remorse.

———

I sit up, groggy, and shut the music box. I blow out the
candles and lie on my bed in the smoky-smelling dark,
hugging my knees to my chest. I wish the ghosts could
touch me, because I want to unlearn everything I just saw.

I reach over and lift the edge of the mattress. There's a
slim pink cell phone tucked between it and the box spring.
I turn it on and see a background photo: Elyse and Dan in
formal wear. I hid this from her so she wouldn't find out
the truth. So she wouldn't leave.

Elyse is downstairs making omelets for the three of us.
I can hear her chatting with my dad. She has no idea this
whole situation is my fault. My fault we woke up with no
memories, helpless, clueless. My fault Elyse is still here,
losing memories and being abused. My fault my father's
in this condition. Maybe even my fault Summer Falls still
exists—that my mother's still enslaved to the founder,
delivering life force from its citizens.

I don't have to tell her. She'll never know what I did.

But I'll know.

It's in the past like everything in that stupid book she's walking away from. Anyway, I've changed. I'm not the same selfish, impulsive person who let her down. I can walk away from this forever, right now.

But I've shared everything with her. If I don't share this, then I'm still that manipulative person I was before. She deserves to know the truth.

I hear her socked feet padding up the stairs. "Here, I think I put too many mushrooms in it." She hands me a plate with a professional-looking rolled omelet. Of course, working at a bed-and-breakfast, she would know how to do that. But I set it down on my desk, too nervous to touch it.

"Elyse, I need to talk to you." Before I talk myself out of it.

"What?"

"When you first woke up, you thought I drugged you. I was all insulted."

"Don't blame you."

"Well, it turns out I did drug you."

"What?"

"With your permission," I add quickly. "I gave you a memory-seal potion. We had a plan; we were going to do a spell together—I don't understand how, since you're not an occultist—and you were going to be the one to go under the waterfall pool to walk the labyrinth. I guess because I can't go twice. And to keep our plan safe and keep you safe from the ghosts in there, I sealed you. Except I . . ." It's hard to justify my actions, especially with her staring at me. "After your memory was already gone . . . I decided not to go through with it."

"But I'd already gone through with my part."

"I know. That's, um, that's what was bad. I think I knew that I was on a bad path, and I didn't want to be that person anymore, or for you to remember me that way."

"So you left me hanging, with no identity? You sabotaged our plan and risked killing both of us?"

"I know I let you down, but—"

"Why?" she demands.

"You were going to leave town after. Without me. You were going to leave me behind." A lump is welling up in my throat. "You didn't think I was worth taking with you."

"I was right, you weren't," she says flatly. "I trusted you." The disappointment in her eyes, in her voice, physically hurts me. It burns from my throat to my belly. Shame.

I want to argue that it wasn't really me.

I want to slink away.

I want to bury my head in her lap and cry and beg for forgiveness.

"But I don't even understand how our plan would have worked. Doesn't matter, you're right. The point is, I screwed up and got us into this mess. But I did change. I became a different person because I didn't have those memories, because I had to find a new path."

"Don't lie to yourself, you're not that different. You

still love power. You still love magic." She holds up the music box, dangles it open. "You've been spending more time with this than with—"

"Careful with that."

"You should have been careful. With me."

"I know." There's a lump in my throat. "Elyse, I was an isolated little kid. I grew up reading magic books in hotel suites in places where I didn't speak the language. My mom's idea of protection for her son was social invisibility. No one ever taught me right from wrong. My mom didn't always know it herself. She always talked about changing the world, but she forgot the world has other *people* in it. People, not pawns. I thought the only real people were my family. And my dad thought being a good person would come naturally to me. But it didn't. When I first got to Summer Falls I don't know if I had the ability to empathize. Other people weren't real to me, or they weren't people. And then I met you."

"Great, so it's my fault," she says. "You were looking for moral guidance in the wrong place."

"No. Damnit. Stop putting yourself down. I'm not saying you don't have problems—how could you not, after all you've been through?—but you're a good person."

She looks at me with pity in her eyes. "How would you know what a good person is?"

A lump is welling up in my throat. "Because being around you has helped *me* get better. And I'm still working on it, I'm still trying. I could easily have kept this from you.

But I thought you deserved to know what happened to us."

"Wow. Am I supposed to thank you?"

"No. But do you think . . . you could maybe forgive me? I mean, after everything we've been through you know there's more to me than that one stupid night."

From her body language, folded arms and stiff back, I know the answer. "Believe me, I *want* to," she whispers. "I feel like I could forgive you almost anything, but not betrayal."

"Betrayal? It wasn't like that." In my head. In reality, from anyone else's perspective, what else would you call it?

"You're not really asking forgiveness, anyway. You're asking me to trust you again. But you crossed a line. And trusting someone is about taking a chance, until you know them. Now that I know the truth about you, every fiber in my body's telling me to walk away. I know you could stop me," she adds. "You could stand up and grab me and hold me back. You could follow me. Or you could stop me with magic. So I'm going to ask you not to do those things. Just sit there and let me leave."

And that's what she does—straps on her backpack and walks out the door, still carrying the music box. I watch her, wanting to run after her. She's going to the bus station, then she'll board a train, and if I ever see her again it'll be years and years from now. She'll be a different person. I know some spells that would hold her here, just so I could talk to her a little longer . . . but then I'd just be proving her point, that I haven't changed. There's no way to win.

CHAPTER 31

ELYSE

PRESTON HOUSE IS DARK AND QUIET WHEN I enter, so I'm hoping my parents have taken the tourists for a mind-clearing hike up at the falls.

I'm in no mood to deal with Liz, let alone Jeffry. But there he is sitting like a lord at the kitchen table, reading his newspaper. Beer in hand, boots resting on the chair across from him.

"How's my princess?" He grins at me like I'm five. Like he didn't just days ago shake me and throw me against a wall. Seeing my backpack he automatically asks, "How was school?"

I clench my teeth. It's Saturday, you abusive jackass. "Super," I say, confident he can't process sarcasm. "Most productive day of my scholastic life."

"Good deal. Hey, since you're here, could you rustle up some dinner for us?" I'm hyperattuned to the tiny cloud of irritation forming around his eyes. "I don't know where your mother's at."

Make it yourself.

I just lost my only friend, the only person I could be myself with. The only guy I could imagine being with forever.

I'm leaving town today.

I'm not going to say any of the things I want to say to him. Thanks to my journal, I've learned the hardest way, time and again, the only safe way to deal with this man is indirectly. Lying to him. Avoiding him. One more lie, then he's out of my life. "Sure, let me go upstairs and put my bag away. Then I'll wash up and . . . roast a chicken."

"That's a good girl." He doesn't even look up from his paper.

I figure I have five to ten minutes before he's breathing down my neck again, so I head into my room and call Joe. "I was thinking," I say. "About that ride you offered, to the bus stop."

"Leaving *right* now," he says. I can actually hear car keys jingling in his hand. "Be waiting outside for me in fifteen minutes."

It doesn't take me long to pack. Two pairs of shorts, two T-shirts, extra socks and underwear. My journal and a pen, my iPod, wallet stuffed with cash. Even with the music box, there's a lot of room in my backpack. I debate bringing my cell phone. It could be useful, but what if I were tempted to call Marshall? Or pick it up if he called? I delete the contacts, delete the video of me urging my future self to trust him. I can buy a new plan when I get to California. Or wherever.

Or just sell the phone.

It occurs to me that I don't know how long it's going to take for me to find a job out there. Maybe I should bring along a few more things I can sell fast for extra cash. Another phone would be nice. A laptop, even, if I can get my hands on one. I feel a quiver of shame. I've already lied to my mother, now I'm contemplating stealing from her. I think of Marshall's unapologetic retort: "I did what I had to do." I finally get it. To get out of this place before it kills me, I will do whatever I have to do. No matter how dirty it makes me feel. Stealthily I tiptoe downstairs to scout the family room for boostable electronics.

Instead I run into Liz coming out of the garage and into the laundry room, keys in hand.

"Honey, you're back!" She beams at me, looking like a little kid in her pink jumper and crisp white blouse. "How was . . . ?" She trails off, clearly unable to remember where I've been the last couple days.

"I'm not back for long." I know she'll have to have this memory wiped, and it'll take her one step closer to insanity, but selfishly I want this moment of honesty. I need it. "I just came to get a few things. I'm leaving town, and I might not ever see you again."

Liz gasps and leans against the door to the garage for support. In a small voice she says, "Well. Well, I shouldn't be surprised. You're almost never at home as it is. . . ." She nods at my guy-jeans and oversize men's T-shirt. "Dan's going with you, right? He'll take care of you."

Dan's catatonic in the asylum, but thanks for trying to stay in touch with my life. "Aren't you even going to ask where I'm going?" I snap, surprised at my own anger. "Aren't you going to try and talk me out of it?"

"I can't stop you, Elyse. You're eighteen. And you've got your father's iron will."

"Don't *ever* compare me to *him*." I can barely recognize my own voice. Then I realize she might not be talking about Jeffry. She could be talking about my biological father. The olive-skinned man at the asylum. Maybe some part of her remembers him still. I think of their faces close to my three-year-old face in that photo I glued inside my journal's front cover, where I'm looking up at him with total trust and adoration. He let me down; he let me fall so hard I broke in two. Those things can never be undone. I want to scream in his face like I did to Jeffry, but he's not here. I turn to Liz. "You just let things happen, don't you?" Though I know in my heart it's not Liz's fault. "You let my dad disappear." What could she do against Preston, against the town, the whole system? "You let Jeffry hurt us." She was a victim too—still is. But right now I don't care. All I care about is my truth, my pain. "You let bad things happen. To me, your daughter. You're supposed to take care of me, how could you let him do that?" I can barely speak through the lump in my throat. "Why couldn't you stop it from happening?"

Even through my tears I can see her recoil from me, can see the person I was just talking to recede from the surface, into the backs of her blue eyes. My answer's wrapped inside my own question. *Couldn't.* She couldn't. And she still can't. "Why shame on you." She sounds robotic; her gaze looks clouded. "Your father would never hurt a fly."

I point to her sleeves. "Why are you wearing long sleeves in the heat? Your arms are covered in bruises from where he grabbed you."

Her eyes dart to her covered arms. Slowly she raises one sleeve and frowns. "I don't . . . remember what happened here, but I know . . ." She shakes her head. "Now what were we just talking about?"

"I'll tell you what happened!" *You've tried to leave him many times. Sometimes you get as far as the bus stop or a motel.*

I pull the book from my bag and hold it up. "I wrote it all down, here, in my journal."

"That book." She freezes. "You and that book." She grabs it out of my hands, her voice turned low and guttural with rage. "Always writing up in your room. What is it about that book that makes you act so strange?" She holds it open and rips it in two, and I dive at her, clawing at her hands, pulling both halves of the journal toward me, twisting her arms in the process. It's only paper and ink, it's only the past, but I've gone berserk. I'd die for this book, I'd kill for it. It's me she's trying to rip into pieces, that's how it feels, and I'll fight tooth and claw to save myself, till with a cry of pain she lets go.

That's when I realize how badly I've scratched her hand with my nails in my fury to save the journal. I stare at the drops of red blood on her wrist. Thick and red and real. Somehow I had thought—why had I believed she wouldn't bleed real blood? That her flesh was plastic doll flesh, that nothing could penetrate to make her feel pain.

I hug the two halves of the journal to my chest, overcome with guilt. Am I becoming like Jeffry, willing to hurt people when they frustrate me? "I am so sorry—"

"No, it's okay!" She holds up her hand, tears running down her cheeks. "Tomorrow I won't even remember where I got these marks, just like I don't remember the others. Everything'll be fine again, like none of this ever happened."

"No it won't." A lump aches in my throat. She's saying she'll forget my abuse, just like she forgets Jeffry's. I'm just another source of bad memories for her, calling the hungry ghosts to her window. Making her crazy. "It won't be fine, because *I* won't forget."

"I know you won't." Her shiny eyes meet mine. "You've always been different from me, from most people. My life has been a blur, but you . . . you see more, you understand more."

Her voice is sad, but there's a spark in her eyes, the same spark as when she comforted me at the bus stop so many years before. "Thank you." I'm not sure why I said those words. I don't even know if what she said was really a compliment. But I'm so grateful to see her—the real Liz, the one from my happy memories. I never thought I'd get to see her again. Unconsciously I lean toward her, dropping my head on her shoulder.

She smoothes my hair, and I feel hot tears glide down my own cheeks. "You shine with a special light. Like you didn't really come from me, just came through me. Passing through, from someplace better. On your way to something brighter than I'd ever see."

After all the wipes, all that she's endured and forgotten, maybe there's only a sliver of a person left inside that body, trapped behind those tired eyes. But that person is real, and suddenly I don't want to leave her behind. "Don't say that. Your life's far from over." I take a deep breath, reach into my jeans pocket, and pull out the Amtrak passes. I hold one out to her. "Mom, why won't you come with me?"

She bites her lip.

"Take it, please. What?"

"You called me Mom."

Did I? "We could go anywhere, start over."

"But why would I want to leave?" Her wrist rubs the wet creases of her eyes where tears have pooled. "I'm so *happy* here."

"Don't do this. Please don't disappear on me again. I saw the real you just now, we had—"

"We had a moment, that's all it was." She shakes her head sadly. "I don't know if there is a real me left." She reaches behind her neck to the clasp of the ruby necklace. Grandma Bets's necklace. She unhooks it, opens my hand, and lets the chain slip down and disappear into my palm. A good-bye present, the oval stone warm from her body. I came down here to steal from her, and instead she's given me everything she had. Like she's always done. Maybe not what I wanted, not what I needed, not enough. Just what she had.

"*Liz!*" Jeffry yells from the top of the stairs. "You home? Hey, wasn't someone going to roast me a chicken?"

"Coming, honey!" she calls back cheerfully, and grins at me as if nothing's happened. "Time for me to go start dinner."

"Good-bye," I say, though she's already halfway up the stairs and can't hear me.

She's bought me time to escape. I swing my pack over one shoulder and sneak out the open garage door just as Joe's car pulls up to the driveway.

I throw my backpack in the back and launch myself into the passenger seat. "Just get me out of here." He doesn't know how close I came to losing it all.

"Don't ever look back," he tells me.

"I won't."

"You're doing the right thing."

"I know." I realize I'm still hugging the two halves of my ruined journal. "I just wish I could have talked my mom into going with me."

"Oh, no, it's way too late for her," he says cheerily. "She's getting close to used up."

Used up. Such a brutal judgment. I can feel a sudden fury heating up my cheeks at the thought of my mother being used up. Of Jeffry using her to cook him dinner. And the founder using her to keep his spell working, and even the tourists using her as some kind of folksy R & R–providing robot that makes beds and serves breakfast, never once seeing her as a real person. And what about me? How long did I take her for granted for all her uses before I finally figured out there was a human being inside? But as harsh as Joe's words sound, I wouldn't be this angry if they didn't contain a grain of truth. It probably is too late for my mom. I tried to talk to her, tried to help her. All I can do for her now is honor her memory. "Don't talk about my mother like that," I say to Joe. "She's not an object, she's a person."

"Oh, of course, forgive me." He gives an embarrassed chuckle and fumbles with the AC. "I'm afraid this assignment hasn't been good for me. Seeing what this place does to people, it's made me cynical."

I nod, trying to calm down. I can't blame him for that, seeing as how it almost had the same effect on me. Even though as a magic user he's protected from the ghosts, he's still a victim of this place too. There's no way to just be an observer. "I hope they assign you someplace better next time."

He chuckles. "They'll probably find somewhere even worse, but it's out of my control. Like the army." Then he cheers up and spends the whole ten-minute ride listing all the wonderful things I absolutely have to check out in California. From the Golden Gate Bridge to the San Diego Zoo to Universal Studios. I don't have the heart to tell him I'm sort of over California, now that I know he's the one who wanted to go there after all—not me.

Then abruptly he pulls over to the side of the road, right under the "Welcome to Summer Falls" sign, beside the copse of aspens that Hazel stumbled out of to attack the sheriff.

"Looks like the new bus stop's over there," he says, gesturing. I can see it, too, the bench and its sheltering overhang, just on the other side of town limits. Across the strange line where dewy green grass all of a sudden gives way to hot, barren rock. Clutching the journal halves tight in my arms, I quickly cross the street and reenter the real world, once again marveling at the eerie transformation from lush garden to forsaken desert. Hot, dry air burns my lungs as I turn back and wave good-bye to Joe, who's still sitting in his car. He waves back at me, an almost tender expression on his smooth, owlish face. Young mothers watching their toddlers wade into the pool on the first day of swim lessons have that look.

He's way more jazzed about my future than I am.

CHAPTER 32

MARSHALL

AFTER ELYSE LEAVES I STAY ON THE FLOOR, where she told me to sit, for a long, long time. I stare at the doorway where I saw her walk away from me without looking back, and after a while I can't even picture her quite as clearly, and I can't remember if she was wearing my khaki jean jacket or just had it tied around her waist. I sit there, still and silent, eyes closed, ignoring my rumbling stomach and the TV blaring from downstairs. I probably look catatonic, like Dan.

Eventually the sun comes up and two birds start chattering outside my broken window. I don't know how much time has passed before I'm aware of the burning pressure of rough carpet branding my left cheek and realize I must have fallen asleep.

Light-headed and cranky, I stagger downstairs.

I can smell the kitchen trash from the living room. Bill's still parked on the couch, chugging generic beer, his eyes glued to a baseball game on ESPN.

"Dad, let me make you some eggs or something."

"I'm good." He raises his beer can, a self-mocking salute. "Breakfast of champions, right?"

I shrug. I decide I might as well take out the trash now—since he can't leave the house, I'm the only one who can do it—but before I can get two steps toward the kitchen, he calls behind me, "Where's Elyse?"

The question makes my chest ache all over again. I turn back. "Gone." And maybe it's not fair, but suddenly I'm pissed at Bill for making me say it out loud. For being so checked out, he didn't know. "Didn't she walk right by you? Didn't you hear the door slam?"

"I, uh . . . must have dozed off." Bill glances at the pyramid of empty cans on the coffee table, then up at me, a troubled look spreading over his face. He sets his can down, smoothes his AC/DC T-shirt, where it was riding up his belly, rakes his fingers along the back of his neck like he's trying to comb his hair, which long ago fell out. You can tell he's trying to will his way into sobriety, into Concerned Parent mode. He pats the couch cushion next to him. "Hey, buddy, sit down. . . ."

I really don't feel like explaining, but I sit next to him and grab a double handful of popcorn from the bowl. It's so stale and dry, it tastes like little pieces of confetti, but I don't care. Then I reach into the cooler at Bill's feet and crack open a beer. What the hell.

Bill meets my eyes and sighs, as if to say, *We both know*

I don't have the moral high ground to stop you. "So what happened?" he prompts. "You two had a fight?"

"I don't want to talk about it."

"Son. Let me give you some advice. . . ."

I can't help it, I snort. Maybe it's more like a snicker, even. Guess there's something about a bleary-eyed, drunk dude in torn sweats offering me advice that just pushes my buttons. Bill looks away from me, clearly hurt. Apparently I couldn't cry to make myself feel better, but I can laugh to make someone else feel shitty. "No offense," I add, though that ship has sailed. "It's too late for advice."

"No, it's not." From his urgent tone you'd think our lives were in danger. But then again, his relationship with my mother was his life. "If you're both alive, it's never too late. Call her. Go after her. Apologize for whatever stupid-ass thing you did."

"I tried, okay?" I gulp down the cold, bitter liquid. It tastes foul. Fine with me. "Hey, why are you assuming it's all *my* fault?"

He gives me a look. "Come on, Marsh . . . I know you."

I blink. Ouch. My own father thinks I'm a jerk. "Know what? You *don't* really know me all that well. I've changed."

"If you say so."

Passive-aggressive Bill strikes again.

The thing is, I can't really argue with him. Because knowing someone means you know who they were in the past. Anything else is just a glimmer of possibility, a distant hope, and probably wishful thinking. He's judging me by my past actions, not my words. That's fair. Which only makes me angrier. I can feel my fingertips turning to ice, my pulse pounding. "Why don't you just say it? You think I'm an ass."

"I didn't say that."

"No, because a nice guy like you would never straight-up call his son an ass. Well, I didn't turn out *nice* like you. I make a lot of mistakes, yeah. But I make a lot of smart decisions too. At least I do something." I fold my arms. Am I really going to say this? "Not like you with Mom. You never even asserted yourself at all. You just followed her around while she did magic." Until magic killed her.

He snorts and reaches for the popcorn bowl. "You don't know shit about my marriage."

"Yeah? I know that if *you* had died, right now she'd be in some cave in New Zealand doing magic. Not sitting on this sofa remembering how great you were."

"She wouldn't have to sit here." Bill stands, but he's had so many beers, he stumbles and has to pull up his baggy sweatpants. "Because she wouldn't need your help to get out of this goddamn town. I never thought you'd grow up to be so selfish."

"Maybe you raised me to be selfish."

"What's that supposed to mean?"

"It means why didn't you ask someone else for help, Dad? Other than me. You couldn't, because Mom was the only other person you were close to. You didn't have a friend in the world."

"You and Eva were my world. We gave each other all we ever needed."

"Bullshit. I needed friends. A *home*. I was a kid, and I didn't know what I was missing. But you should have known. You two took me all over the world, and what do I remember? All my memories are of hotel suites with us in them. Like our own cozy little space pod. Nothing could touch us. No one could even see me. And because of that, I never thought of reaching out to anyone else either." Until I met Elyse. "I'm not saying it was right that I didn't help you break out of here. But I *understand* it. For once I didn't *want* you to drag me away to the next place."

His eyebrows sink down sadly, and the knuckle of his right index finger finds its way between his lips. "I knew you needed a home, but your mother needed to travel for her work. If she had one true love it was magic."

"Then why are you so hell-bent on remembering her?"

"Because I loved her, you dumb kid." He turns away from me, drunk tears in his eyes. "I loved her, even if I came second. That's what love is."

"Well, that's very moving, Dad. Too bad you were so busy being in love with a dead person, you didn't notice your son turning into a monster."

Maybe I went too far, or maybe he'd just had enough, because he turns from me and walks away. I can hear his bare feet clomping around on the kitchen linoleum and figure he must be getting more snacks, when a shaft of sunlight illuminates a strip of the carpeting and the front wall.

"Dad?" I hear the back door creak open. "What are you *doing*?"

I race into the kitchen, but he's already stepped outside onto the back porch step, into the brilliant sunlight. He throws out his arms in front of him and mutters something, and I hear him sigh.

Then his body crumples and he collapses on the wooden deck with a sickening *thud*.

CHAPTER 33

ELYSE

THE BUS IS HALF EMPTY AND TAKES AN HOUR TO get to the hot, loud, crowded train station. The people look startlingly different here. Different from Summer Falls people, different from me. So many more shapes and sizes. So many dark jackets and scuffed shoes. Their skin and hair look dull, as if they've never seen the sun. There's a sadness weighing each and every one of these people down—I can feel it emanating from their cores—yet they seem to move faster than I do, with an energy I'm unused to seeing. Their faces look sharper, more alert. Tougher. It's a whole new world, just like that first morning, sun and grass and dandelions. Only this new world isn't beautiful. It's gritty, gray, and ugly. A man in an overcoat leers at me, then goes back to whispering about concert tickets to anyone who'll listen. The dank corners smell like urine. I disappear into the crowd, just another anonymous traveler with sunglasses and a backpack. No one knows who I am;

no one cares. I couldn't have asked for more.

I scan the Arrivals and Departures. There's a coach to Denver leaving in an hour. Whatever. Sure. Fine. I present my pass, buy a bag of chips, and don't eat them. On the train I listen to music on my headphones until I get sick of playing the same old songs over and over. I leave the headphones on as a "Do Not Disturb" sign. The last thing I want to do right now is talk to anyone. Eventually I fall asleep, and someone has to tap me when we arrive.

It's late, after nine. There's a motel across from the train station, but it's got no vacancies. The bald guy behind the counter tells me to walk ten blocks to a Radisson. It has revolving doors, like in the movies.

At the front desk, I attempt to register for a room. It's going well until the glossy, black-haired clerk named Clarissa asks, "May I have a credit card, please?"

Credit card? "Um, I'll just pay, if that's okay. You know, with money."

"I'm sorry, we need a card for incidentals."

Incidentals. I don't even know what those are.

The other clerk, a bored-looking blond boy, looks up. "Ris, it's okay. We can turn off pay-per-view in her room, and she won't have a tab for room service, but we can do cash."

I thank him and hand over a staggering $109 for the night. I feel like I got mugged.

"Room nine-oh-nine has a river view," he says, "if you stand on your tiptoes. Here's your key." He slips me a flat envelope. Too flat for a key.

I open it and see a single plastic card, like a credit card. Huh?

"Something wrong with your key card, miss?"

"Key card," I mutter, feeling like a prize idiot. "Um, no."

"One more thing, did you do valet parking? Because—"

"I took the train," I say.

Clarissa purses her lips and *mmm*s softly under her breath. I wonder what sort of theories and judgments are brewing in her head: train, cash, doesn't know what a key card is. Clueless hayseed in over her head.

Or maybe I'm just judging myself again. It's hard to tell the difference sometimes.

In the hotel room's shower I wash off the grime from the train and put on clean clothes, feeling a little surge of panic at how quickly my supply of money *and* clean clothes is being depleted.

I lie on the enormous bed and flip through TV stations. Cop shows. Courtroom drama. Shows about families, always with a tinny laugh track. The channels are endless, but the offerings are disappointingly familiar. I bet Marshall isn't watching TV right now. I bet he's working on a spell, doing something important. I miss him.

He crossed a line. You have to have standards. Limits. You can't just let people do anything to you.

I pull the music box out of my bag, wind it up, and open it. Of course I can't use it, even if I do have more memories left. I can't do magic. It's not one of my gifts.

Maybe I don't even trust magic, really—it feels, on some level, like a lie. A manipulation. But taking the box away from Marshall was spiteful, and I'm not proud of that.

I'm not proud of leaving Liz behind either.

What the hell *am* I proud of?

Other than my pride itself, which is the reason I deleted his phone number from my phone and why I won't call information now and get it back.

The laugh track on TV blends with "America the Beautiful." Is this why I left town, to be alone in this hotel room I can't afford, watching the same inane shows I could have watched at home?

Maybe I should just give up and go back. The only person who'd be disappointed in me is Joe. He said he was just giving me a little push with the dreams, but he was *so* thrilled about my leaving town. . . . I remember his oddly tender look as I crossed the invisible line that separated Summer Falls from unincorporated county.

I blink. The line out of town. That was the same line Elizabeth couldn't cross, even when the sheriff tried to force her. Why couldn't she? I'd spent enough time working with Marshall to know it had to be magic. Yet what were the odds that these two strangers, a mild-mannered young occultist and a non-occultist street person, would be bound up in the same magic spell?

I pull out the Preston House brochure, remembering the old photos in it. But there's no clear picture of W. P. Preston's face—of course there wouldn't be. He'd make sure of that. My eye's drawn to the famous shot of President Coolidge and his wife relaxing in the Prestons' backyard. Then I zero in on Mrs. Coolidge. Her neck. My hands rush to my own throat, to the hard ruby pendant. I reach into my bag and dig out Marsh's Swiss Army knife. I slide out the magnifying glass and check out Mrs. Coolidge's necklace. It's the same . . . the one Grandma Bets passed down to Mom. Was it a gift from the Coolidges to the Prestons? If so, then why did Grandma Bets have it?

Well, it could have just appeared in the antique store after Mrs. Preston's death.

I run the magnifying glass over Mrs. Preston's image. Her profile looks so familiar.

And why was that homeless woman helping to support Grandma Bets in the wedding photo? Why would a random acquaintance go out of her way?

Because she wasn't a random acquaintance. She was family. Probably Grandma Bets's own grandmother. Elizabeth Preston. Who still looked the same after a hundred and twenty years, thanks to thousands of other people's unwilling sacrifices. Including her descendants.

Including me.

I'm descended from the Prestons. Liz never bought the house that is now the B and B—she grew up in it.

And if I'm descended from an occultist, that means I was born with at least a touch of his talent for magic.

Excited, I turn off the TV and wind up the music box. I don't have candles. Even if I did they'd probably set off the hotel's smoke alarm and I'd be fined the rest of my money. But the book didn't mention candles specifically—the flames were just for concentration. And I remember the words he said. Not words. Sounds. The spell itself.

I lie on the hotel bed, open the box, and stare as the baseball player begins revolving around a single point. Then I'm staring at the halo around him, and soon after, I jump into amber waves of grain.

———

"Hey."

The guy startles me so much, I drop my book into my locker, the book I just fished out of there. The blue-and-green journal.

"Don't you remember me? It's Marshall."

Now that I've gotten a better look at him, I do remember seeing him before. Those intense eyes, the playful mouth. "You stayed at the B and B, right?"

"Yeah, just last week. Now my parents are renting. They really liked it here, for some reason." His mouth looks downright devious now. Hard to look away from those ink-black eyes. "Anyway, the thing you asked about." What thing? I asked this boy about something? When? My hands clutch the book, but I don't want to open it here. Not here. Not safe. "The house we're staying in, it has . . . protections." What's he talking about? "If you play your cards right, I'll let you come over tonight."

"Excuse me?" I know my voice sounds a little snobby, but seriously, I've gotten less ridiculous come-ons from football players. Aren't out-of-town boys supposed to be more subtle?

"You seem stunned and overwhelmed by my generosity," he says, deadpan. "Women often are. Don't worry. You can pay me back in any number of—"

"Are you crazy?" I cut him off. "Why on earth do you think I'd want to set foot in your house?"

He leans against the lockers, his brow wrinkling in confusion. "Because it's safe . . . ? Hey, you're the one who asked me to . . . wow, you don't even remember, do you?"

I shake my head. But now he's got me, I'm intrigued. "Hold on." I pull open the book. It parts to the middle, the first open page bookmarked by a pen. Quickly I page back, watching the dates, until a week has slipped by in reverse. I spot his name, read the whole entry. His story checks out. I flip back to today. Quick as lightning, my hand scrawls, Marshall, safe house.

He leans forward, arms crossed, an amused smile playing on his lips. "Did you just write about me in your diary?"

I snap the book shut, hug it to my chest. "None of your business."

He leans even closer, the devilish smile spreading to his eyes. "Can I write my address and phone number, so you don't forget me?"

"I don't let other people write in it." Not that anyone's ever wanted to before.

Marshall nods, clearly not the slightest bit taken aback. "Eight-six-three Finch Street," he says, backing away. "Come over tonight."

"Maybe," I whisper.

CHAPTER 34

MARSHALL

UNLIKE JEREMY AND RUTA, UNLIKE ALL THE other people I've witnessed having heatnaps, Bill doesn't wake up seconds later. He doesn't wake up minutes later. I have to drag him into the house, and he stays passed out. Minutes pass, and I keep checking his vitals and reassuring myself that he's not catatonic—not rigid and staring into space like Hazel was—he's just sleeping. In the living room I build a ward circle around him and check his vitals again. When my screaming, empty stomach can hold on no longer I slap together a cheese sandwich in the kitchen and rush right back to check on Bill. In my heart of hearts I know that obsessively watching him isn't going to magically cure him. But I don't know what else to do. And whatever's happened to him is my fault.

Night falls, and I cover him with blankets and keep a vigil in the living room, watching the TV shows and baseball games he'd been reduced to watching endlessly to pass the time without human contact.

My fault too.

Around dawn I'm dozing off in front of a hockey game when I hear a groggy voice from the floor. "Marsh, what time is it?"

"Dad!"

He's sitting up, looking bleary-eyed, the blanket pulled up to his neck.

I sink to my knees and throw my arms around him, clapping him hard on the back. "I'm so glad you're awake."

He glances around the living room floor, looking sheepish. "Guess I must have been tuckered out. Your mom already up?"

At first I think I must have misheard. Then my heart sinks. He doesn't remember Eva's dead. That painful memory's been wiped from his mind and turned into . . . what? A new stained-glass window for the church downtown?

"Let me guess, she went straight to her office without getting a healthy breakfast in her."

"She's . . . she's not here," I say, feeling a lump in my throat. My fault, my fault.

"Well, I feel like making pancakes." He nods and glances at the cupboards, which I know haven't been replenished, except for cans, for eight months. "Think she'll be home in time to eat them hot?"

I can't look at him. "No. She won't be."

"One of those manic days, huh?" He whips out his cell

phone. "No problem, I'll talk to her. Even geniuses have to eat," he adds cheerfully. He's such a different person, without her death. Happy-go-lucky, sweet, and mellow, the person he was in my memories. But Eva's never coming home to eat his pancakes. How long until her continued absence starts to worry him? How long till he freaks?

"Put the phone down."

He gives me a funny look but hits Send again. "Calling to see if she wouldn't mind stopping at the market for blueberries." He hangs up. "I don't understand. Something's wrong with her number. Did I forget to pay online?"

I feel like a monster. "Dad, hang on. I'll go . . . look for her. You stay here in the house, okay?"

"Well, of course I'm going to stay in the house," he says, and chuckles at my stating the obvious. "I wouldn't want to . . ." He throws back his head and closes his eyes, mimicking a heatnap.

I hate to admit this—I mean, really, really hate it—but I've screwed things up bad and I'm in over my head. I need help. Magical help.

It takes me half an hour to hike to Joe's cabin.

"Marshall, you finally came to visit!" He smiles at me, then pushes up his glasses and looks at me carefully. "Oh, I see. It's a something's-wrong kind of visit. I'll make tea."

I sit at his antique, unfinished wood table, drink the tea, tell him what happened . . . leaving out the part where Elyse left me. "How can I get my dad his memories back?"

He shakes his head sadly. "It's impossible."

"Nothing's impossible," I say. "I'll do anything. Anything it takes."

"The only way I know of would be to free the place of power . . . but that's too dangerous."

"It's not the danger I'm afraid of. It wouldn't work. I've already been down there once."

"Oh?" His face is impassive. "So you recovered memories, then?"

"Yes, well, some of them. Enough to know it would kill me to go under a second time."

"That's true," he says, nodding earnestly. "Of course an occultist of your skill might have time to complete the ritual before . . . well, before. But it doesn't bear thinking about. Because risking your life . . . well, that's something only heroes do."

Hero. That's what he called me back at Mollie's after the fire broke out.

"I don't blame you for being scared of death, Marshall." He ducks his head. "I'm . . . not much into danger myself. Guess we're two of a kind."

I pull back, repulsed by the idea of us being the same. He's the kind who sits around drinking tea and looking worried. I'm the kind who considers grand sacrifices to make up for my grand mistakes. When it comes down to it, I'm not actually that scared of death. Maybe it should scare me how little death scares me—but after all those dreams. . . .

My whole body feels cold. The dreams, dying underwater. My dreams of being a hero. Those dreams were made in someone else's factory. Someone who was good at influencing, not doing. *"You can't force people to learn. You can only try to be a positive influence."* He'd already admitted to sending Elyse dreams of California. He was trying to influence her to leave town—but whoever sent me the underwater dreams was trying to get me killed. And why? For the same reason. My palms have started to sweat. "Is that how you neutralize threats to your power?" I say. "With a dream spell? Because no offence, that's kinda Magic 101."

He smiles. "Did you enjoy your heroic deaths?"

"I don't like being manipulated."

"But you sure like the idea of being a hero, don't you, Marshall?" His voice is soft. "Especially after you spent your whole life being a sneaky, selfish little shit. Just like your mother liked the idea of proving herself worthy to a cruel world that ignored her genius. Everybody who's unhappy longs for *something*." Joe takes off his Coke-bottle glasses, but this time his blue eyes are cold. Shrewd. Old.

Joe is the magician my mother worked for. The founder.

"He is the town. He's the man."

"You killed my mother."

"Please, I admire your filial piety, never having had any myself, but let's remember who we're talking about. Eva Moon was a victim of her own greed."

I shake my head. "She wanted to restore the environment. She was a hero."

"She was a glory hound. She wanted to go under a

second time and claim the treasure for herself. No one goes back for seconds. History's a one-way street."

"But you lured her in. And you didn't even pay her the fifty thousand dollars, you cheap bastard."

"Because she failed. Oh, she tried—she practically froze to death in my labyrinth, trying. But all she did was destroy my poor mill."

"Maybe she had a better idea for what to do with it. You said she was a visionary."

"Vision isn't always a plus," he says. "Eva was like a great chef who can't boil an egg. Literally could not do magic unless it changed the world, and I was asking her to help keep things utterly the same. My spell clashed with her signature. Be like asking you to do a spell that isn't sneaky and selfish. Face it, my boy. Your mother was a loser. A sore loser."

Before I've even processed it, I've thrown out my left hand and cursed him. He rocks back as if I've punched him, laughing as bright red blood spatters from his nose. But instead of hitting the floor, the blood runs backward, flying up and vanishing into his nostrils like a horror movie on Rewind. His face looks fine, as if I'd never made contact. "Thank you, Mrs. Edna Brooks of Mulberry Street," he says, sweeping a bow. "Who just forgot smothering her little orange kitten under a couch cushion while watching TV. His name was Charlie." He holds up his empty teacup. "To Charlie! It's a beautiful machine I've created, isn't it?"

I back toward the open door. "You're crazy."

"No, son, just a hundred and twenty years ahead of you."

The door slams shut. I'm trapped here with him.

My heart's pounding out of my chest, but I try to stay calm. "Why did you make this place? To live forever?"

"I just wanted to be with the woman I loved," he says, and his face becomes Joe again, nerdy, eager to please. "Elizabeth was going to die if I didn't do something. History proved that; the cure for tuberculosis was decades away."

"Your wife was sick?"

"She wasn't my wife yet. Just a maid my parents dismissed when her pregnancy started to show. Our baby, Elyse's great-grandfather. It was a scandal, you see. I was a son of a wealthy industrialist, engaged to a well-bred girl. But Elizabeth captured my heart because she saw what others couldn't see."

"Ghosts." The homeless woman was Mrs. Preston?

"We just wanted to be together, somewhere we could be married and my family wouldn't judge her for being low-class. My father thought he was punishing me by sending me out west. But the west was our ticket to freedom.

"The Indians who lived here had no concept of the resource they were sitting on, its true value. Harnessing its power was child's play—I'm just lucky I got to it before anyone else. You may think I'm a monster," he adds, "but compared to many occultists, I'm a goddamn philanthropist. My subjects are happy, because I made this place a perfect little nest for them too. Happiness is built into my system. A beautiful town where everyone's content . . . and where Elizabeth and I never had to lose each other. *That's* magic."

"That's bullshit. If you didn't lose her, why isn't she here?"

"Oh, she's here. Hasn't spoken to me since the sixties, but she's bound to me still. In this long life together, we have been mayors, we've been police officers, we've been criminals, we've been teachers. The ghosts are our eyes and ears all over town, so she can't escape the bitter memories any more than I can."

"Seems pretty obvious she's not happy being bound to you."

"She'll come around, by and by." He's slipping into older language. "She's feisty, but I can afford to wait a hundred more years. Unlike you. You see, Elizabeth has no choice, in the end. She can't hold out forever, and she can't break my spell. She never had a whit of talent in the occult."

"But Elyse does," I say, realizing it for the first time. That's why the unseal spell worked, even though she poured the water. "When you found out about our relationship, you pushed her out of town so she'd never be a threat."

"She *wanted* to escape. I just helped her along. I couldn't have made her quit town if she didn't want to. Just as my spell on you wouldn't have worked if you didn't on some level want to die." I start to tell him I didn't want to die.

But hadn't I killed my old self, in a way? "I couldn't even have closed that door if you didn't still want to talk to me. I don't force people."

Manipulation, not force. That's *his* signature; it's all over his spells. I keep my face blank, but my mind is racing. With hope. Because he's wrong: I *can* do spells that aren't sneaky and selfish. Maybe not in the past—my old self couldn't—but now, yes. All the time. The grease fire. Warding Elyse. Could it be that my signature has changed, since losing my memories? In which case . . . the water spirit wouldn't remember me. It wouldn't know I'd been there before. It wouldn't kill me.

"How do you think I imprisoned the elemental?" he brags. "I merely suggested to it that its time had been long, that it was tired now and ready for something new to take its place. It submitted willingly. And what about you, my boy? Elyse is gone, you have no money, no future, your father's damaged beyond repair, your mother's trapped here for eternity . . . Isn't it time you gave up?"

I can still be sneaky when I need to be. I look down. "No. You're wrong. I have a lot to live for."

"Name one thing." He laughs.

I turn away from him, covering my face in my hands. The door opens automatically and I walk out, hunched over, copying Jeremy's posture. I walk up the trail to the falls and duck into the cavern. I don't care if he's watching. I hope he is.

In front of the pool I start to tremble. This is real,

not a dream. It's finally happening—will it kill me or not? Preston's right in a way; I'm not as scared of death, of becoming a ghost, as I probably should be. But it's not that I want to die. I'd rather live. Even if it's just drinking beer and eating popcorn on the couch and playing video games, life is decent. It's just that—like in my dream—I feel like my decent life is a very small thing. Smaller than the good I could do with my death.

If this works, and Elyse ever calls her mother from California, she'll know Liz's different. She'll visit home and find out what happened.

My shirt's so baggy, it would go over my head underwater, so I take it off. I'm wearing heavy black work boots, just like in the dream. I look at the pool's still surface, trying to push away the image of Dan's peaceful, spinning back float in the circle of feeding ghosts, and then I can feel it. Hear it too. The low, vibrating hum of the spirit. A lullaby to its prey?

Out of nowhere, Preston appears before me. "Mind if I watch the feeding frenzy?"

"Suit yourself. I'm not doing this for you."

"Still, it saddens me to think of you dying all alone. Just like your mother."

Is he trying to rattle me so I can't concentrate, so I'll fail to make my way through the labyrinth before the spirit tears me limb from limb? That could mean he knows I have a chance.

"Thanks for your concern." If there's one thing I can

do, it's pretend to be more confident than I feel. "But I'm not alone," I add. "My mother's spell still protects me, even after her death."

"How sweet." Preston laughs. "But I own your mother. Her soul works for me now. Her magic is mine." He raises one arm, points his thumb at my heart, and twists it. My breath catches in my throat as brutal coldness seeps through my core. A string of blue light ripples in front of me like a snake, its trail growing faint and disappearing into the wind with a soft rustle.

I look down at my chest. My tattoo's gone.

I'm unguarded.

A low howl of outrage emanates from deep below as I back slowly away from the pool and onto the main trail. As if the water spirit is grieving with me, grieving the loss of my mother's gift to me. Is that even possible? Can the spirit sense my presence, the way I sense its presence? Did it feel my magical protection being stripped away?

While I'm contemplating this, a slow movement in the soil catches my eye. Double wheel tracks like a stroller, approaching. I start running.

When I get to Main Street I look for Elizabeth, but for once she's not there. Has she moved on to yet another identity?

By the time I reach the town square I force myself to accept the truth: I'm never going to make it home without one of them getting me. They'll be drawn to my bitter memories, hungry for the taste of them. Even if I run in a zigzag, crossing streets at random, I couldn't make it as far as the front door.

I pull my drawstring bag of Chinese coins from my pocket, sit down, and start the incantation under my breath as I spread the coins around me in a circle. I try to calm myself, comfort myself. I just need time to think. There's a solution to this somewhere, somehow. But I can't think of any way to solve this alone. I'm not even good at brainstorming on my own. My magic never got innovative until I started talking about it with someone who liked to argue with me.

I'm no longer invisible when Sheriff Hank stops by to inquire what my business is. He tells me to move it along, his boots disturbing the ward circle. I stand and gather my coins, but the second he turns his back I hide behind the statue of Preston and set up my spell again. I feel like I'm cowering, but what else can I do? If I'm caught, there'll be no one to remind me of what I've lost.

Night falls. Bill's probably freaking out, unable to find me *or* her. He's going to go out again and lose more memories. He's going to be used up fast, because he's alone and confused. The ground of the square gets cold and I rock back and forth and hug myself to maintain body heat.

That's how she finds me.

CHAPTER 35

ELYSE

I'M CUTTING THROUGH THE SQUARE ON MY WAY to Marshall's house, ready to break into a run at any sudden shimmery movements, when I spot the crouched figure shivering behind the statue of W. P. Preston. I would know those broad shoulders anywhere. "Marshall?" I stand over him. "What are you doing out here?"

He looks up at me—for once. "God, I'm glad to see you!"

I realize he's sitting in a ring of coins. Convenient. "Move over." I step into his ward circle. "What do *you* need this for? Something wrong with your tattoo?"

He hangs his head. "Gone." In that word I can hear his grief for a mother he now remembers. He tells me about his dad going outside, how he broke down and asked Joe for help, only to realize what I had, that Joe was none other than William Phillips Preston. "Not that I'm complaining, but what are you doing back in town? It's not safe for you here. Or for me, now. I'm not protected anymore. I'm just like anyone else."

I take that in. Marshall is no longer protected from ghosts. He's as defenseless as I am—more, because he can't see them. He's as bad off as any resident of Summer Falls, except worse because he knows what's at stake. The worry shows in his eyes. They look dull, watery. Standing just inches away from him, I have to fight the urge to reach down and take his hand, to comfort him like he used to comfort me. But he's the one who did this to us. To himself. I force myself to stay cold. "It's interesting. To see how you deal with being powerless."

He exhales a growl. Then his face softens to resignation. "I don't blame you for hating me," he says. "After everything that's happened to you, you deserved to have one person who wouldn't let you down, and I failed. Miserably. I hate asking, but will you please help me get home?"

I bite my lip.

"I need to make sure my dad's safe. He thinks my mom's still alive; he's probably going to start looking for her soon if he hasn't already."

"Of course I'll help you get home." Why does he have to be selfless now? It's hard to be mad at him when he's so different—but if I don't stay mad, I'll trust him again, and then I could get wiped. Erased. Killed, even. "No guarantees we'll make it though, and you have to pay close attention to what I say. When I see a ghost, I'll tell you right where it is and which way to run." I look around and see a white nightgown that shimmers. "Right now, for example, the little girl who was in my room is peeking in the window of Frieda's." I'm starting to recognize individual ghosts.

"Poor kid probably just wants some candy," he mutters.

"No, she wanted candy fifty years ago," says a cranky voice. "Now she wants your memories, and if she gets them you're cooked." Elizabeth's strolling over to us barefoot, in her brown patched dress. My smooth-skinned, red-haired great-great-grandmother.

"Mrs. Preston?" Marshall says.

"Not that name." She waves him off. "A hundred years is too long to carry any man's name, let alone that bastard's. I'm just Elizabeth now. Or, 'Hey, you, stop defacing public property.'"

A thought occurs to me. "When you destroy something in the town, does he lose some of his power?"

She nods. "We both do. But I don't care about myself anymore. I just want this to end."

"Then will you help us?" I say. "You've had lifetimes to come up with a plan."

"You think I haven't waged my share of revolutions against him? But every time I come up with an idea, he finds a way to use it to make himself stronger. Like when I wrote that children's book about the Indians who lived here before we made a mess of things."

"*You* wrote the storybook?" I ask.

She nods shyly. "Forty years ago, I had it illustrated,

317

printed up, and sent to the library without his knowing. Townspeople who read it would get ideas in their heads that maybe this place was better off before the mill and the tourists. But he got wind of it. Tore out the last few pages so it ended the way he liked it, and that's how people know the story now. What feels right to them, what they're used to, is him winning."

"Still," I say, "you could have done more. . . . I mean, you've had all this time, and the ghosts don't take your memories."

"They don't take memories away from me," she agrees, "they give them. Misery, pain, all the time. I think of it as purgatory, a punishment for all my sins, but Preston enjoys it. He says it keeps him human."

"You really feel all our bad memories?" I ask. If she knows everything that's happened to us, to me . . . "Then why don't you help us? Or . . . wait . . . are you the one who gave me the journal?" I think I wanted it to be her, to think I had some kind of guardian or fairy godmother watching over me, even a crazy one. But her perplexed expression tells me all I need to know. Even when I was a child, the only person watching over me . . . was me. "How can you just sit back and watch it destroy us?" I ask. "Your own descendants are being sacrificed to keep you alive."

"I'm as much against it as you, but I don't control any of this. *He* did it, long ago, and without my say-so."

It's not like I think she's lying or something, but it's

not good enough for me. Maybe Marshall's right that I'm not capable of forgiveness. I turn away, but I hear him say, "Elizabeth, you can help us right now if you're willing. We can use a second pair of eyes on the way home."

We barely make it home, and Marshall instantly sets about creating a ward circle while I search for his father, calling his name. Instead I find a note on the kitchen counter.

> Eva and Marsh, I'm worried. You're not answering your phones. I can't remember where you said you'd be. I'm going to look for you. Call me if you get

He never finished his sentence or signed it. He must have gotten distracted.

Marshall frantically runs to the phone and hits #3 on speed dial. "It's just ringing," he says. "I probably haven't paid the bill in months."

He looks miserable, and I can't tell him his father will be okay. I can't tell him it's not his fault.

But this time I do squeeze his hand and just say, "I'm sorry."

"Me too." He blinks away tears. "You never told me why you came back."

Once I've determined there are no ghosts in the house, we sit in the kitchen, where I make him a cup of tea he'll never drink and one for myself. "I realized a lot of things," I said, "when I left Summer Falls. But the main thing is, this isn't really about the two of us. I mean we're just two people. Whatever issues we have between us, it doesn't mean five thousand other people deserve to live their lives as happy batteries."

"And that's not counting the ghosts, like my mom," he adds, "and the people who haven't been born here yet."

"Exactly. So, we're going to have to find a way to work together."

"I'm willing to do anything that has a chance of working." He tells me about his confrontation with Joe/Preston and how he'd been about to jump in the water when he realized he had no chance of success. "I'm not telling you this so you'll see how selfless I am—well, maybe a little. I'm hoping you have an idea I haven't thought of. Because no matter how I see it, we can't do this. If either one of us goes in, ghosts kill our minds. I realize there's no way you're ever going to let me do the memory-seal spell on you again—"

"You got that right." I'm pretty sure I'd choke on the potion. "But even if I did trust you, you're not protected now and you can't see ghosts. There's a pretty good chance you'd be nabbed before we even got to the falls, and then Preston would know about our plan."

Then we're both silent.

"I'm pretty sure you're thinking what I'm thinking," he says.

"Seal *you*."

He nods. "Make me a blank again. Then show me the plans I wrote up and guide me. Tell me what to do, where to go . . . Any strength you have as an occultist, it might not be much, but it'll add to mine."

"Or maybe it's a lot, and that's why Preston didn't want me in town."

"The ritual my mom wrote up, the one she was presumably in the middle of when she died, was to claim the place of power. But my mother's plan was unethical. I mean, it was environmentally sound. But then the ghosts, including her, would still be stuck here. I have my own plan that would free the ghosts and set mortal time moving again for the Prestons and the town, but it wouldn't restore the damage that's already been done to people's minds. And Preston could always find another place of power and set up his system somewhere else."

"Still, it would be something." It would be huge. "Are you willing though?"

"Yes," he says quietly.

We decide to make it simple in the video we record for him. He sits on his bed and faces my phone's screen. "I'm Special Agent Marshall King," he says, clearly trying to hide a grin, "and I've voluntarily taken a drug that will seal off my memory, for my own protection, during this mission. My partner, Elyse Alton." He turns the phone toward me and I wave. "She'll be here just to guide me along, smooth the process for me, and give me detailed, minute-by-minute instructions."

We crack up laughing as soon as he hits Record off.

"That sounded like bullshit," he says. "What if I don't believe myself when I hear it?"

"I think when you recognize your voice, you'll have to believe it. Or at least believe it's for your own good to believe it."

It takes him more than an hour to mix up the potion. He shows me the thick red liquid at the bottom of the chalice. "The color's from the wine. I remember it tastes awful."

"I don't even remember." Bitterness.

He drinks it down, his face twisting in pain. "It's fast-acting, I remember that too. I'll start to act drunk, then I'll fall asleep. This could be the last time I ever talk to you as me."

"Marshall, don't—"

"Let's not dance around the truth. Preston could kill me before I get my memories back, and even if he doesn't I might never be myself, this self, again. And there's something I need to say to you." His voice cracks.

"Nothing you say is going to make me trust you again."

"Give me *some* credit, please. I get that. I know you don't believe you're a good person, Elyse, but you're wrong. Here's how I know it. *I* trust *you*. I know that, even though you hate my guts, you will take care of me tomorrow."

"I don't hate—"

"You'll be a great guide. You'll make sure this gets done right. Because, Elyse, you're a hero. I always wanted to be one, I even got the pecs and the magic powers, but you're the real thing."

There's a long pause, and I can feel my anger melting when he says, "God, I really want to kiss you."

"What?" I spit. "You're joking, right?"

"Sorry, just, I'm instantaneously buzzing." Right, the potion's stifling his inhibitions. He gives me a sly smile and settles back on the mattress. "Maybe you should tie me to the bed. You know, in case I flip out and try to kill you when I wake up with no memories."

"This is really bringing out your perv side. Luckily *I* have morals."

With a chuckle he lifts his head off the pillow. "Sometimes."

"Are you trying to goad me?"

"Yeah, is it working?" This time when he tries to lift his head, he's too tired and it falls back.

I can't help laughing. "Good night, Marshall."

Less than ten minutes later he falls asleep.

I lie beside him, unable to fall asleep myself.

I keep thinking of how he said this was the last time he'd be talking to me as himself. And how he already wasn't the self he used to be before we did the first spell. Who he is keeps changing, and the Marshall I'm mad at seems to no longer exist. But that doesn't make me any less mad, and my anger's firmly attached to the face and voice and body I think of as Marshall. What if he had never regained that memory? What if I'd found out some other way what he did, by finding my phone, for example? Would I still be this distrustful? In some ways more so, because at least now he'd told me what he did. Which couldn't have been easy, or fun. Just the fact that he confessed suggests to me that the latest version of Marshall, integrated with all his old memories, would never have done what his predecessor did. I let myself kiss the top of his sleeping head, inhaling his sandalwood scent, and wonder who he's going to be in the morning.

CHAPTER 36

SPECIAL AGENT MARSHALL KING

"WELCOME BACK, AGENT KING." A VOICE FROM above my head. A girl's voice. Crisp. Confident.

I force my bleary eyes to open. The room is dark. There's a heart-stoppingly beautiful girl standing over my bed, her face bathed in lamplight. Spiky hair, piercing green eyes focused on me. One arm's folded across the front of her oversize khaki jean jacket; the other hand's holding out a steaming mug.

"Here." She passes the mug toward me, and without thinking I reach out my hands to accept it, its warmth between my palms instantly comforting. "I thought this might help you wake up faster than last time."

The aroma of coffee perks up my senses enough that I can speak. "Thank you." My voice creaks with grogginess. I groan and ease myself up, careful not to spill coffee on myself. I take a sip of hot coffee—it's got milk and a little sugar in it—and let it slide down my throat.

Then another. And another.

That's when her words finally start to sink in. *Last time*. Last time what? She's acting like she knows me. Why don't *I* remember *her*? The impression she gives is military, or maybe NSA. Definitely badass. What did she call me? Agent . . . something. The clock behind her says four a.m. "I don't remember falling asleep," I say.

"If you really start to think about it," she says calmly, "and I don't particularly recommend doing so, you'll realize you don't remember anything at all, including me. That memory loss is only temporary."

"What happened to me?" I ask. She seems to know everything.

"You drank a memory seal last night, in preparation for completing a task that requires you to be . . . a blank slate."

I blink. "Memory seal?"

"This video will explain everything." She slides a cell phone onto my lap, hits Play on the cued-up vid.

"I'm Special Agent Marshall King," says a dark-haired guy. "I'm you. Look in the mirror." On cue, the girl holds a compact mirror in front of my face . . . his face. "I've voluntarily taken a drug that will seal off my memory, for my own protection, during this mission. This is my partner, Elyse Alton." The guy in the picture turns the phone toward someone else, and suddenly the beautiful girl is in the frame. She waves. "She'll be here just to guide me along, smooth the process for me, and give me detailed, minute-by-minute instructions. Don't ask what it's about. I've already agreed to it."

The video ends.

"I know it sounds crazy." The look in her eyes now is gentle and compassionate.

"It sounds off-the-hook insane," I agree. Like I should throw off these covers and run from her as fast as I possibly can. But it's definitely my voice in the video. And more important, something about this girl's sureness feels natural, trustworthy. I just don't think she would lead me astray. "All right, brief me on this mission, please."

She tosses me a pair of jeans and T-shirt and looks away while I dress. "My part of the mission," she explains, "involves distracting the enemy while you perform the actual task. The cabin where he lives is on the way to where you're going, so I'll go and visit him first and make sure he's not looking out the window or otherwise noting where you're headed until it's too late."

I nod. "And what is this task I'm doing?"

"A magic ritual." She hands me a notebook. "You're very skilled in magic. Take some time to read through it."

I open the front cover and see a diagram of what appears to be a circular spiral labyrinth. It's only one page long, and it doesn't take me long to understand the general idea. It's simple but crazy.

I point to the diagram. "Can I ask you a few questions about this?"

"Actually you're kind of the expert in this area."

"Me?"

"You wrote all this," she says.

No way. I grab a pen from the desk and scribble, *I did???* on the page. The handwriting matches, deep-pressing and right-slanted and practically illegible. The handwriting of someone crazy enough to come up with this ritual. "I wrote this," I repeat, trying to get used to it.

"Well . . . some of it you adapted from the work of another agent."

"Can I talk to him, then?"

Her lips form a sad line. "I'm afraid that's not possible."

Twinges of alarm burn the pit of my stomach. "How dangerous is this mission?"

She looks me in the eye. "We're both risking our lives."

I think about dying, my life being cut short today, and realize with a shock that I'd be willing—for the right cause. "In your opinion, is it worth it?"

"Yes." She says the word with longing, with passion. "Yes, it is."

"And I believed that too? Last night, for example, before I lost my memory."

"Yes. It's what we both believe."

I nod. "Then I'll do it."

Not long after, the doorbell rings and we head downstairs to see a redheaded young woman standing on the doorstep.

"This is Elizabeth, our consultant," my partner explains.

"Hey." She nods at me.

I take in the redhead's dirty face and brown patched

dress. She's either in deep cover as a street person or she's a street person.

Trust my partner. "Hello." I stick out my hand for the redhead to shake.

"You are to stay with her at all times," my partner goes on, "until you dive into the pool. She'll lead you there and her job will be to steer you clear of any obstacles—so if she starts to run, you follow."

I nod. "What kind of obstacles are we talking about?"

Elizabeth and my partner look at each other.

"What, is that classified information? Do I need a higher clearance or something?"

"Ghosts," Elizabeth says.

"Ghosts?" I repeat dumbly. "Is she kidding?"

"I wish," my partner says.

She hands me a flashlight and the three of us walk along the main road. We get to a trailhead just as dawn is breaking. The trail begins to climb quickly, and soon I can see the sweeping panorama below of the calm lake, a town with trees and lawns and buildings, and the surrounding land—a lifeless desert stretching endlessly in all directions. It's a weird sight to behold, but then again it's a pretty damn weird night.

Abruptly, my partner splits off from us. "Wait here ten minutes," she tells us. "Then run for the pool."

The ten minutes is interminable. I keep thinking about this enemy she's distracting. About what kind of danger she might be in that she's not even telling me about. I guess that's the thing about being partners. My risking my life is one thing, but I'm not comfortable with her risking hers.

"Walk quickly," Elizabeth says, when the time's up. "We don't want the person who lives in that cabin to see us together—or to see you at all."

We race the rest of the way up the trail and come to a roaring waterfall, but Elizabeth points behind it, to an overhanging rock structure. Inside, quietly hidden like a secret, is a natural pool.

I know what I'm supposed to do.

I'm about to dive in when I hear footsteps approach.

"Oh, no," Elizabeth mutters. "It's him. We're cooked."

I look up to see a man in a morning coat grinning at me. "Well, well," he says. "I always enjoy watching a good death."

"Ignore him." My partner appears behind him. "Just follow our plan. Trust me!"

I don't know why, but I do trust her.

I plunge into the clear, cold water, my jeans and heavy work boots soaking it in, my skin sprouting goose bumps in protest as I look below at a circular spiral made of rocks. Water insects and tiny fish swim in between the stones. A low roaring vibrates from the bottom of the pool, sending a shiver down my spine. What's down here with me?

I swim down toward the bottom. As I get closer I can see tiny model buildings in the labyrinth. All elaborately designed and new-looking. A church. A library. A school. Houses painted white, yellow, green.

I feel a strange urge to walk the labyrinth from start to finish. It's drawing me in, but that's not what my mission is. Not what the piece of paper with my handwriting said. All I have to do is walk a circle around it, until I'm free. I find my footing in the mud below and start walking awkwardly because I have to hold myself down or I'll float to the surface.

What does that mean, until I'm free? Free of what? How will I know?

I figure I'll find out soon, but I'm running out of breath fast. Should I come back up?

Maybe "free" means the girl's going to come rescue me or take my place for the space of a breath. Freeing me of my responsibility here, sharing the burden like partners do for each other.

I keep walking, though I'm desperate for a breath and it makes me feel light-headed. I remember the strange man in the morning coat's words: "I always enjoy watching a good death."

What if it's my job to die here? Is that part of the ritual?

What if freedom doesn't mean I'm getting rescued? What if it means being free of this mortal coil? Free of life?

It doesn't matter. She said the mission was worth dying for. Worth it to both of us.

Another second and I'll have to breathe in, only I can't. My vision blurs, colors shift to red, and I keep walking.

CHAPTER 37

ELYSE

AFTER I LEAVE MARSHALL AND ELIZABETH behind on the trail—with instructions to wait ten minutes—I walk up to Joe's log cabin and take a deep breath. It comes out shaky. My heart feels like it's exploding in my chest. How am I supposed to outsmart my hundred-and-fifty-year-old evil occultist ancestor? But I have to. I need to distract him, keep him from noticing Marshall.

I take a second deep breath and knock.

No answer, then Joe/Preston finally comes to the door, wearing plaid pajama bottoms and a T-shirt, his Coke-bottle glasses askew on the bridge of his baby-smooth nose. "Elyse?" He's deeply disappointed to see me here, and he's too surprised to hide it. "What are you doing here? I thought you'd be in California by now."

"I realized I couldn't leave this place," I say. "Not yet."

"Don't tell me you're homesick?" He shudders, and I wonder, Is he playacting for my benefit? Pretending to be

Joe, the hapless occultist sent here by coldhearted higher-ups? Or is a part of him honestly sick of being stuck in this paradise he created? After all, is it really paradise if you can't leave?

"More like I have unfinished business here."

His eyebrows go up. "Are we talking about a boy?" he says with an indulgent smile.

"Maybe."

"I'm not the best person to be asking for relationship advice," he warns. I remember Elizabeth's account of their century-long marital feud and think, Yeah, you're not kidding there. "But, come on in." He sighs, and moves aside in the doorway, gesturing for me to join him inside. *Success.* "I'll make us some tea and try to convince you that no boy, no matter how cute, is worth you being stuck here."

He means it. I'm sure, this time. He wants me out for reasons of his own, but he also genuinely wants to help me do what he no longer can: move. Move on.

"Excuse me while I put a kettle on for tea."

I look around the one-room cabin, at the old-fashioned wood-burning stove in one corner and a single bed (made) in the opposite corner. It's primitive but looks comfortable at the same time. Joe/Preston puts a kettle that looks more like a witch's cauldron on the stove and busies himself setting up teacups for us. "So, is it Dan?" he asks. "Because that was a terrible tragedy, but you can't sit here and dwell on it forever."

"Not Dan, but you're close." The polished wooden

table's set with mustard-yellow velvet-covered chairs. Their high backs are shaped like keyholes. I quickly choose the one facing the window.

"Another athlete?" He sets down our cups and sits across from me. "Anyone I'd know from school?"

Behind him in the window I can see Elizabeth and Marshall dart past along the path to the waterfall.

I feel a tiny, tiny bit sorry for Joe. I have to remind myself that he's done horrible things. He's been indirectly and directly responsible for horrible things happening to me. But he's also my great-great-grandfather. If it weren't for him, I wouldn't be alive.

"It's not about any one boy," I say. "It's about all the boys, and the girls, and men and women, and children. Like Dan. And Pete. And my father. And that woman Hazel. All the people in this town who've been sacrificed. I can't leave Summer Falls until I know that won't happen to anyone else."

Joe sets down his teacup hard. "You don't sound like yourself." His voice sounds odd, and my pulse pounds. Did I give away our game too soon? Did I ruin everything? "It's obvious to me who's been influencing you." He waves his ring finger at himself and suddenly he's dressed in his old morning coat and top hat, just like his statue in the square. Gone are the Coke-bottle glasses, the hair sticking up, the clashing clothes. All vestiges of Joe are gone. "Come on, Elyse." He walks over to the door and opens it. "Let's go finish your unfinished business so you can leave town."

"What are you going to do?" I scramble to follow as

he marches up the path toward the waterfall, desperately grabbing at his arm, but he's too strong and keeps walking. The waterfall's so loud here, we have to yell to be heard. "What are you going to do to him?"

"Nothing!"

"I don't believe you!"

I dive at his knees, trying to stop him, but he's so pumped up with life force, he's almost like a god. My hope sinks at the sight of Marshall still standing next to Elizabeth by the pool.

"I just want you to see," Preston says, "the futility of trying to mess with someone else's kingdom. He can't touch my spell. He's just a pawn. The water spirit's going to recognize his signature and eat him for lunch.

"Well, well," Preston greets them. "I always enjoy watching a good death."

"Ignore him," I say to Marshall. "Just follow our plan. Trust me!"

Marshall takes a deep breath and dives in.

"Well, it was swell knowing him." Preston turns to Elizabeth. "Nice to see you here, beauty. I lost my mind the first time I saw that hair."

She turns from him, but her long red curls still blow toward him in the breeze.

Thirty seconds pass, the longest thirty seconds of my life.

"Son of a bitch, it should have spat him up or eaten him by now." Preston takes off his hat. "Why isn't it picking up his signature?"

"Because he's *changed*." I stare at the pool, desperate for a sign that something's working. Come back up, Marshall.

"People don't change. Water spirits play with their food sometimes. But just to be safe, I'm going to end this now," Preston says. "I'm sorry, Elyse, but you'll forget him soon." He pulls a crystal from his pocket.

Quick as a snake, Elizabeth throws her arms around him and kisses him full on the lips. Preston closes his eyes, a look of ecstasy on his face, just as she knocks the crystal out of his hand. It falls onto the rocks below, and I don't even hear the end of his hissed curse. I have to get Marshall out of there, even if it means abandoning the mission.

I run up, launch myself at the pool, and dive in. I'm still midair when I glimpse something pale and shiny breaking the surface of the water. *Ghost.* I barely miss crashing into it.

Then I'm submerged. Cold stuns every cell of my body, and my skull throbs with an instant ice-cream headache. My eyes can't focus, it's blurry . . . then I realize why: all around me, the water is cloudy with ghosts. Fast-moving ghosts. A sparkly swirl of them, exploding upward like a geyser from the depths. No way I can escape this many at once. My heart pounds as images of drowning fill my mind.

The ghosts close in on me. Their limbs brush against my trembling skin, their touch as light as smoke. I thought I'd be repulsed, but they seem so familiar by now, like neighbors. The little girl with sad eyes. Hazel in her peach frilly apron. The 1920s swimmer with his cap and goggles.

The warrior with feathers in his hair. Tomoko pushing her empty stroller. Eva with her dark mermaid hair. And then I realize how many ghosts have swept past me and kept moving, soaring to the surface like shimmering birds. And that I'm still awake, alert.

They're not feeding off me. They're not hungry for my pain.

They're free.

We did it. *Marshall, we did it. Please be okay.*

I swim down after him, through the rising sea of ghosts. As I race for the bottom, a spiral of stones comes into view. A maze. Marshall's lying in the center of it, facedown.

Suddenly the rock structure starts to crumble, and I grab hold of him and push off the bottom, carrying his unmoving body upward. He's deadweight, his eyes closed, but my lifeguard training's taught me how to carry dead-weight. Above me more and more ghosts are evacuating as I push toward the surface. The moment we break it, he grabs a lungful of air. He collapses on the rocks, coughing.

I feel around in my zipped pocket. The vial containing the antidote is still in there, thank god. "Drink this." Without a moment's hesitation, he uncaps it and downs the thick red liquid.

"Didn't think we'd meet again till hell," Preston greets him. But something's wrong with Preston's voice. It's strained and gravelly. He's popping coat buttons, spreading, his face lining with creases, his hair shedding. Elizabeth's red hair is turning rusty, then white, her face wrinkling like crumpled notebook paper. It's like watching a fast-forward video of a tree's leaves in autumn.

Above the roaring of the falls, I hear a horrible rumbling from the valley. Like an earthquake, downtown buildings are falling over. The lights have gone out. Neighborhood streetlights too. I think of Liz and all the people I know in town, how scared and confused they must be.

"It's finally over," Elizabeth mutters, her voice an old woman's now. A look of peace comes over her face.

The hum coming from inside the pool is now a roar. We watch together as behind Preston House, the once-glassy lake roils and bubbles, dark blue waves punishing the shore. Then a deafening sound and Preston House itself has fallen, caved in on itself. "Mom!" I scream. "No!" And then my legs turn to jelly under me, and I crash. Memories. Not just thirdhand memories from the journal to the music box. Real, in my gut, memories. And all of them hurt so much, I sink to my knees on the rocks, racked with sobs.

I feel a hand on my back, and then Marshall reaches out his hand to help me up. "We did it." I can tell just by the slightly devious spark in his eyes that he's back, fully back. "Mission accomplished. I knew you'd be unable to stop yourself from rescuing me."

"Wait, what? You planned that part? *That's* what you wrote down in your notes, 'She'll come rescue me'?" The sneaky bastard held something back from me *again*?!

"If either of us knew the whole plan, it would have

been compromised," he says. "I had to be willing to trust that you'd come in and rescue me, or be willing to die if you didn't. I looked at the part of my mother's notes where she was trying to get them to switch from being memory-junkies to being methane-eaters. And then I rewrote it so instead they craved nothing."

"You freed them," I say. "I saw them go, Marshall. I saw your mother. She's free."

"And the water spirit's finally free from Preston's rule."

"So now the place of power is yours." Old Man Preston sneers at Marshall, grudging admiration in his ancient blue eyes. "What are *you* going to do with it?"

"You mean what are we going to do without it," he responds. "Didn't you hear me? The spirit is free." He reaches out his hand to me and I take it without hesitation.

"You're just going to walk away, that's your plan?" Preston throws back his white head and laughs. "It won't last, you know. Won't be long before someone just like me or your mother comes to claim it."

"They'll have to get to it first," Marshall says with a grin. "And it won't be easy, thanks to the protection spell I came up with. Consider it the anti-Summer Falls effect."

We hear a deep, low cracking sound as the glacier over-looking the falls starts to rumble forward. The ice flows over the cliff like the falls themselves, in slow motion.

"So you really are giving it up!" Preston's crazy laugh carries in the now chilly wind. "Eva's son and my great-great-granddaughter throwing power away. I guess blood is no thicker than water after all."

But even as he says the words his voice cracks. His and Elizabeth's wizened flesh shrinks and peels away to bone that crumbles to dust and blows over the cliff toward what was once the town below.

A cold gust of wind howls from the encroaching wall of ice. Marshall and I cling to each other and watch as, below, individual tiny lights appear on the dark streets of Summer Falls. Flashlights and candles, thousands of them, slowly drifting closer to one another. Then we run together down the trail, racing ahead of the ice as it swallows our footsteps.

NINE MONTHS LATER

ELYSE

WHEN I SWING THE MINI IN FRONT OF THE STATE mental health facility, Marshall's waiting for me out in the sunny cold. With a smile, he opens the passenger-side door and leans over to kiss me hello. He buries his hands in my spiky, short hair, still wet from the pool where I teach swim lessons every afternoon.

I kiss him back, then hand him something small covered in a denim-blue cloth napkin. "Here. It's carrot-ginger this time."

He unwraps a golden-topped muffin, still steaming from the oven, and takes a bite. "It's good. Thanks for keeping it warm."

Ever since Marshall started working part-time as an orderly and shift manager at Mollie's, he's become hyper-attuned to making sure people feel appreciated for doing tasks and services that are sometimes thankless. Some-times he grumbles about the way customers treat waiters, especially since these days Mollie's isn't just a hangout for locals but for kids in Green Vista and Eagle's Point too. They still remember the days when Summer Falls was a well-funded, verdant garden, and their homes were poor and dry as dust, and many are still bitter about losing all those football and basketball and baseball games. That's the dark side of memory. But this is a community that needs rebuilding, and rebuilding takes leadership. Marsh's already been promoted in both his jobs, but he's still getting used to the fact that strangers notice him whether he wants them to or not—they flag him down in fact and ask him for things, like extra ketchup or napkins or to clean up a spill. Sometimes a spill that's done on purpose. Another dark side of memory. Vengeance.

Yesterday I parked in the visitor's lot and went up to visit my father and Dan and the others, as I do several times a week. Dad's doing better all the time, and now he always recognizes me. The younger patients, like Dan, are recovering fast. Last month Dan spoke his first word. It was *Pete.* We still don't know what happened to him after he was taken away from the Ferris wheel accident. Dad himself hasn't spoken yet, and sometimes his eyes still look vacant, but we have hope, now that the former asylum is a real, cutting-edge, working mental hospital. The old doctor quit and disappeared after a state investigation found him guilty of fraud and gross misuse of state funds.

It doesn't hurt that Marshall uses his orderly job to practice healing magic on the patients he works with.

After work four days out of five, we take the bus to Green Valley Junior College, along with Jeremy, Carla, and Ruta, who's working hard to get accepted to Colorado State in two years, where she plans to study neurobiology and find a cure for the victims of Summer Falls. Four days out of five.

But today is the fifth day.

When Preston House fell in on itself, the front parlor collapsed into the basement. Jeffry was downstairs, watching TV in the basement, when the ceiling opened up over his head and plaster rained down on him. What killed him, they say, was the pink high-backed chaise from the parlor that cracked his skull. Mom—who was outside, thankfully, watering her flowers when it happened—says she hopes he died instantly. But I like to think that in Jeffry's last moments he experienced the type of acute mental clarity that only fear can bring.

Shelly says it'll be a long time before I'm done working out my anger and confusion. She's one of the counselors who set up a temporary practice downtown in Main Street Clinic. When the United States government first declared Summer Falls a disaster site, they sent emergency-aid workers to help rebuild our homes. What the aid workers discovered was widespread depression, odd memory problems, hallucinations, and mass hysteria. There were also injuries when people suddenly regained their worst memories. Sixteen people who were driving their cars crashed them. One ex mill worker is still in a coma after a bar fight, and an old man ran over his own foot with his lawnmower. The news camera crews that were already showing up to ogle the glacier that had suddenly doubled in size and grown to cover the old falls turned to us as a human-interest story. As the climate-change debate raged around us, we became a kind of natural curiosity for viewers, a symbol of American innocence cruelly smashed. CNN reporters shoved microphones in our faces and asked us to comment on how the tragedy had torn our community asunder. Yes, they used the word *asunder*. Millions of dollars poured in from text-fund lines. Eventually the government issued a grant paying for psychiatric counseling for every man, woman, and child in town.

Liz went to see a counselor too for a while, but then she got too busy running Two Bears Lodge. Our tourist industry dried up when the glacier doubled and the ghosts and heatnaps disappeared. Wilderness tourism popped up as the consolation prize, and my mother made a grab for it first. She opened Two Bears and runs it all by herself. She says she's not ready to start dating and may never be. Marshall's dad, Bill, says the same thing, though he's been known to show up for dinner at Two Bears with his son and linger with the innkeeper over coffee. Since Eva's death was finally ruled accidental, her life insurance paid out fifty thousand dollars. It's what she would have earned had she succeeded in preserving Preston's spell, and it's enough that Bill can afford to work part-time in Summer Falls and be near his son.

In my bedroom at Two Bears Lodge, we change into our winter wilderness gear, starting with thermal underwear and ending with snowshoes and poles. Marshall grabs another muffin before we leave and insists I split it with him. Even with extra calories beforehand, the trek always leaves us exhausted, every muscle fiber singing with pain, collapsed in each other's arms on the giant beanbag in front of the fireplace.

"You ready to face the cold again?" he asks.

"As much as I ever am. The others are on their way," I add. "Carla just texted to say she and Jeremy might be a few minutes late."

At first we had searched for the guardians. The legendary tribe that for thousands of years had hunted deer and fished near the waterfall, watching over the place of power before Preston arrived. But they were gone, disappeared.

It wasn't that they had died out; one of the other orderlies at the asylum was descended from them. He was kind enough to give us names and phone numbers of others too, cousins and friends of his. But they turned out to be accountants and salespeople and car mechanics and, in one case, a Methodist priest. There was awkward silence or laughter on the phone when we tried to talk to them. None of them believed in, or had any skills or interest in, defending magical waterfalls. Outside of Preston's museum, the world had moved on, for better or for worse.

That was when we realized that being part of the tribe had nothing to do with the past, with where someone's ancestors came from and what they did. It had to do with responsibility in the here and now. We were the spirit's protectors. We were the new tribe. That's what we'd inherited, or won. Not the privilege to use this power for whatever we want but the privilege of keeping it safe. We don't understand everything about the place of power. We know it's too much—too great—for us to ever allow ourselves access to it, but it trusts us. We're its caretakers. We'll fight to the death to keep what happened here before from ever happening again.

Every time I see it, it still makes me feel a funny thrill. The majestic ice-capped mountain. The handrails gone. The trails gone. The wintry world I see around me is real in a way that the world I grew up in never was. Despite the frigid air, I can feel the warm presence of the water spirit all around us, building its strength after its long years of servitude.

In a hundred years, the glacier protecting the spirit will melt. Ninety-nine and a half now. Maybe by then, when our spell is faded, the world will be ready to handle more power. It won't be our responsibility then, because we won't try to live past our own time like the Prestons did. But right now it is our responsibility, and one we don't ever intend to forget.

We snowshoe to where the mouth of the old falls used to be. Marshall and I smile at each other as a snowy fox crosses our path and skedaddles away.

"Still think we made the right choice?" he asks,

reaching out for me. "I know it's not the most glamorous life. It's not California."

"California was never real." I lean into his arms. "It was a dream somebody else put in my head. This, here, with you . . . this finally feels like a place I belong. What about you? You've been to Paris, Africa, all around the world. You really think you're going to be happy staying in one place?"

"I was never happy *before* I came here. Before Summer Falls, before you, I never had a home."

I pull him close and gently press my cold lips against his, savoring his responding kiss and knowing that the warmth spreading through us both has nothing to do with magic spells.

I hear our friends in the distance, but they can wait.

ACKNOWLEDGMENTS

A HEARTFELT THANK-YOU TO MY EDITOR, KRISTIN Daly Rens, whose notes are always spot-on and at the same time genuinely encouraging. What an amazing and rare combination of talents that is! Her insights forged GLIMMER into a stronger book and helped me grow as a writer.

As for my agent, Jim McCarthy, he continues to be the best partner in publishing I could imagine: supportive, knowledgeable, and awfully witty too. Some days I cannot believe my good luck in having the opportunity to work with him now on multiple books.

I want to give a shout-out to book bloggers Raila Soares and Kari Olsen, who tirelessly promote YA books in their spare time. Ladies, your dedication and profession-alism are inspiring, and you're permanently on my ARC send-to list.

And to my husband, Robert Brydon, I'll just say this: happiness *is* being married to your best friend.